D1006956

SPLIT

Also by Stefan Petrucha

Teen, Inc.
The Rule of Won

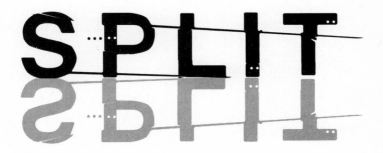

SPLIT

STEFAN PETRUCHA

Walker & Company
New York

First published in the United States of America in March 2010 by
Walker Publishing Company, Inc., a division of Bloomsbury Publishing, Inc.
Visit Walker & Company's Web site at www.bloomsburyteens.com

Coleman Bark's translation of Rumi's Quatrain #1245 appears in the collection
Open Secret © 1999 and is used here by permission.

For information about permission to reproduce selections from this book, write to
Permissions, Walker & Company, 175 Fifth Avenue, New York, New York 10010

Library of Congress Cataloging-in-Publication Data
Petrucha, Stefan.
Split / Stefan Petrucha.
p.   cm.
Summary: After his mother dies, Wade Jackson cannot decide whether to become a
musician or a scholar, so he does both—splitting his consciousness into two distinct worlds.
ISBN 978-0-8027-9372-0
[1. Consciousness—Fiction.   2. Space and time—Fiction.]   I. Title.
PZ7.P44727Sp 2010   [Fic]—dc22   2009008889

Book design by Nicole Gastonguay
Typeset by Westchester Book Composition
Printed in the U.S.A. by Worldcolor Fairfield, Pennsylvania
2 4 6 8 10 9 7 5 3 1

All papers used by Walker & Company are natural, recyclable products
made from wood grown in well-managed forests. The manufacturing processes
conform to the environmental regulations of the country of origin.

Once I, Chuang Tsu, dreamt I was a butterfly, fluttering here and there; in all ways a butterfly. I enjoyed my freedom as a butterfly, not knowing I was Chuang Tsu. Suddenly I awoke and was surprised to be myself again. Now, how can I tell whether I am a man who dreamt that he was a butterfly, or whether I am a butterfly who dreams that he is a man?

—Chuang Tsu

SPLIT

PROLOGUE

I'm staring at Mom's face, a face I've seen at least as often as the sun or the moon, only something's gone from it now. She lies in a rented hospital bed, pointed toward the window that looks at the little gray bay out back and the bright sky beyond. It's her favorite sight in all the world, but she's not enjoying it. Something's missing. She's missing. She's dead.

A hospice nurse gets her ready. For what? I didn't ask. Probably for the funeral parlor to come get her. Mom's getting ready, going places. It's the most excitement she's had in months. Somber and respectful, the nurse removes the IV, then squeezes out a big wet sponge over a bowl. For a while, the only sound in the world is the trickle of water from the sponge hitting the metal bowl. That, and the drone in my head.

It's a funny thing, the drone. It's almost constant now. It started a few hours ago, when Mom could still talk. It started just when she finished what turned out to be her last words.

To me, anyway. She may have said something else to Dad. I don't know. But this buzz has been there ever since, a constant conversation.

Like, I'll think: "She looks like she's asleep, peaceful."

But I'll also think: "No. She looks dead."

It's not quite like that. It's faster and the words blur over each other.

Couldawouldashouldadonesomething.

Likewhat?NotlikeshewasfallingdownsomestairsandIcoulda-caughther.

Dad's on the phone with the funeral parlor. His voice shakes at the end of every sentence. He looks as white as the walls. And I'm thinking: "The parlor. Why are they called parlors? Makes me think of spiders and flies."

Why? Because that's what they're called, okay? Just accept it.

A month ago, when the doctors were finally sure we'd be losing her, Dad said he was afraid he'd start drinking again.

He's afraid? Imagine how I feel.

How do I feel? I don't know. How the hell should I know?

I'm hungry, haven't eaten in a day. I need some food.

How can I think of food at a time like this?

Dad looks at me from the phone. "Wade, eat something."

But I want to run and keep running, jump up on a wall, do a crazy mourning dance.

But I want to curl into a ball at the bottom of the sea and never move again.

Maybe I'm passing out. Maybe I should eat something. Okay, I will.

My head feels about a mile away from my body, but I drag both of them toward the kitchen. On the way, I pass the big workroom, drenched in sunlight from mirrors and crystals and a gorgeous day. I stop to take a look, which may have been a mistake, because it hurts so much to see.

This is where she keeps . . . *kept* . . . her unfinished projects. That means *all* of them: half-carved wooden boxes, sculptures, paintings, plays, scrapbooks, furniture she picked up at tag sales planning to stain but never got around to. It looks like she never finished *reading* a book, let alone writing one. All her hardcovers have a bookmark, some covered in dust they've been unfinished so long. But they're all neatly stacked, like stones in a graveyard. Other people would never get half as many unfinished things into this space. It's an ordered chaos.

She never could finish anything, ever, no matter how hard she tried.

Don't talk about her like that. She did finish. She finished life.

She knew. When she found out she was dying, she said at least she wouldn't have to worry about what to be when she "grew up" anymore. Therapist, marine biologist, activist, poet. She wanted to be so many things. I worried that raising me held her back, but she said she was like that long before I was born.

Was it a good life? Was she happy?

Of course she was. She loved me and Dad. Always did. She'd do anything, sacrifice anything, even her dreams. That's what gave her a life.

Of course she wasn't. She was trapped and stuck like the spider's fly, almost exploding from longing for all the things she wanted to do but never did.

I make it to the kitchen. A newspaper's open on the

table. There's a headline about Prometheus, the huge particle collider where Dad works that was just built outside Rivendale. It's being fired up for the first time today, and some weird group's afraid it'll end the world or rip a hole in space/time and open up a new dimension. I used to think that was silly. The world can't be that fragile. Now, I know it can be. My world, anyway.

I pick an apple from the basket the Callwells, our neighbors, brought yesterday. I bite, roll a piece of Granny Smith in my mouth, chew, swallow. My stomach hurts.

Throw it out. Forget it.

No, keep eating. It'll give me something to do.

I carry the apple with me as I pad up the carpeted stairs.

Stay downstairs, Dad needs your help!

No, I need a minute. I need to put this scene behind me, just for a second.

Why? This isn't something I can leave behind. It'll just come into the room with me.

Christ! Can't I even get a second, please?

I make it to my room. It's like the workroom in a way, a mix of clean and sloppy. Dirty laundry mingled with clean. My guitar's on the floor, buried in a litter of carefully handwritten songs. I never wanted guitar lessons. I didn't want lessons to mess up the noises I made. But I play for an hour every day.

On the bed, my laptop's next to a neat pile of school notes written in a sloppy scrawl. A notice from that new computer teacher, Mr. Schapiro, sits on top. He's looking for someone with soldering skills to help fix some circuit boards. Could be me. I don't know jack about programming, but Dad taught me to solder when I was ten.

That, at least, is something I can fix. I could make it work.

What, am I nuts? Go back to school? Why? I never want to see that damn cage again. Schapiro's probably as bad as the rest.

Oh? And do what instead, exactly?

Quit. Take the guitar, go to that new coffee dive with the big rat on the sign.

I wouldn't last a day. Besides, Dad would kill me, or worse, kill himself.

Screw him! Live!

Screw you! You can't just do whatever you want!

You? Who are you talking to, exactly?

Me. I'm talking to me. It's freaky that I have to remind myself. I can't believe what Mom said before she died, that it was so important to her. I can't even decide whether to sit on the floor or lie on the bed, and the buzz in my head just gets worse and worse.

Stay in school! There was that girl in class I wanted to talk to. Denby.

Quit. Sing. I can still talk to Denby. Be easier to hook up with her if I'm a rebel guitarist.

No. Hold it together. For myself, for Dad . . .

The guy who already said he felt like drinking again? What does he care about me? Besides, that particle collider might end the world any day now.

He's sick. He needs my help. Even a particle collider can be fixed.

Mom was sick, too. I sat by her side for days and what did that do? Still dead, isn't she?

Mom, what am I supposed to do?

CHAPTER 1

About Three Years Later . . .

Denby thinks too much. Other than the ability to live my life the way I want, she's my favorite thing, but I have to face it, she's a thinker. Oh, on the outside she's as serene as wildflowers on a rolling hill, with blue-sky eyes and a dirty-blond breeze. Inside? Her brain's a dark electrical storm.

Like right now, we're at The Rat. The whole point of being here is that there's nothing to think about. That's why people come. Yeah, they come to see me, but it's also about *not* thinking, not studying, letting the air out of your shoes. No one cares what you do, long as it's legal, and, hey, if it's not, just take it out to the alley. It's The Rat!

But Denby? She's not sitting ten minutes when she reaches behind the coffee bar and grabs the card deck that time forgot. Hey, I love games. Life's a game. *I'm* a game. But I know she's up to something else. Only, what?

She slips them out of the cozy cardboard and I can't take my eyes off her. I'm logjammed with her and the cards. Then she makes them all face the same way, which is anal even for Denby. I should know. We've been together, what? Two years? She's perfect except for this . . . this . . . *thinking*.

I try not to watch. I let my gaze wander through the wonderfully dim open room full of brown round tables and disaffected teens. Everyone's thought-free, sipping java, hanging, looking forward to the steam from my music machine.

The damn cards call me back, though. The abstract reds and whites mess with the table browns and bad-lighting yellows. Bit by bit, row by row, I sit and watch her card house grow. No metaphor, an *actual* house of cards.

"What are you doing?" I finally ask.

"Playing a game," she says, her sky-eyes riveted on her hand's machinations. "You like games, right? This is a game, that's a game?"

"Yeah . . . so?"

"So I've been thinking about this poem we read in English class, by someone named Rumi. It's all about games. It reminded me of us. I even memorized it:

Since we've seen each other, a game goes on.
Secretly I move, and you respond.
You're winning, you think it's funny.

But look up from the board now, look how
I've brought in furniture to this invisible place,
so we can live here."

She gives me a smile and a wink.

I quit school, but I'm not dumb. I get it. That's what she's been thinking about, moving furniture into that card house. It's a metaphor for commitment. A commitment from me to her. I bet she was waiting for me to ask, so she could recite that poem and suck me into the same conversation we've been having for months.

How many times do I have to tell her that long-term planning is not where I'm at? It's unfair to keep bringing it up, not Rat-like. Denby is not one with The Rat.

"Well, I'll tell you," I say. "All you've got there, Denby, is a skyscraper for ants. And I'm sure there are lots of other ants ready to commit and commute to it, get ant-jobs with ant-benefits, lead lives of quiet ant-desperation, ant–day in, ant–day out, until an ant–particle collider wipes 'em out and they spend their final ant-moments wondering what the ant-hell it was all about. Or maybe they just eat their dead. I dunno. Who can figure bugs? But I am not one of those ants, okay?"

"They shut down that collider, remember?"

"They'll build another, I'm sure. Not that it'll do Rivendale's unemployment rate any good. You know how many people lost their jobs? See how silly it is to plan?"

She ignores me. Keeps building. Worse, she starts whistling.

I have to knock it down. Not out of anger, or revenge, but from a selfless need to liberate Denby from this notion that it's somehow important to build and plan things, like card houses and relationships.

It'll take time. I'll have to wait for the right moment.

Knock it down too soon and it won't matter. She'll expect it, and then she won't care. If I wait too long, though, she'll be finished, and then she won't care either. And if she doesn't care, what's the point? It'd be like writing a love song after you've forgotten you were in love. I have to wait for the moment she cares the most, then yank it away from her.

I wait for a sign to tell me the time is nigh. Finally, it comes: the last card, the last one she has to place to finish her house, happens to be a joker. The only one in the deck, too. I know, because sometimes I play poker with the owner, Po. No worries. I'm here. I'm the missing joker.

I stand like I'm going to the can, but only walk two steps away. I face her back and give myself a moment to appreciate the scene. She's beautiful. Her arms are spread, bare elbows on the table. The loose flaps of her kelly green shirt form enticing armpit hollows, perfect for my needs. The tip of a black and emerald tattoo in the small of her back juts from the lip of her jeans. Her sneakered foot taps, trying to burn the excess energy in her body so she can keep her hand steady for that one . . . last . . . card.

In silence, I wave my hands over my head. I'm the main attraction here, so The Rat's many heads slowly turn to me. There are times, like this, when The Rat becomes a single creature; loner stoners, dreaming emos, chic-geeks, and lock-and-stock jocks, all melting into one big blob. I know that creature well.

"What are you up to?" The Rat wonders. "Will you make us laugh again?"

I nod toward Denby and the card house. In true silent-film comedy fashion—Charlie Chaplin, Buster Keaton—I widen my eyes and wickedly rub my hands together. The Rat grins. The Rat understands. The Rat wants it, too. It's Trickster's business.

Trickster is the Clown-king, the god of messing things up to remind us that nothing lasts. I used to hate him, back when I lived in the suburbs with my parents. These days, I like to think we're buds, that I am the herald of his truth, that it is better to break than to be broken.

Only Po, The Rat's Barista/Keeper, rolls his eyes at me as he stands behind the coffee bar. Buzzkill. Thinks he knows what makes me tick, what makes me tock, but really, I'm the one who gives this place myth and meaning. I'm the one who started the rumor that this place was originally called The Rat because of the giant momma rodent living in the basement. Even Po bought into that one. So let him roll his eyes. The momma rat is real enough. Po brings a gun whenever he heads down there.

Hee-hee. Denby's too wrapped up to notice how the world has subtly shifted, how everyone's staring. But, hey, when you're thinking too much? Anything that doesn't involve anxiety's object—gone. Dead as the dead themselves. That's when the Clown-king comes to mess with you.

Index fingers out, I cry, "Hail, Trickster!" and jam my wiggling index fingers into the soft spot below her armpits. The results? A slo-mo explo, like the Hiroshima A-bomb, only there's no lasting damage to the environment, no mutilated survivors or increased cancer rates. The plastic-coated rectangles erupt into the air. Denby lunges forward, a laugh escaping from her mouth before she can swallow it. A stolen laugh. Better than a stolen kiss.

It is done. Oh, Denby, I've wrested you from the tyranny of your own hopes and wishes, set you loose in the greater world! Behold the wonder that is me!

Or not. Slo-mo stops. Real time resumes. Airy sounds rush in where fantasies fear to tread. From behind, I see Denby's cheeks burn with realization. She rises, spins toward me, and pounds her fists into my chest so hard I can imagine the bruises.

"Son of a bitch! Bastard!" she says. After that, her screams go wordless. Just the raw feeling rushes out of her mouth, vague vowels that make my eardrums crackle.

Words of explanation gurgle up my throat like water from a tap, but, let's face it, I'm screwed. She's stronger than she looks and angrier than I've ever seen. What to do?

I . . . laugh. I can't help it. The Rat laughs, too. When she realizes they've all been watching, surprise and hurt mix with shame and she storms off to the bathroom. She's so loud that despite the ringing in my ears from her screams, I hear her feet pound on the floorboards.

"Oooo . . . ," says The Rat, like the kid sister I never had. As in, "Oooo, you are in *trouble* now!"

Ah, The Rat. They don't just think I'm an asshole, they know it. I don't disagree, but I also like to think

(a) I'm not *just* an asshole and (b) assholes have their uses.

I follow her. I've won the game, but I want to be sportsmanlike. In an odd moment of theme coordination, the ladies' room door has a tile on it with a stylized card-deck queen. Much as I love signs from the gods, I *hate* signs from the owners.

The Rat gasps as I open the door and walk in.

So here I am in the ladies' room, impressed at how much cleaner it is, how it doesn't smell as bad as the one we Men Must Use. It's a one-woman space, so the only privacy I interrupt is Denby's, and we both know she wants to yell at me some more. She looks at me, card-red around the eyes.

"Why? Why'd you frakking do that?"

I think about saying sorry, but I don't, since neither of us would believe it and I never apologize about anything anyway. No commitments, no regrets. Instead, I laugh again, hoping she might join in. She doesn't.

She turns from me, like she can go hide in the sink. I pull her back, saying "Hey, hey, hey . . ." as if that's an explanation. When she faces me again, I feel the heat of her rage coming off her in waves.

"Hey, hey, hey," was all I had, so I fake something. I talk so fast, I kind of hope it's real. "It was . . . an answer to your poem. You want to build things but . . . what's the point if everything falls apart?"

She doesn't skip a beat. "Bullshit. You just like breaking things."

"That, too."

She sniffles, wipes her face, looks down. I look down, too. I don't know what we're looking for.

"I hate you," she says.

"You love me."

"That, too," she admits. "But everything falls apart, right?"

Ow. Nice one.

"I'd like to be alone now," she says.

"Sure," I say. A beat, then, "Oh. You want *me* to leave?"

She rolls her eyes. At least she didn't punch or scream.

"That was a joke."

"So are you."

"I like to think I'm more of a parable."

"You *wish*. You know, you *could* be something special if you grew up, if you ever bothered writing one of your songs down, or finishing one. Until then, you're a joke, a *bad* joke, like the guy who walks into a doctor's office with a duck on his head."

I give her the punch line. "And the duck says, 'Doc, can you get this guy off my ass?'"

"Exactly," she says, not smiling. "I graduate this year, and I know you love me, but I'm not spending the rest of my life hanging out at The Rat with someone stuck on my ass, got it? That's *my* poem, Wade Jackson. Take us seriously, take *yourself* more seriously, or we're over. How's that hit you, Clown-boy?"

I blink. She nods, reading something in my face I'm unaware of.

So I leave.

I should feel chastened, but I don't. I don't believe for a second she'll leave me. I suspect that's what annoys her most.

I snag my guitar and sit on a stack of wooden plat-
forms, the kind the delivery guys move around with
forklifts. They're called pallets. Po calls them a stage. I
like to call them the Center of the Universe, so I can feel
better about where I'm singing. Alone at the Center of
the Universe, I strum and mumble to myself, working
on a little song about life as a duck with a person stuck on
his ass.

Po, knowing Denby got the best of me this round,
smiles. Funny guy. Thin, nearly hairless. Bits of African,
Asian, Anglo-Saxon all shoot out at you, depending on
his expression or the way the light hits him. "Mixed" is
an insult; Po's an "intersection" of humanity, rich and
strange. He's like a mythical creature.

He doesn't pay much, or at all sometimes, but neither of us really understands money. Mostly I get to
sleep in the storage closet upstairs and swipe sand-
wiches, as long as my singing brings people round. And
it does. I'm not a huge star, but I bring in a fair crowd. Po
won't admit it, but I think I keep the place in business.

I even have a stalker of sorts, Ant. Not the bug kind
referred to earlier, but short for Anthony, his name, and
for antennae, which he has. His fashion claim to fame
are these two ultralong locks of bristly red hair he keeps
stitched together in what he thinks look like dreadlocks.
He's always jerking his head, making those antennae
shimmy and shake, as if he can't look at any one thing
for long. The guy has the attention span of a flea.

The first night he came in and heard me play, he
said, "You've *got* to record, man! Get some MP3s out
there!" It was easy to distract him. I just said, "Hey,

look at that shiny light!" and he'd stare at that for a bit, but eventually he'd turn back and say again, "You've *got* to record, man! Get some MP3s out there!"

Took ages to explain what Denby still won't accept, that I don't do studio because I never play the same thing twice. I don't think Ant believed me until he came by regularly for about a month and kept hearing different songs. Now, Ant's someone who struggles to stay *in* school. Should be graduating, but he's a year behind. His doting mom keeps hiring tutors for him, but none of them ever work out.

Not that he doesn't enjoy life. Give him a rubber band and he'll amuse himself for hours. Lately, he and his high school homeys have been taking turns seeing how many pennies they can catch off their elbows. They play for money and the kitty gets pretty big. Ant's king of penny catching. He wins so often, it's like his salary. He's so damn proud of it, he talks about it like it's an Olympic sport. *That* he can focus on.

Denby slips out of the bathroom, hoping no one will notice. I can't let that happen. I stand at the mike and clear my throat into what I like to call the Unsound System, because even when it works it's awful, and because I'm fond of naming things.

"This is for Denby," I say, "who worries too much." And I sing:

Oh, I know I burst your bubble,
Brought down your house of cards
Dunno why I'm so much trouble
Or why we're so at odds.

But when I say I love you
The world comes crashing down
And there's nothing left to see no more
But Denby all around.

Each time I build a sentence
The words get swept away
I only want to talk to you
But don't know what to say.

'Cause when I see you smiling
My world comes crashing down
And there's nothing left to say no more
But Denby all around.

It's kind of an antifolk thing, not too inventive melodywise, but I strain my voice just right on the end notes. It sounds so full of feeling I even get a little choked up myself. *Am* I full of feeling? Dunno, but it has the desired effect.

Denby leans against the wall, teary eyed but for different reasons than before. When Ant starts a standing ovation, Denby comes running, jumps, and throws herself at me. I barely get the guitar out of the way before we fall backward on the stage. My chest still hurts from where she pounded me, but not so bad I don't forget about it when our lips meet.

I turn my head sideways and look at The Rat. It's on its feet hooting and hollering, Ant the loudest. Maybe I *did* mean it.

Either way, life's a game and I won this round.

Pulled a song out of my ass and it pulled my ass out of the fire with Denby. Things fall apart, then they come together, but you can't plan it the way Denby wants. Her days could be more like mine if she went with the flow instead of against the current.

Speaking of currents, a strong one steps in, ruining the mood, big and meaty and kind of dumb. His name's Alek. I can smell his leather duster and too-much cologne all the way from here. He stands behind Ant, not applauding, not smiling. We both know what he wants: the money I owe him. Two hundred bucks. It's the end of one game and the start of another.

"Gotta go," I whisper in Denby's ear.

"What?"

I nod toward Alek. She knows the score, so she stands, not too fast, adjusts her clothes, and makes herself scarce.

I rise and nod at the crowd. I even bow. I take a few slow steps toward Alek, like I'm going to talk to him, then run like hell out the front door. *Hakuna matata.*

CHAPTER 1

CHAPTER 1

Two Years, Eleven Months, Twenty-eight Days Later

Great. Perfect. Denby's not thinking hard enough and we can't afford it. Yes, it's not fair to her, she's typing programming code that she doesn't get, but what's fair got to do with it? It has to be right. There are no do-overs when they give Rivendale High School students access to the main computer at the Prometheus Particle Accelerator.

But try telling her that. Even before I hand her the corrections I know she'll start playing around with some game she's invented, like *no, you.*

"I know it's tough . . . ," I say.

"No, you. *You're* tough," she says, as she brushes back her straw blond hair and smiles. She's great, really. Love her so much I want to marry her.

". . . even impossible . . ."

"No, you. *You're* impossible."

". . . to type something you don't understand, but please focus. A colon out of place changes everything. This isn't poetry."

"*You're* not poetry."

We're in the computer lab, my home away from home, working hard, working late, and we're all a little punchy. Anthony, my partner in this mess, picks his head up from his laptop. "Actually, a colon out of place in a poem changes everything, too," he says.

"Not helping," I tell him. "We have to finish and we've only got until morning."

Morning. Oh, God. How many hours left?

Denby sees the paper shaking in my hand. "Wade, calm down or *you'll* be the one with a colon out of place."

I hold one hand steady with the other. "Please. The devil's in the details."

"I get it," she says, taking the paper.

Okay, so sometimes my hands shake and sometimes I get dizzy spells and actually faint. I try to hide my hands when I can. I haven't told anyone about the fainting, not Denby, not even Dad. I know it's a panic attack, but I figure I have reason to be anxious.

"Clean your colon, save the world, Captain Ahab," Anthony chimes in. He's been calling me Ahab since he was assigned *Moby-Dick* for AP English. Sometimes I call him Starbuck. Not the coffee franchise, but Ahab's first mate. Only, I don't think Starbuck was pudgy or had two red dreadlocks that stuck out from his head like antlers.

"You're trying to make it sound stupid, but it's true."

Complicated, but true. Denby doesn't understand the math, but Anthony should know better. I can't believe he treats what we're doing like it's all abstract, just numbers. But I get it.

Like all particle colliders, Prometheus shoots subatomic particles at one another in a huge ring miles long. When they *collide*, they either break into smaller particles or fuse into bigger ones. This lets us see the basic building blocks of reality. That's the whole point of a particle collider—it's one big science experiment. Once we smash enough atoms to study *all* the particles, we think we'll understand, well, everything.

But knowledge has a price. In this case, if those collisions ever create a particular particle called a "strangelet" (specifically a negative strangelet) and if it happens to travel across the vacuum inside the ring and touch the ring itself, it would, bit by bit, change whatever it touched into more strangelets: the ring, the administrative building, the parking lot, the surrounding forest, the streets, the strip mall, the town of Rivendale, the next town, the state, the country, until the entire Earth and everyone on it would become a molten mass of . . . strange.

Things don't get much more intense than that, so yeah, my hands shake.

Hard to believe? Well, in 2000, before the smaller collider at Brookhaven was activated, they believed in the problem enough to study it. They concluded that even *if* a negative strangelet were produced, it'd have to exist more than 10^{-9} of a second to reach the ring. Strangelets don't live that long. 10^{-9} of a second is centuries in strangelet-years.

But—and there's always a but—the very first day Prometheus was turned on, it produced the first strangelet *ever* seen. It wasn't negative, so the Earth survived, but even so, they shut down immediately. This brought all of Rivendale to a standstill, since most people here work for Prometheus.

An outside group of prestigious physicists and mathematicians was rushed in, headed by the ultra-prestigious Dr. John Finley. Despite the production of a positive strangelet (which won Prometheus all sorts of accolades *while* it was shut down, btw), they calculated there was only a one-in-a-*billion* chance of a negative strangelet being produced that could last long enough to touch the ring— statistically speaking, that's less than a snowball's chance in hell.

They'd have started up the collider again after that, had not a far less prestigious group of scientists and mathematicians called the Wilson Group brought a lawsuit that kept Prometheus closed for another six months. That cost my father his job at the collider, so I have a certain bias against the Group. Their leader, Judith Wilson, wasn't worried about strangelets, oh, no. She, more *Star Trek* fan than actual physicist, had her own wacky theory that Prometheus might open up a rift to another dimension and suck us all in. Some members of the Group even went so far as to theorize that this other dimension might actually be the hell spoken of in the Bible. I don't know if they thought we'd find snowballs there.

The science was bogus, but the nationwide panic it created was real. To satisfy the Wilson Group, a super-special "anti-interdimensional, anti-hell" shielding was placed inside the ring. It was made of a new aluminum alloy that probably helped contain the vacuum but, really, it was an expensive joke. Prometheus has been running ever since, without incident.

Which brings me to today, my shaky hands, and a small detail I happened to notice. The math behind that one-in-a-billion calculation? Since the math was done *before* the shielding was installed, it didn't take its thickness into account. With the shielding, the distance a strangelet has to travel before touching the ring is *shorter*, changing the odds. I'm no Einstein, but no slouch either. When I recalculated, the odds looked more like one in *ten thousand*.

One in ten thousand. Those odds sound great if they're the chances you'd survive a life-saving operation, but for the survival of Earth itself? Not so much. The day my mother passed away, the very day a strangelet was first produced, I learned that the things you think can never happen sometimes do, that the world really can fall apart. On the lighter side, if I'm right—and I'm sure I am—to fix it, all they have to do is strip out the stupid shielding and it's back to a billion to one.

But (and here's another of those buts) I'm just a high school senior with an hour to prove it, which is why everything has to be absolutely, positively, completely right.

As if she hears me thinking, Denby lifts her coffee cup and points to the small wet ring left behind on the table. "Eep! I could've just saved a microscopic universe from death by cappuccino heating!"

"Anthony, please help me out," I say.

"Yes, Ahab," he says, wheeling back from his laptop. Antlers dangling, he recites, " 'There is a theory which states that if ever anyone discovers exactly what the Universe is for and why it is here, it will instantly disappear and be replaced by something even more bizarre and inexplicable. There is another theory which states that this has already happened.' That's Douglas Adams, from *Hitchhiker's Guide*."

"Not helping. You know, you've been a pain in the ass ever since you've been on Ritalin."

"You're just mad because my average is almost as high as yours."

"No, *you*," I say. I look at them both through bleary eyes. "I know you get the *idea*, but you don't believe it can actually happen."

Denby scrunches her face. "Anthony, do *you* think it can actually happen?"

"Does it even matter? Isn't it enough I'm working my ass off because if we're successful it's my *only* chance to get a Prometheus scholarship, wind up in a decent college, and have a life? Honestly? One in ten thousand strikes me as *great* odds. And that's what it is—odds, a game. It either happens or it doesn't. I'd hate to think I have *that* much control over anything, except maybe my bladder."

Junior year, Anthony was the first student I ever tutored. I was getting nowhere with him, no matter what I tried. He seemed smart, so it didn't make sense. Turns out he's textbook ADHD. When I showed him the questionnaire I found on the Web, he started nodding so fast it looked like his antlers might come off. It was as if it was written just for him. Ritalin worked like a charm. Calmed him and now he's straight As. Of course that doesn't means he understands *everything*.

"All right, let's get this straight, kiddies," I say. "I will now take valuable time away from our work to prove a point. *Nothing's* really random, it just *looks* that way."

I pull a penny from my pocket and toss it. "Flipping a coin, right? Random?"

It spins up six, seven, eight times before it falls. Six spins . . . seven . . . after the eighth spin down, I catch it. Heads.

I show it to Anthony. He grunts. I show it to Denby. She slaps the sides of her face with both hands. "Holy crap! I had no idea you could flip coins! Of *course* I'll marry you!"

I do it again. Heads. They're still nonplussed. I do it again. Heads. Again. Heads. After the fifth time, I've got their attention. It's an old magician's trick. You just have to make sure it spins the same number of times before you catch it.

Anthony's delighted. His antlers jiggle. "Cool! Why waste time programming when you could be out on the street making bets?"

"Because," I say, tossing the coin, "someone has to save the world."

I'm about to catch it a ninth time, when someone's long fingernails jam themselves into a sensitive spot on my ribs, tickling me. I try to fight it, but laughter bursts from my mouth. The penny hits the ground, rolls, lands. Tails.

Should've known better than to turn my back on Denby. She's all over me.

"Tickle, tickle, tickle! Who's the big man who's gonna save the world?" she says as I twitch and guffaw.

"Geez, guys, get a playpen," Anthony says.

I laugh so hard I wheeze. "Cut it out, Denby! Seriously!"

I don't sound angry, so she doesn't. But then I snap forward, out of control, and accidentally hit the keyboard, leaning in on the keys. Random characters spit into the programming code followed by a long, long stream of x's, like little kisses on an Xmas card.

"Denby! *Damn* it!"

"Sorry! Sorry!" she says, pulling back. "Oh, Wade, I'm so sorry!"

In a flash, Anthony rolls over and scans the screen. "Two hours' work at least."

Denby whimpers. Hurt, like a puppy that accidentally bit its owner too hard, she runs out. I wait until the gray metal lab door clicks shut before I even say her name.

"Denby!" I know she can't hear me. I turn to Anthony. "Should I go after her?"

He shrugs. "Wouldn't know. That's even more abstract to me than the end of the world. Never had a relationship. Just soda."

Of course I go, but I hate leaving the work behind. You have to tend things or they fall apart. Speaking of falling apart, when I open the door the school smells hit me: sneakers, sweets, sweat, old lunchroom food, mold, and a hint of cleaning fluid. I look up and down the row of lockers crumbling with rust. At the end of the hall, a fluorescent bulb crackles on and off over a half-dry puddle of cola, like in a horror movie. A lovely reminder that the lab and the computers in it, provided by the Prometheus Corporation, are the *only* new things in RHS.

The swinging door to the girls' bathroom thuds closed, so I know where Denby went. I walk up and knock.

"You okay?"

A muffled voice behind the door says, "Fine."

"Come on out. Please."

"Can't I pee?"

"Sorry."

I step back. I should bag this. Morning approaches. Time's running out. I eye the steel gray computer lab door, a trapezoid of light spilling from the bottom. Anthony will try to patch the data, but I have to check it. He's good, but he makes mistakes.

Denby or the lab? Denby or the lab? For one hour tomorrow morning, our code will run a simulation on the Prometheus computers to see if any negative strangelets come up. It's just one shot. Denby will understand that, she'll have to. I turn to go.

She must have heard me thinking again, because she comes out, leans against the wall, and looks up at me. "You don't forgive me, do you?" she says.

"Of course I do. I just . . . wish you weren't messing around tonight."

"*You* were flipping the coin."

"I was trying to make a point."

"Well . . . so was I!"

"Oh? What kind of point were you making?"

"I could be studying for my math test tomorrow, you know," she says.

"I know . . . I'm sorry . . . I just . . ."

She puts her hand up to my cheek. It sends a pleasant shiver through my body.

"Well, that's distracting," I tell her in a singsong voice.

"Yes," she says softly. "That's the point I was trying to make. Sometimes you work yourself up so much you look like you'll pass out."

I try to soften my voice. "Well, at least *my* point didn't screw up the data."

Her hand stops moving. Her face scrunches. "I really screwed it up, didn't I?"

Oh, Denby. Should I lie and say she didn't or just tell her the truth? You'd think I'd know how to react to her now — we've been seeing each other for years — but she's still the only one I know who can get to me so fast and so easy, in good ways and bad. That's why I gave her the engagement ring. Graduation's coming and, assuming the world doesn't end, if I wind up in another state for college, I'm afraid of losing her. Dad says fear isn't a good reason to get married. I, on the other hand, have always found fear to be a great motivator. She hasn't answered yet, though.

"I don't know. Anthony's fixing it."

She gives me a little kiss. "And you have to check everything he does ten times. Can't you just trust him a little more? He's almost as smart as you."

"I don't think I'm smarter."

"Yes, you do."

"Just more . . . motivated."

"If you keep going full out all night isn't it more likely *you'll* make a mistake?"

I stiffen. I can't afford to think like that. Not tonight. I say, too loud, "I've *never* made a mistake by paying too *much* attention. Paying attention got me here in the first place."

I should know better. I expect her to back down when I bark, but she gets all riled up, too. Comes from having two older brothers. Denby always stands up for herself.

"You are impossible to talk to!" she screams.

"Then don't talk to me!" Not the best comeback.

"Fine," she snaps. She starts walking away. "Thanks for making my mind up about the ring. Nice job controlling that, Wade!"

"Denby, wait!"

She spins, waits.

I walk up and pull out a crumpled piece of paper. At least my hand's not shaking now. She eyes it with great suspicion. "You want me to do more corrections?"

"No . . . it's . . . I was going to show you tomorrow, if the demo worked out."

She raises her eyebrows, unfolds the paper, and reads: "The Denby Factor?"

I shrug. "Does it sound stupid? Do you prefer The Denby Parameters or maybe just Denby 1.0?"

She's genuinely surprised. "You're naming your programming code after me?"

"Well, yeah. I hope you don't think it's as stupid as . . . you know, thinking I'm saving the Earth from evil strangelets."

She looks up into my eyes and says nothing for a long while. I'm half-expecting a clever quip or a comment about what a nerd I am, but she stretches up and kisses me. While she does, everything in me stops shaking. As she pulls slowly away, our lips are the last things that come apart.

"No," she says. "I don't think it's as stupid as believing you're saving the world."

That went well, except for the part where she still thinks what I believe is stupid. But we can work on that. Maybe tomorrow, when it turns out I'm right and Prometheus shuts down to strip out that ridiculous shielding, it'll be an even better present.

We'll see how she feels about it then.

CHAPTER 2

I dream all the time. I dream I'm someone
Denby might like better but I don't like at all,
someone who never quit school, someone who
works his tail off, someone who—get this—keeps
trying to get her to *marry* me. My drunk, dead-
beat father's around, too. I take him to AA
meetings. I help pay the mortgage. Yeah,
Prometheus, that particle collider, is even up
and running and I'm trying to fix that, too,
trying to stop it from destroying the world. I
must be nuts.

I wake with stiff muscles in a hazy chill-pill of a morning. The dream images do a sticky thing, like someone
opened my skull and poured maple syrup in, drowning
the waffles of my thought. Hmm . . . must be hungry.

Dreams, go figure. Denby says they're where you act
out your hidden desires. But I keep telling her I don't

have any. That's the point, I act them all out. Life's what I want it to be. I'm exactly who I want to be.

I sit up on my cozy park bench, stretch, and yawn like a good homeless person. In the dream the bed's comfier—I'll give it that. Even better than the one I had before I left the suburbs. Comfort. That's how they trap you in those ant-skyscrapers and McMansions. The park I slept in is in a better part of Rivendale, so I bum change until I have enough for a decent coffee, then drink it nice and slow. Now *that's* dreamy!

It's late afternoon by the time I saunter Ratward. The building, a two-story card-shaped rectangle, sits on a steep hill in exactly the kind of neighborhood you'd expect: old, worn, abandoned, *iffy*. Like you shouldn't be here *if* you scare easy, or maybe you should *if* you like a little challenge. I hear it got even bigger after a lawsuit shut the collider permanently. There's only one other business, a greasy spoon across the street. The Rat's the draw, pulling disaffected suburban kids from three counties. Kids just like me, before Mom died and I went off-grid.

With Alek's hearse-black SUV nowhere in sight, I figure I'm in the clear and head on in. And I am totally wrong. I practically bump into the big leathery lug.

"Alek! Been a whole month?"

He looks like he waited all night for me and isn't happy about it. But, if everything's a game, so's Alek. The rules for Alek are (1) Keep things light, (2) Keep things moving, (3) Keep your eyes on the nearest exit.

Mine's the door right behind me, but Alek shifts, blocking it. Good move. There's also the side door to an alley, and the rear door to the kitchen. The only way out through the kitchen is into the basement, then through an old storm door. But the basement's where that big momma rat lives, right by that door. Yeah, even though I started the rumor, she freaks me out a little, too. More than Alek does, anyway.

"Guess. What. I. Want. Wade," Alek says in his thick voice. Like it's a riddle.

"A sense of purpose?"

He points a meaty finger at the rear exit and says, "Alley. Now."

I gesture for him to go first. If he buys it, I'll just bolt out the front and maybe stay in the park a few days straight like I did last month. Between drug deals and nightclubbing, Alek rarely visits. I'm not worth the effort. Or so I thought.

"No. You. First."

Hm. There's something different going on. He's talking one word at a time, like he's trying to remember what he was told to say. Loan-shark lessons from Daddy? Bad. Alek's dumb and lovable. Daddy's Russian mob.

Why borrow from such risky quarters in the first place? It was fun! All I did was ask, and he pulled out a wad of bills, flipped off two, and handed 'em over. I spent most of it on candy. Still got a crate of Crunch bars somewhere. Denby was furious, but even she figured Alek for a big teddy bear. She wants me to pay him back because it's the "right" thing to do. Plus, she's worried his dad beats him when he screws up.

I suss the possibilities as poor abused Alek and I enter the alley, our official no-man's-land. It's where the elite meet to smoke joints, swap spit, beat each other up, or whatev. Not Po's property, not Po's business. The only cop who comes within a ten-mile radius of this neighborhood is another bit of local myth: Officer Smelser, and he's in cahoots with Klot, a psycho drug dealer. Klot's supposedly a frustrated artist. I don't know what medium he worked in, but these days it's the art of terror. Just mentioning their monikers puts fear into the hearts of everyone, everyone except me. Po says it's only because I've never met them, which gives me an idea.

I nudge Alek, point at nothing, and shout, "Oh, no! It's Klot!'

Ha! Alek nearly jumps out of his skin. What little color he has drains from his Slavic face. He looks around like a car's about to hit him.

I pat him on the shoulder. "Just kidding, man."

He glares. "Don't."

He's pissed, but it served its purpose. We both know Alek's no Klot, and it's always nice to have a little humility in the air.

It's still afternoon, but here in the shadows of two buildings, it may as well be dusk. I realize why I didn't see Alek's car. It's parked here, blocking off the head of the alley. More advice from Dad?

Turns out we're not alone. Brosius, a real stoner, leans against a sticky brick wall like he's holding it up. He always looks like he's focusing on some mountain range just out of sight. No point in saying hello. Don't think he understands the word anymore. Alek, still pissed because I mentioned Klot, grabs Brosius by the shoulders and shoves him toward the head of the alley.

"Move."

Bro, stick of a guy, stumbles forward like a floppy marionette, muttering "Oh, wow" over and over. He heads

out, leaving his pot-haze hanging in the air. I stand in it
and inhale deeply, hoping for a contact high. Not that I
envy Bro's otherworldliness, but I can always use some
stray thoughts.

When Bro reaches the SUV he stares at it for a while,
like he can't figure out how to get around. It's wedged in
pretty tight. Finally, he shrugs, opens one door, climbs
in, and gets out the driver's side. Sometimes the only
way around things is through them.

Alek rolls his eyes, then steps up close, showing me
his height, his strength, his dull eyes.

"One. Thousand. Dollars. Now."

A grand? Geez. High interest rate. But things are not
so bleak. I just move to the Advanced Rules for playing
Alek. When he thinks, he does it slowly. If I talk fast,
time it right, give him something to do, it's like his brain
can't keep up. It'll start to confuse what I'm saying with
its own thoughts.

"Alek, you got a pen?"

He pulls out a Bic. I slip it into my pocket. See how I
did that?

"Been. Ten. Weeks."

I put two fingers against my lips and nod toward a
crumpled pack jutting from his duster pocket. "Can I
bum one? A cigarette?"

He pulls out the pack. "No. More. Time. Tonight."

I nod vigorously. "Light?"

He hands me a yellow disposable lighter, also a Bic.
"Nothing. Personal."

I light up, puff, pocket the lighter, and wonder if
he'd give me his watch. Wait. Better idea.

"Hey, Alek, got another hundred I can borrow?"

He almost does it. His hand moves toward his wallet, but then he stops, bundles up a fistful of my T-shirt in his hand, and pulls me toward his face.

The next sentence is his own: "You think I'm an idiot, Wade?"

"You? No. No way." But, yeah, sure I do. I do think he's an idiot. Big and stupid as they come. I mean, who has the pen, the lighter, and the cigarette, me or him?

"I need that money. I did something that really pissed off my father, okay? If I don't make up for it by tomorrow, he takes the car keys. I need that money to help make up for it."

Bingo. The last puzzle piece. Alek's life is nothing without the wheels.

"What'd you do? Forget to take out the recycling?"

He pulls me closer, his hamburger breath dispersing the pot smell in the air.

"You *don't* want to know. I need the money tonight."

"Okay, but really, man, what'd you do?"

He tightens his grip. Whatever it was, it's not as easy to get out of him as a pen or a lighter.

"Got it," I say. He lets go, leaving behind a rumple the size of his fist's inside. He pats it down. I'm about to ask to borrow his jacket, but don't get a chance, because he slams his big fist up into my diaphragm.

"Just. To. Make. Sure. We're. On. The. Same. Page."

Daddy again. Alek's not a hitter. He was even holding back. I crumple against the wall just to make him feel better.

"Hey, Alek?" I moan. "Got that extra hundred?"

He pulls a single bill from his wallet and tosses it. It

flutters, lands at my feet, touches my sneaker. I think, like Bro, "Oh, wow." I could probably get him to jump off a cliff.

"Tonight."

"No problemo."

Like they say, where there's a will, there's a way. Alek steps aside. I snatch the cash, pretend to give my body and my self a moment to get reacquainted, then head back in. What did he do to get Daddy so pissed? Ah, screw it.

No need to pretend to hurt anymore, so I straighten. The crowd's picked up in my absence. Having customers to deal with doesn't keep Po, who apparently watched me leave with Alek, from telling me how wrong I am. "Going to get yourself killed this time, Clown-boy."

"Po, man, I know what I'm doing. Trust me."

"Trust *you*?" he says. His laugh sounds like a small animal wheezing. "One day you're going to wake up in a motel with a kidney missing, just like my uncle!"

Right. He loves to tell me about his stupid kidney-free uncle.

Denby's not here. Good. She works after school doing data entry to pay her rent. Left home a few months ago, after a big fight with her folks over, well, me. That's when all her commitment thinking started. She keeps inviting me to her place, but I won't go. It'd be like a first step toward a real relationship. Hell, I didn't ask her to leave home.

And right now it's easier to move without her sense of right and wrong, easier to feel my way through the ether, easier to just ask, without judgment, "Oh where, oh where could a thousand bucks be?"

There. Good old Ant is playing pennies-on-the-elbow. The pile in front of him is even bigger than before. It's at least a thou.

I saunter up. "Gambling again, Ant-man?"

He smiles widely, unable to hide the fact that he's happy I'm paying attention to him. "It's a living, Clown-boy."

I want to grunt. I generally only allow Po and Denby to use that nickname, and then only when they're mad at me. But I want him to keep smiling.

"Want to try?" he says, antennae wiggling.

Hm. I was just going to ask him for the money, but winning it could be more fun. It's a weird game, the penny-elbow thing, but I've seen them do it often enough.

I grab a copper with my left hand and bend my right arm so the elbow's up and my wrist is near my ear. It's almost like a yoga position. Then, with my left hand I carefully place the penny flat on my right elbow. Now all I have to do is move my right hand forward fast enough to catch the penny while it's in midair. I do—*snap*—only I don't.

The penny hits the floor where the light doesn't go.

Ant loves it! Finally, something he can do that I can't.

"Slow down," he says.

I balance, slow. I wait, slow. I snatch, slow. Thud. Falls just as fast.

"No, no," Ant says. "Watch. Imagine yourself catching the penny, then do it."

I've never seen him so focused. He'd probably be a doctor or a lawyer or a computer geek if his brain let him stay on the same subject for more than a minute.

Snap! One second the penny's on his elbow, the next it's not, like a magician palming a card. Where'd it go? Did it . . . disappear? Ant unrolls his fingers, revealing the penny in the center of his palm. I whistle.

"Ant-man, what's the most you've ever caught at one time?"

He shrugs. "Nineteen. Twenty, once."

"Twenty, ha! No one saw that except you," a sniggering penny-snapping pal says.

"Fine. Nineteen," Ant says, vaguely deflated.

"Now, now," I say. "He is an Ant of honor. He says twenty, it was twenty. But the thing is, Ant, would you give me ten-to-one odds if I did twenty-*one*?"

He blinks for a second, not sure he heard me right, then his antennae set to shivering. "Geez, Wade, I'd give you twenty to one!"

He laughs. I laugh. His friends laugh. We're all laughing our asses off.

I put the hundred down on the table.

"Ten to one's good enough."

"Ooooo!" say his pals.

Ant twitches and stares. "Wade, this is *my* game. Don't throw your money away."

One of his friends pats me on the shoulder. "I think he's challenging you."

"Then it's a hundred easy bucks for you, Ant-man. Unless I win."

I'm not hustling him. I really *did* miss twice. I've

never caught a single thing off my elbow. I'm just count-
ing on Trickster to side with me because, well, because
it would be funny.

Ant looks at my money. "No. Forget it. I'm saving
you from yourself."

I push it. "What are you, a penny-wimp? Wussy?" I tap
him on the shoulder. "Pound-wise and penny-foolish?
Penny saved is a penny earned? Penny for your thoughts?"
I tap him harder and harder, trying to get those antennae
to move. I'm not making any sense, but it doesn't matter.
Everyone's snickering at him. He's totally embarrassed,
almost beet red, and he doesn't even know why.

"Fine!" he shouts, swatting my hand away. "Your
funeral, Clown-boy!"

He counts his money, then realizes he knows exactly
how much he has. He pulls a twenty off the top, then
pushes the rest toward me.

"When you gotta go, you gotta go, Ant-man."

He grabs some pennies, counts, and stacks. I eye the
little tower and say, "Drumroll, please."

The gang at the table pounds with fists and fingers on
whatever's handy—*didididididididididididididididididididi*.
Soon, the whole Rat joins in.

I pull up my sleeve. I narrow my eyes. With great cer-
emony, I lift the stack. I practically hear Ant thinking,
"He can't do it . . . Can he? Nah . . . Can he?"

The drumroll gets faster, louder. The Rat-people add
eerie hums and cymbal crashes. You can't pay for inci-
dental music like this. I'd better get this over with fast
before someone starts playing air guitar and I feel like
busting a move.

I put the stack on my elbow and remove my fingers.

The second I do, I realize there's no way that penny-pile will stay balanced for more than half a second. Uh-oh. The tiny tower already flops, ready to fall like a house of cards when I . . . *snap!*

The drumroll stops. And?

The pennies are snug in my palm. Twenty of them. One, just *one*, separated. But I haven't dropped it yet. It's wedged between my fourth finger and pinky, threatening to slip out. I pivot my wrist. It stays.

"Hail, Trickster!"

The Rat *cheers*! There are thundering claps and stunning air-guitar riffs. They like this better than my songs. Ant-man? He looks like I ran over his mom. Well, he's old enough to make his own decisions. Game over.

I snatch the bills and turn to my adoring Rat. "I'm here every night through Tuesday!"

I head back to the alley. Alek's there, talking on his cell, probably about that thing I don't want to know about. Whatev.

"Calm down, I'm not scared. My dad won't *let* me bring it myself, Sergei. I'll get you the money, but why can't you meet me? Wait, got an idea. A messenger okay?"

"Al?" I say. He looks up like he doesn't remember me until I hold out the wad of bills.

I put a hundred in his hand. "That's what you just gave me." I count. "Here's another nine hundred dollars. That makes a thousand. So we're square, right? All paid up?"

He looks at the pile. For a second I think he may figure out I'm only paying a thousand when I owe him eleven hundred. But he doesn't. He just grins, says, "All

even," and goes back to his call. I pocket the extra hundred and head back inside, free as a bird.

Ant-man's gone. Probably licking his wounds but,
geez, you'd think he could shake it off. Any gambler
knows you win some, you lose some. It probably just
stings a little more because it was me.

Po eyes me from the bar. "Trickster. Ha. You think
you're a cartoon, like Bugs Bunny or SpongeBob. You
think Trickster loves you like a brother, but sooner or
later he's going to do to you exactly what you do to everyone else—take you apart, piece by piece."

He shows me his back, makes a motion like a knife
slashing against the skin of his lower abdomen, where I
guess the kidney is. "Just like my uncle."

CHAPTER 2

After days of trying to do the right thing, I always
dream I'm doing the wrong thing, that Dad's van-
ished, probably drinking, that our house is gone,
and that I am smug and stupid. I quit school, play
lousy songs in a coffee-bar dive, and think it's the
center of the universe. I don't want to commit to
anything—not to my music, not to friends, not even
to Denby. Something's always falling apart, but
I'm too stupid to worry. I just think it's funny, like
life's a game. A game? Only in my dreams.

The next morning, by the time I stumble downstairs after
about an hour's sleep, Dad's at the breakfast table, reading
Entertainment Weekly and biting a piece of soy bacon with a
look of infinite grief. He hates the soy, wants the real pig,
or at least turkey (it's like something *has* to die for it to
be tasty), despite what I keep telling him about his choles-
terol. I figure if he can manage to stay sober almost seven-
teen years, he can eat healthy, too.

Behind him, through the picture window, I see the little bay and Mom's bridge. The hard part about still living here is all the reminders that she's gone. Dad says that'll be a comfort eventually, like it is for him, but it's been almost three years and I'm still waiting.

I let loose a sound a moose might make, which Dad recognizes as a yawn.

"Same dream?" he says, slapping on a smile. "Means you're working too hard."

I'm better at taking that you-work-too-hard stuff from him than from Denby. But today, I bristle just the same.

"I know," he says, sucking soy from between his teeth. "Today's the big day when you get them to fix Prometheus and save mankind. I am proud of you. Really."

I know he is. I also know he's a little worried that if I'm right, they may shut down again. His job there wasn't much, but he lost it when they closed the first time. These days he's still connected to it, like everyone else. Literally. He manages a Jiffy Lube on the main road leading to the collider, changing oil for his former fellow employees. If they go, so does his business. Hates the job, but it's all he's got right now.

Yet not once in all the time I've been working on this, not once has he spelled that out for me, warned me of the economic consequences for us or the town. So yeah, he can tell me I work too hard.

"Right or wrong, Wade, when it's done, do me a favor? Cut school and spend a day with Denby, okay? A day where you just kick back and don't mention *marriage*, which, by the way, even though you are eighteen, I am still against."

He may manage a Jiffy Lube, but all those AA meetings

make him more like a therapist with all his healthy-mind talk. He quotes the Twelve Steps to me so often, I keep telling him he should hang a shingle.

"Like I'm really going to cut class in my senior year. Right."

I pour a cup of coffee, slouch down into a chair, and change subjects. "Just once, I wish I could dream about things being the way I want."

Dad gets up and pats me on the shoulder. "You probably do. You did play guitar once upon a time. Maybe you miss it."

"Please. Everyone thinks if the subconscious says it, it must be some deep truth. What if it's just a kluge?"

"Kluge?"

"A clumsy solution. Maybe that's how our brains evolved. Maybe there was this totally efficient lizard brain and our human consciousness just got stuck on top of it at the last minute. Dreams? The result of a bad design."

"So when you're done saving the Earth, you're going to work on evolution?"

I sip my coffee. "Maybe. It's not very efficient."

He knows I'm kidding, so he laughs as he walks to the garage door. In general, I try not to argue with him too much. It's gotta be tough on his ego knowing he comes up with only half the mortgage, and the rest comes from his teen son's automated Web-based tutorial business. Aside from saving the world, I'm also, like Anthony, really looking forward to the Prometheus scholarship. Then Dad won't have to deal with my college bills at all and *he* can take some time off from work and go spend it with a girl.

But all of that comes down to the next few hours.

Wouldn't it be weird if that negative strangelet were being generated right now? I look around and try to imagine the edges of the world disintegrating. There'd probably be just one strangelet at first, but it would bump some other sub-atomic particle, then there'd be two, four, eight, sixteen, and eventually one would touch the outside ring and it would all be over. If someone noticed early enough, there might be time to shut the collider down, and the strangelets might die out, but you'd have to catch it fast. Brr.

Denby's right, I'm on overload. Is the code correct? Did I go over Anthony's corrections carefully enough? Even the fact that I didn't find anything wrong makes me nervous, like I didn't look hard enough. Sometimes it's only finding mistakes and fixing them that calms me down. Should I check again, if only to help myself chill?

No, no time.

One of Mom's projects hangs in the kitchen, an old window frame with a mirror stuck behind it. She never painted it, so the old finish on the frame is peeling. We kind of like the way it looks. I look in the mirror and try to do a little trick the Samurai used before going into battle: I stick out my tongue and make the most ridiculous face I can. It's supposed to remind you how silly life is, how silly you are, but I don't feel silly, just scared. And my hands still shake.

I head to school in my hybrid—another gift from the Web tutorial business. It also earned me a great mattress, a skylight, and mobile Internet connections for our comput-ers. Car's the best. If I keep it under thirty it runs on bat-tery and doesn't use a drop of gas.

What if I did miss something? For the want of a nail, the war was lost.

Wait. I can have the computer voice read the code out loud to me. That way I can check it while I'm driving. I flip open my rig on the seat next to me and press Start. It's a slow boot. The code takes up nearly my whole drive, but it finally kicks in. Hearing it read by a robo-voice makes it tough to follow, but if I focus I can manage. Details, details. So far, so good.

For ten minutes, as I drive, I don't hear a single mistake, but then *I* make one. I almost run a stop sign.

I slam on the brakes. Tires squeal, everything lurches forward. From the corner of my eye, I see the laptop fly toward the edge of the seat. I lunge to catch it. I manage to clamp my thumb and forefinger on the corner, but I'm a fraction of a second, just a fraction of a second, too slow. It slips from my fingers and slams to the hard floor with a gross crack of metal and plastic.

Damn! Damn!

I sit there, paralyzed, my heart pounding like the jackhammer beat of the lousy seventies music Denby likes to dance to. I hate that stuff. I feel so light-headed. I hate that even more. Did I just ruin everything?

I don't want to look, but I force myself. I pick up the rig. The display gives me the blue screen of death—a really bad sign. I try to reboot. As I do, I feel the keys wobble. It's cracked down the freaking middle. The best I can manage is a shutdown.

Don't panic. Don't panic. It's not—ha—the end of the world.

That's right. It isn't. Anthony has a copy on his laptop, with all the changes from last night, and there's an earlier version on the school mainframe. Two backups. So, no problem, no problem, other than my laptop being destroyed.

That should make me feel better, but it doesn't. I still feel like I'm going to pass out.

As I sit there freaking, a squirrel runs in front of the car. It looks at me, runs back to the sidewalk, then back in front of the car. Now he sits there like he's waiting for me to run him over, the little white furs on his chest rising and falling with his quick breaths. We're both frozen in the face of danger. Where's the evolutionary advantage in that? Gotta be a kluge, in the squirrel, in me.

I know it's weird as we stare at each other, but kind of peaceful. My pulse slows. I shake my head and get back to myself. I fold the broken laptop and put it in a safer position on the floor. The squirrel's still there, so I honk, lightly. He doesn't budge. I honk louder. Still nothing. I open the door, planning to scoot him away personally. The second my foot hits the ground, he scampers off, darting among the trees.

Much like the squirrel, I speed to school, letting the gas engine kick in. I park, nearly fall out of the car, and run, pushing my way through the morning crowd of students, earning a few curses, and finally stumbling into the lab.

Anthony and Mr. Schapiro are already there, looking up as I enter. Without a hello, I say to Anthony, "Got your rig?"

He holds it up. "Yours?"

"Don't ask. We'll use your copy. Boot and hook it up."

"Oh crap!" he says. Now he's tense, too, antlers bobbing. Having someone else worried makes me feel better, but not much.

"It'll be fine, just fine!" Mr. Schapiro says. He smiles,

but I can tell he's worried, too. A balding short guy with rimless glasses, he blinks whenever he's excited. Right now his eyelids flutter so fast it looks like his head may take off. So the three of us stand there worried until the code shows up on Anthony's laptop.

"You make any more changes?" he asks.

I shake my head. "Didn't find any mistakes. What you've got is what I had."

"Excellent!" As Anthony connects a cable from the laptop to the school's mainframe he and Schapiro visibly relax. Me, I go straight to the next part—will any of it work?

"Where's Denby?" I ask.

Anthony's face twists in an odd way when I mention her name. "She waited until the late bell, then said she'd check in as soon as her math test is over. Asked me to kiss you for her, but that's not going to happen."

As Zero Hour approaches, Mr. Schapiro steps up and grabs my hand in both of his. He briskly rubs the back of my hand to calm me down. "Steady, Wade, steady. It'll be fine and, even if it isn't, at least it will be over, right?"

He's trying to help, but "it will be over" can be interpreted in more ways than one.

He backs off, slapping his hands together in a concluding clap. "Look, boys, I can't stay. I'm just here to wish you the best. I hope you're right, Wade. I hope you shut down the whole freaking Prometheus system!"

Anthony and I give him a look. "Mr. Schapiro, that's not what we're going for. I just want them to fix it."

He swallows, straightens. "Of course. Of course."

I'm starting to understand why he isn't allowed in the room when we connect to Prometheus. He and his ex-wife were involved in the Wilson Group, the people responsible for the stupid shielding in the first place. I assume he left because he realized how ridiculous they were. He swears his activist days are over, but little comments like that make you wonder. It's also a sign of how much power Prometheus has in Rivendale. They can kick teachers out of their own classrooms.

But Schapiro shakes it off and gets excited all over again. He pats me hard on the shoulder, like I'm justifying his entire teaching career in one fell swoop. Done with me, he slaps Anthony so hard his antlers hit his eyes. Then, finally, he leaves.

"Worse than Mom," Anthony says. "And she makes better cookies."

As the clock clicks down, I breathe quickly again. Surprisingly, when Anthony's laptop announces, right on time, that the connection with Prometheus has been made, I actually calm down. It means things are working so far.

A window opens and we're greeted by the visage of Dr. John Finley. He headed up the group of prestigious scientists who originally calculated the one-in-a-billion figure, then he stayed on to work as chief media liaison at Prometheus. He's essentially the collider's public face.

"Wade and Anthony! Good morning. Good to meet you!"

His voice is clipped, hurried, but there's an affable calm to his demeanor, like he's not just rich and important, he's also balanced and self-actualized. Dad's wrong. Dr. Finley's who I want to be, not the guitar-playing parasite of my dreams.

"It's an honor, sir," Anthony says. Sounds lame, so I'm glad he said it, not me.

Finley doesn't answer. He looks like he's glancing at the time on the screen, thinking about wherever he has to be next. This is probably just a PR thing for him, proving yet again how safe Prometheus is.

"Shall we get on with the science project, guys?"

"Sure," I say.

All we have to do is click Start on the program on Anthony's laptop. Everything's automated after that. He moves toward his rig, then hesitates.

"You take the wheel, Ahab."

"Sure thing, Starbuck."

I lean over to move the mouse but, all of a sudden, I freeze. My blood pressure shoots up and my heart pounds. My hand vibrates so much it looks like I'll miss the key if I try. Seeing this, Anthony surreptitiously reaches up and clicks the button for me. Thank you, Starbuck.

The programming code winds its way through sundry firewalls and into the simulator on-site at Prometheus. I'm a little disappointed that there's no huge power hum or other exciting sound effects. It's totally silent as our data uploads, a small indicator bar rising.

Finley looks bored, even as our simulation starts to run. Not us. Now Anthony's freaking, too. His antlers shake as much as my hands.

Whenever there's a theoretical collision, colored pixels smash each other and make more colored pixels. We're set to do ten thousand runs. If just one produces a negative strangelet that lasts long enough to reach the shielding, I'm right. The whole process will take about an hour. Time passes like molasses.

The first six thousand times, nothing happens. It's

possible I could be right and *still* nothing will happen. How about that, huh? I could be completely correct and this could still amount to absolutely nothing. The ten thousand and first run could produce the strangelet, and we'd never know, until it happened for real, in which case, it would be too late.

I tap my tongue against my teeth. I try to think about anything except the fate of the world, but it's hard, you know?

At run 7,267 something does happen. We get ourselves a bright green pixel. It's lighter, a different green than we've see before. I'm not sure what it is, but when Finley doesn't look bored anymore, I suspect. He looks curious, then perplexed, then fascinated. Everything the light green pixel touches also turns light green, until the whole screen goes light green and freezes. Now, I'm certain.

Anthony looks at me, eyes widening, like, *Does that mean what I think it does?*

I don't say anything. I don't think I can. I wait for Finley to finish scanning his screen, wait as a weird, befuddled smile plays across his face.

He looks up into the webcam and says, "Gentlemen," as though he doesn't believe it himself, "it looks like your calculations are correct."

"Yes!" Anthony shouts. "Yes!"

I was right. I don't know whether to be thrilled or terrified.

"We have an important discussion ahead of us," Finley says. "I'm at the Marriott Conference Center, two minutes from you. Can you meet me? And I'd appreciate it if you didn't discuss what you've seen here with anyone from the press until we do."

Discuss what we've seen? I can't even talk.

"We are so there!" Anthony says.

I clear my throat and manage, "I'm sure under the circumstances we can get a pass from school for the day."

"I'm sure you can," Finley says. "I hope you like strawberries."

His com screen vanishes.

Anthony leaps out of his seat and dances around the lab. "Strawberries! He's giving us strawberries! Never liked them before but I love them now!"

He hoots so loudly that Schapiro, who was probably waiting right outside the door anyway, rushes in to hug him. I lean back and exhale for what must be twenty minutes. They'll have to strip out the shielding to make the collider safe, but that won't take too long, will it? They'll probably want to shut down immediately.

I grab my cell. First I'll call Dad, then Denby. I'm thinking Denby 1.0 is the better title. The Denby Factor is still okay, though. Wonder which she'll pick.

As the cell connects, it dawns on me that Finley was two minutes away all along, so maybe this *wasn't* just a publicity stunt to him. Maybe he knew I was on to something. And that, that makes me feel so damn good, I actually manage to stop worrying for a while.

CHAPTER 3

CHAPTER 3

I, Super-Wade, concoct a computer program proving not only that Prometheus is dangerous but showing how to fix it. With loyal hunchback assistant Ant by my side, I present it to Powerful Particle Dude. He's like, "Thanks, Super-Wade and Hunchback-Ant for saving our undeserving world! You shall be bestowed with fame, fortune, and fresh strawberries!"

Sometimes the comic-book colors of my dream bleed into reality. For instance, right now there's a hellish pit to my left and Death itself to my right. I balance on crumbling brick. I stand on one bare foot. I hop, I turn. Flecks of red rock tumble as I sip from Po-provided Styrofoam. I do not spill a drop. It's like tai chi, only unstructured and undisciplined, which means it's not like tai chi at all. It's *my* chi.

"Will you get down from there?" Denby says,

annoyed. She's being a bummer again, thinking. Worse, thinking about me.

"No," I say back.

She clenches her teeth and slams her school books against her hip.

We're in the Alley-Oops, on the opposite side of The Rat from where I met Alek. It's too small to be a real alley. It looks more like a mistake. So, Alley-Oops. Usually no one comes here except me, but today Denby rushed over during the school lunch break just to bring me down.

"You could fall!"

"No, I can't."

I'm in my favorite duds—a worn bathrobe and boxers. Denby's in tight jeans and a light blue shirt that are hard to keep my eyes off. Fortunately, the robe's grand, a multicolored thing she got me at the Salvation Army. The loose threads are like little decaying rainbows. I love the way it flops around as I move. Makes it easier to ignore her.

"Are you trying to kill yourself because I'm pissed you stole money from Anthony?"

"Nope. Do it every day. It's my morning thing. Though, technically, since I've slept in, it's an afternoon thing. And I didn't *steal* it, I *won* it!"

She's right about one thing, I could kill myself. To my left there's a ten-foot drop onto concrete. If I fell that way, I could crack my skull or break my leg. The other side's the real charm, though. There, the hillcrest that The Rat sits on ends in a sheer drop.

After ten feet of brick wall, there's another fifteen

of fieldstone and sloppy cement. It looks like a mountainside and ends in a huge pile of rusty car parts, microwaves, baby carriages, broken glass, and black plastic bags full of God-knows-what. It's the edge of a huge junkyard.

"You should have seen him this morning. He was so crushed he looked sick! He's practically being thrown out of school because he's failing everything already, and that stupid game was the only thing he lived for. You took it from him! And all he ever did was idolize you!"

"His problems are *not* my responsibility."

Things live down there, among the garbage. Sundry vermin slither and crawl in the many in-between places. Some believe the junkyard is where the Basement Rat was born and that the rest of the rodents are kept in check only by Death, the junkyard dog. He's kind of like Klot, the way people talk about him. Not the wannabe artist stuff, just the psycho-killer part.

I named him Death myself, called him that in a song I did about the birth of The Rat. He's a thick-muscled mongrel with a big floppy face, always lying in front of the huge tire pile that forms the hollow cave where he lives.

I point him out to Denby. "They say that dog killed a man, tore out his throat. That's why Death is now forever held by that chain driven deep into the earth by a single spike. It's the very same chain the Greek gods used to pin Prometheus, the jerk who gave fire to man. So, Ant could have it worse. He could be the dead guy, or the dog, or the chain."

Denby does not groove on my story. "Fix this, Wade. Play him again and *lose!*"

Sounds like fun, actually, but (i) I only try to fix things in my dreams and (ii) . . .

"Can't. Already used the money to pay back Alek."

"Look . . . can you . . . I don't know . . . can you stop hopping around like a jerk for just one second?"

So I stop. I stand straight. I look at her in all seriousness. Then I go back to my dance. "Done, now."

She shakes her head, looks at her watch, and walks away.

"Hey, if you like Ant so much why don't you marry him?" I call after her.

"He'd be more reliable!" she shouts back, picking up her pace.

These Denby encounters have been happening more often lately. It takes me a good five minutes to dance her bad vibes out of my head. Even when I do, things don't stay calm.

Out of nowhere, Death tenses and snaps his head to the side. I look where he looks—along the uneven wall below, across fields of sleeping consumer bones. Nothing. It's so still, when a dollop of Death-drool hits the ground, I hear the *plp*. What's he on about? Must be something. Denby back?

I raise my gaze to the Alley-Oops and I listen. From the narrow strip of visible street, I catch a slight rush. It could just be the early-afternoon air stirred by a passing car, but it gets louder, regular. Footsteps. Someone's running into Alley-Oops, kicking things out of the way as he goes.

"Ant?"

He's not alone. Two men chase him. Not kids—men, with rough facial hair and a Slavic pallor that matches their long gray coats. If I'm in Technicolor with my rainbow robe, they're black and white. They're big, too, the size of doors. Door-men. Looks like Ant was worried about more than losing to me when Denby saw him this morning.

Ant's strides are long and steady. The Door-men? Not so much. The lengthy coats hamper their legs. Even so, by virtue of brute strength, they gain on him.

"Anthony!" a voice calls. It's Alek, up near the street, all out of breath. This is his show? What's he doing with Door-men? Daddy buy him some for his birthday? Oh, this is starting to make sense. I hate it when reality does that. Means it's up to something.

Seeing me, Ant cries, "Wade! Help!" Like I'm super-powered or something.

"Don't you 'Wade' me!" I say, wagging a finger at him from my perch on the wall. "You borrowed money from Alek, didn't you? What'd you do that for?"

Stopping in front of me, he manages a quick antennae-shaking shrug of remorse. "I was trying to be like you!"

"So this is *my* fault?"

He reaches out and grabs my ankle. Some of the coffee leaps over the Styrofoam, splashing my knuckles with heat and sticky cream. The pain sends me lurching and I . . .

. . . fall.

I go over, bathrobe flapping like the wings of a

flightless bird. Not toward Ant and the concrete, either. Toward Death.

Falling's something you really want to be there for. The slightest thing can be used to great advantage, a flash of an outcropping, a soft spot you can try to land on . . . or . . . not.

Whunk! The back of my head whacks the ground. So do my back, arms, and legs. What's left of the cup-guts spill, pouring steamy liquid onto me. Vapor rises as my exposed chest produces a lobster-red map of the coffee puddle. Ow.

There's a heated argument going on above me, but I can't make out the words. My head's ringing so loud I wish I could put it on vibrate. I figure they caught Ant, though. As for me, only my butt seems to have survived intact. I almost wish it hadn't. It landed on a overstuffed trash bag, bursting it. Whatever was inside, wet, cold, and rank, has already soaked through my robe, into my boxers, and up against my butt skin.

Then, throat-ripper Death starts calling, and his barks, I understand.

My neck muscles screech "No, don't turn me!" as I angle for an eyeful of the mongrel. He's gone dog-loco, spittle flying as he runs toward me, looking at me like I'm manna from dog-heaven. He's probably been waiting for years for me to fall.

I always try to laugh at my own pain, because I feel it gives me permission to laugh at the pain of others, but this, this is a toughie.

Thankfully, Death reaches the end of that chain pretty quick. His feet keep going as his head is pulled back. You'd think he'd quit but, no, he keeps pulling. The stupid dog keeps tugging and tugging, like he's going to drag the whole Earth forward to get to me. I'm about to turn away and check out the rest of my wounds, when I see the spike shimmy, ready to slide on out.

Duh. It's just in *dirt*, right? Another tug and it comes free.

This would be a really great time for me to stand and run, but my body disagrees. While I struggle, wide-eyed with pain, Death chugs, drool trailing in the air behind him in long sticky strings. His jowls dangle, flapping so high they slap his dull eyes. Three feet from me he just can't wait anymore, so he leaps, chain and all.

I see big teeth, smell dog breath. I bring my arm up, to offer it to his fangs instead of my face, but I'm not fast enough for Death. He's on me. I brace for the feel of canines shredding my nose or twisting out chunks of cheek. I stiffen, I shiver, I wait.

There's no biting. No blood. Instead, something that feels like wet sandpaper rubs all over my face, real sloppy, and I hear the unmistakable high-pitched whimper of doggy concern. Death is licking my face. Aw. He was *worried* about me.

Trickster's got my back.

I put my hand on Death's head and pet him. "Good Death, yes, you are. Good Death! How come everyone's afraid of such a big silly puppy?"

Speaking of silly puppies, above the fieldstone, I hear the sound of one Ant whining. Death looks at me like I should do something.

"Hey," I tell the dog, "I've got nothing *against* the guy, but he's like this . . . this puppy always following me around. If I feed him, he'll keep coming back!"

Death stares at me. He's worse than Denby.

"Oh, fine! I'll check it out."

Moving has been easier. Getting my manhood accidentally stuck in my zipper as a kid was easier. My right arm works, so I use it to prop myself up. The rest of me seems more bruised than broken. I stand, balancing on wobbly trash bags as the cold and slimy thing on my butt drips down the backs of my legs.

I don't want to look at what I landed in, but Death does. He stares at it like it's the solution to a mystery he's been trying to solve all his life. I follow his gaze to a rank and rotting pile of spaghetti. It's bursting through the shredded black plastic of an old garbage bag like fake intestines in a bad horror movie.

Still, it's not as gross as it could be, not until Death saunters forward, shoves his snout in the bag, and starts eating. Now it's totally gross. And the smell. I feel like I'm going to toss my cookies. I reach over and unhook his Prometheus-chain.

"Go on," I tell him. "Get out of here! Go catch a particle accelerator!"

He picks up his head, moldy spaghetti strands dangling from his lips. It takes a second before he seems to finally realize how easy lifting his head was without the chain. Then he barks and runs off toward the patch of flat land in front of his tire cave, kicking up clouds of dirt. And what does he do next? Make a beeline for the exit and freedom? No. Death runs in circles so precise, so regular, he may as well still be chained. That's commitment for you. Hey, I should tell Denby that one.

"I lost the money in a bet, okay? I need more time!" I hear Ant say, an octave higher than usual.

"No. More. Time. Got. Job. For. You."

I scramble down the bag pile and hobble to the gate. I'm not exactly running, more like tripping forward. The steep sidewalk back up to The Rat is tougher, but I make it in time to see things aren't as bad as I thought. They're worse.

The Door-men are trying to shove a struggling Ant into the spacious storage area of Alek's SUV. As he fights for his life, Ant sees me, glowing in my rainbow bathrobe and dripping spaghetti gunk. His face lights up with hope. This, of course, distracts him, so they get the better of him. One second later, a single antenna dangles outside the door. A Door-man folds it in. The door slams and the SUV rattles on its suspension from whatever it is Door-people do to captives.

"Keep. Out. Of. It."

Alek's at the head of Alley-Oops, fishing for his keys.

"Hey, Alek, take the money I gave you last night for Ant's debt. I'll get you more today. You know I'm good for it, right?"

"No," he says. "I. Need. Him."

What? Did he say no? "Need him? For what? Something I can do?"

"No. Not. You. Him."

"I'm insulted. Is it the bathrobe? I can change into my tattered jeans, y'know."

He hops into the driver's seat. I walk up and rap on the window. "Can I at least bum a cigarette?"

He puts the car in gear and pulls out, tires squealing. Spaghetti drips from my butt as I watch the SUV vanish on the long, straight, trafficless road.

Damn. Never could do the same trick twice.

CHAPTER 3

CHAPTER 3

I may be calm, but my body worries without me, giving off anxious waves, clingy stress-relics that say, "Remember me? I'm not letting you off *that* easy!" Each wave carries a piece of dream, a flash of my imagined life, where everything's sloppy and wretched and all out of place. I dance, up on a wall, in a filthy alley, wearing filthy clothes while Anthony's chased by Frankenstein mobsters. They drag him off screaming, and I'm scared. I can't help him, can't help anyone. It's ridiculous, out of whack, out of place because in the real world I may have just saved everyone, in the real world . . .

No dream gets better than this.

I did it! We run to my car and leap in. Anthony tries to toss his victory music up on the sound system, but he's too giddy, too busy pounding his feet and slapping the dashboard. When he finally gets it going, he bounces his head to the beat so fast it looks like his antlers will fly off. I'm smiling, trying to show how pleased I am, but it's not enough for him.

"Scream, man! Scream! Don't you *ever* scream?" he asks.

"Not usually."

"Just this once? Denby'd want you to."

He's right. She would. So I do. *"Yeahhhhhh!"*

We both scream as I drive along, nearly drowning out the thudding bass and drums that rattle our feet.

"Faster! Faster!" Anthony howls. "I want strawberries! I want them *now*!"

"I'm five above the limit," I say.

"Oooo! Five above the limit! Go, Speed Racer, go!" He grabs at the wheel, just enough to scare me.

"Anthony!"

He sighs, slumps back, then screams some more. He's so scattered from excitement he reminds me of what he was like when I met him—hyper, with an attention span equivalent to the nanosecond life of a strangelet.

"See how it pays to worry?" I say.

"What?" he says, too into the music.

I want some credit for my fear. I want him to know this is all a testimony to fretting details, even how I managed to get in touch with Finley in the first place. I had tried to call but couldn't get past the switchboard. After twenty tries, I'd *guessed* the right format for his e-mail. Boom—he wrote back, eventually offering me an hour on their simulator. I brought in Anthony to help with the coding and Denby volunteered to key in corrections. The rest may be history, if I don't pass out.

Near the strip mall at the outskirts of Rivendale, the Marriott Conference Center rises, a big glass square, reflecting morning light like a second sun. Why didn't Finley just invite us to Prometheus? It's only another ten minutes. Ah, now I think I *am* looking for things to worry about.

Ignoring Anthony's continued pleas for speed, I cruise into the lot at five miles per hour.

"A valet! A valet! Use the valet!" he begs. "I'll pay. Come on, you *know* we're going to be famous and rich. Spend some of it!"

"Neither's happened yet. And it's not about the fame, right?"

"Right, right. We're saving the world, yada yada yada, Captain Ahab."

"Have you ever even read *Moby-Dick*?"

"What? Sure. They kill some fat white guy, right?"

"A whale."

"That's pretty insulting, to call a fat guy a whale."

"A real whale. And they *don't* kill it. That's the point."

Did he skip his Ritalin? He does seem off his meds. I hope he doesn't act strange during the meeting. I'll have a hard enough time keeping myself under control.

I find a spot. We walk through some glass sliding doors into a posh art-deco lobby and introduce ourselves at the desk. The clerks whisper to one another, ogling us like we're Bill Gates. A cute redhead among them gives Anthony a wicked smile that seems to put him into shock.

She leads us down a long hall, past a gym, to a huge conference room. With another wicked smile, she opens the double doors and reveals a huge table with a really nice spread—fresh strawberries and cream, other fruits, croissants, even a cappuccino machine with a barista standing by. The place is so grand, I barely see Finley sitting at the head of the table. I'm almost sorry I didn't use the valet.

Finley, looking exactly as he did on the webcam, only with better resolution, sips some tea. I'm thinking he should be at least a little worried that the particle collider isn't as safe as everyone thought, but he doesn't seem to be. He smiles warmly as we walk in.

"Wade! Anthony! Grab some grub, pull up a chair."

Anthony laughs as he fills his plate with gusto. Four croissants and a ton of strawberries, drowning in cream. He's already embarrassing me, but what the hell, I don't think we'll get points off for sloppy manners.

"I love it!" Finley says. "Couple of bright high school guys find what all the big dogs missed. It's like Dell computers coming out of a garage."

"Wade did most of the work," Anthony offers between gulps. I appreciate the humility, but then he spills some coffee on the table. Before he can wipe it, the barista steps over with a cloth.

"So, will you be shutting down Prometheus soon, Dr. Finley?" I ask.

The smile fades a bit. "That's a *little* premature. This was just a short simulation. The board will want to check your code, run it over a few times, vary the conditions, and so on, before they decide what to do and when. Some of them are on vacation right now. It'll probably be a week or so before any decisions like that get made."

I tense up. "A week or more? But what if in that time . . ."

He gives me that warm smile again. "A strangelet devours the world?"

"Well . . . yes. Isn't that the point?"

He nods. He pats his hands together. He taps his fingertips against his lower lip. "I'll give it to you straight. What you've done is amazing. We owe you our thanks, and under the right circumstances, you'll receive those thanks."

"But?"

Anthony, still chewing, nudges me and whispers, "Heh-heh . . . you said 'butt.'"

Christ. Thank God Finley didn't seem to hear him.

"Computer simulations aren't reality. Prometheus has been operating for years without incident. And I'm sure you know the Earth has been bombarded with colliding particles from space for thousands of—"

"But—"

"Ha! You said 'butt' again!"

Starbuck's definitely off his meds, and that time Finley *did* hear him. He chuckles good-naturedly as I shoot Anthony a glare.

I clear my throat and hope I don't sound whiny. "Dr. Finley, natural conditions aren't the same as the Prometheus environment. And there *was* a strangelet produced, on the first day."

"Stop there. You're right. Absolutely right. The shielding has to be taken out. Never should've been there. You know the story. We had to do it to get the entire town moving again. I *am* taking this seriously. I've scheduled a call with some board members in about an hour, but . . ."

We both look at Anthony. He says nothing, though he does stifle a giggle.

"Because of that lawsuit, they're going to resist. They'll be terrified the Wilson Group will sue again, and this time destroy our funding. They'll test it every which way, try to poke holes in it any way they can. And *then* and only then, if your parameters prove absolutely correct, they'll want to fix it *quietly*. You don't want the collider shut permanently, do you?"

"No . . . ," I say. I'm afraid to add the "but" with good old Starbuck at my side.

"If you'll be a little patient, do it my way, the board will be *extremely* grateful. I'm not exaggerating when I say your work easily qualifies you for the scholarship program—"

"Yes!" Anthony hoots. He clenches his fist and brings it down to his chest.

But Finley ignores him. His eyes are on me. "We want the same things."

I sigh. "Every minute Prometheus operates with the shielding in place is another minute the dice roll on the end of the world. Doesn't that make you nervous?"

He shakes his head. "Honestly? No. Those dice have been rolling for years and nothing has happened. I'm only talking a few more months. At ten thousand to one, the odds are in my favor. Let me talk to the board. Can you and I at least agree to discuss this further tomorrow?"

What are my choices? Go to the press? I could wind up making the entire town jobless. What's a month or two? Sounds okay when he says it.

"Fine."

"Thank you. I appreciate your faith. I really do. So let me get started on living up to it. Gentlemen?"

He rises. So do we. Then he snaps his fingers as if remembering something.

"Aside from the school mainframe, are there any other copies of your code?"

"Just on Anthony's rig," I say.

"I have an unusual question. Can I have it?"

Anthony practically leaps out of his seat. A piece of strawberry flies from his mouth and rolls across the table. "No! Why?"

"Please, relax. I only want to be able to reassure the board you've abided by our agreement and that all the data involving your project is secure. It will help immeasurably."

He holds his hand out, calmly, like he's trying to feed a squirrel.

"But there's . . . personal stuff on it!"

I shrug at Finley sheepishly. "He's a little tense today."

Finley nods. "I won't look. Promise. I'll have you a brand-new laptop by morning. E-mail me your specs for a dream machine, and let's see how close I can get. Meanwhile, call me John."

"Let him have it, Anthony. It's okay. You want the scholarship, right?"

"Yeah . . ."

"And you liked the strawberries?"

"Yes . . ."

I reach over and gently tug the laptop from his hands. He lets go. Then we leave, quickly.

I manage not to shake until we reach the parking lot. That couldn't have been more frightening and embarrassing than if I'd planned it that way. Can I trust Finley? Did I get this far just to hand the whole thing over to the wrong guy? And what's up with Anthony? By the time I pull out of the parking lot, he's still stone silent, and I realize I need someone to talk me down.

"Of course you did the right thing," Denby says on my cell after I explain. "You keep saying Finley is one of the good guys."

"I know, I just—"

"Need something else to worry about?"

"Yeah."

"Oh, Wade, forget it for an hour! You did it! I am so proud of you! I bet Anthony's thrilled."

I glance over at him in the passenger seat.

"No. His antlers are drooping. Still upset about his laptop."

"Geez, guys! Maybe I can at least cheer *him* up. Once they heard the news my friends started fighting over who gets first crack at him. I can get him a hot date and we'll all go out to dinner. Let me talk to him."

I hold the phone toward him. "She wants to get you a girl."

He waves it away. "No. I don't want to date one of her friends."

"What's wrong with you?" I mouth at him.

"Wade, hang up. Just hang up."

"Talk to her."

"No. Hang up!"

I pull the phone back. "Apparently my anxiety is contagious. Call you back."

I flip the cell shut and look at my increasingly morose pal. "What'd you have on that laptop, Starbuck? Naked pictures of yourself and SpongeBob SquarePants?"

"It's not *just* the laptop. It's . . ."

"The butt jokes? You were nervous. Believe me, I can empathize."

"No. I mean yes, yes I feel stupid . . . but not because of that."

"Look, the sim worked. We'll get the scholarships, and you were never worried about the rest anyway. Apparently I'm the *only* one worried about that."

His face gets even darker. Without Denby's calming influence, my mind tenses, rattling off anything there might be to worry about, trying to synch up with Anthony. In a few seconds, I've got it.

"*You* didn't find a mistake in the code, did you? And then not tell me?"

I can tell I'm right from the way he shivers. "Yeah. I seem to sort of remember something a little . . . wrong. A small mistake, you know?"

"What? Why didn't you say something?"

"There was no time. And it's probably nothing. I took an extra pill yesterday to keep up, and today I'm running on empty, so I'm probably misremembering . . ."

"Misremembering *what*?"

Antlers in front of his eyes, he rattles off a few lines of code in a voice so low you'd have to know him *and* programming to understand. Unfortunately, to me he makes sense and he could be right. If he is, the whole sim could be off.

I'm sorry I never told anyone about the dizzy spells, because they're getting serious. My head spins. It's like a squirrel has run in front of my car again. In front of my life. A really big squirrel.

Finley's words echo in my head: "Then, and only then, if your parameters prove absolutely correct, they'll want to fix it . . ."

CHAPTER 4

Move along, nothing to see here. Just doing some daydream believing. Job done, Hunchback-Ant and I drive off in my blue electric future car. But something's up. "What's wrong, Hunchback-Ant?" I ask. "I screwed up!" he says. "Your world-saving program may contain certain errors that are my fault! What shall we do, Super-Wade? What can we do?" "Fear not, Hunchback-Ant!" says I. "I'll fix it! It's what I do!"

That was weird, like a little blackout. Woozy from the fall? I do tend to daydream, and sometimes it gets hard to tell where the fake stuff ends and the real stuff begins. What can I say? I've got a wandering mind. Ooh, look! An SUV! It's a blur, a few blocks away.

With timing so perfect it makes me wonder if I'm still dreaming, a cab pulls up and a cranky Po clambers out. Not that he's ever *not* cranky. He usually shows around now so he can pretend to clean The Rat before opening. Seizing the moment, I dive into the backseat.

Po grabs the door before I can slam it. "Where're you going? Time to set up!"

"Gee, 'Dad,' I'll explain later." I shake the door free from his grip and close it.

But Po's not done with me. He bangs on the window. "You pay that man, Wade! You *pay* him!"

Ignoring Po, I point to the SUV and say to the driver, "Follow that car!"

The cabbie, face frayed and wrinkled as an old wallet, looks at me. "For real?"

"Yeah! Come on. Haven't you always fantasized about someone leaping in here and saying 'follow that car'? Don't all cabdrivers secretly wish for that?"

That's all it takes. The cab accelerates. I'm pressed hard into the seat. Wallet-face probably figures I'm here for a roller-coaster ride, so that's what he gives. He makes a hairpin left, taking the corner so fast it feels like the wheels have left the ground.

"Where are you going? He's that way!"

Wallet-face chortles. "Drive right behind him and he'll know we're following. This way we keep parallel, keep track, and you can surprise him."

"You really *are* into this, aren't you?"

"Yep," he says. The cab bounces as its tires skim the curb. "Now you're supposed to say there's an extra twenty in it for me if I don't ask questions."

"Oh," I say. "If I tell you that, does it mean I have to *do* it?"

He looks at me. Amazing how they can keep an eye on you *and* the road. "You got *any* money?"

I could promise him a hundred once we get back to The Rat, but I'm not sure what I did with that bill Alek gave me. Sadly, I hesitate long enough to break the spell. The taxi goes from sixty to zero in two seconds. My head slams the plastic barrier, reigniting a whole series of painful bells and whistles.

"Out."

"But . . ."

Wallet-face reaches under his seat, *the* spot where cabbies keep their protection, and I'm not talking condoms, I mean crowbar, mace, or gun. So, I get out, but I'm miffed. Death wouldn't treat me like this. If I find that money I'm going to buy that mutt some doggie treats in the shape of human arms and legs.

The cab squeals off, leaving me in the center of the street, surrounded by giant shoe-box warehouses. I'm feeling all emotionally vulnerable in my robe and skivvies, but there are no cars around so I stroll down the yellow line.

My Trickster-luck holds. At the next intersection, my eyes land on Alek's SUV, parked by its lonesome in front of a particularly dilapidated warehouse. I'm just adjusting to this new information when the big old iron gate on it that passes for a door yowls on its hinges.

Three figures emerge. Alek. Two Door-men. No Ant.

Eep. I don't really feel like talking to Alek right now, especially if he just maimed or killed Ant, but I'm less than half a block away, in the middle of the street, wearing a rainbow robe. Put a neon sign on me, why don't you? The only place to hide is in plain sight. They saw the robe earlier, so I strip it off and toss it on the ground. I spin, slouch, make my voice low, and start singing to myself:

Oh, why be half-assed
When you can be the whole damn thing?
I used to be like now you are
Thinking I could go real far
But why be half-assed
When you can be the whole damn thing?

It's my disguise: wacky half-naked homeless guy. Not that big a leap, really, but it works. I saunter along, wavering, singing. A verse later, an SUV-blur races past. I keep up the song and dance until it's gone, grab my robe and put it back on, then head for the warehouse.

"Ant-man!" I call. "Anthony?"

Shadows shift and he comes strolling out, carrying a big black case and a manila envelope. He's shaken, but aside from one slightly bent antenna, he seems none the worse for wear. He smiles when he sees me, totally thrilled.

"You came after me!" he says.

Oh, God.

"No, just passing through." Recalling Denby's rant, I narrow my eyes. "You couldn't possibly blame *me* for any of this, could you?"

"No! Why?" Good. Of course that doesn't mean I forgive him for screwing up that computer thing in my dream.

He walks toward me, then sniffs the air. "What is that god-awful smell?"

I shrug, sit on the sidewalk, cross my legs, and slap his shins. "Never mind. What's with the attaché case, James Bond?"

He looks at it like he almost forgot he was carrying it. "Alek wants me to deliver this to pay off my debt," Ant says. I'm not sure if he's really not worried or just oblivious. Either way, he sits down across from me.

"Easy enough. Why didn't he just ask?"

"Dunno. I think he wanted to impress me. Plus he seemed real nervous."

"His dad's been getting medieval lately. Clean your room, collect your loan-shark debts, nag, nag, nag. But you know how that is, with your mom, right?"

Ant purses his lips and shakes his head. "Yeah . . . but . . . it wasn't just that. Alek stole this from a thief who stole it from somewhere else. Now I have to get it to a paranoid guy named Sergei. He's what they call a 'fence,' someone who sells stolen property, I think. It's weird and *complicated*."

"Look for the simple in the complex and the complex in the simple, dude. What's in the manila?"

He holds the envelope open and points it toward me. It's stuffed with cash. Then he looks in the envelope himself and shakes his head. "Funny, last night some of this was mine, then it was yours, now it's Alek's, and soon it'll be Sergei's."

"That's the flow of capital for you. But why *pay* a fence?"

"Dunno."

"And why not deliver it himself?"

"Dunno."

"Cool. We know nothing about nothing. It's totally Zen. I'm sold. I'll help."

Ant smiles. "You'd do that for me?"

"Oh . . . sure. Why not? It's a little drop-off. They happen on TV all the time. It's not like we have to worry about cops in this part of town." I nod toward the case. "What kind of drugs are in it?"

His smile widens. He looks practically gleeful. "It's not drugs. You're not going to believe this. You're not going to believe what this is about."

I'm totally curious. The box is perfectly flat. Strong like steel, shiny like an iPod. Ant presses two latches I didn't even notice, creaks it open a fraction of an inch, then stops. For a second, his face gets all adult.

"Look, but don't touch."

"What, you kidding me?"

"No, I'm serious, Wade. Look, but don't touch."

"Whatev. Open it up, will you?"

"Promise."

"I don't do commitments . . ."

"Come on, Wade, promise."

I rake my finger across my chest. "Cross my heart and . . . ow! Damn!" I hit the spot the coffee burned. "I promise. Just open the box."

So he does. He's right. I don't believe it, but there it is, the "hot" item, sitting in a little carved space made just for it. A car. A toy car. A "hot" Wheels, if I'm not mistaken, embedded with tiny diamonds all along its "hot" little body. I grin ear to ear.

"Is it real? If it is, that's the coolest thing *ever!*"

"Alek says it's real. Says it's the most expensive toy car in the world. Two thousand, seven hundred blue, black, and white diamonds on an eighteen-karat white-gold frame. The gems and gold alone are worth a hundred and forty thousand dollars."

"Hee-hee! It's even got little diamonds on the little wheels!"

Ant smiles. "You sound like you're ten."

"Tough talk from a man who catches pennies off his elbow."

I reach over to put my finger on the car. Ant slaps me away.

"You promised. Really, Wade. Alek told me if anything happened to it, he knows where my mother lives. And he said it weird, like, one word at a time."

I flash back to asking Alek if I could switch places with Ant. Makes sense now. He knew he couldn't trust *me* with that pretty little thing.

"That's just his dad talking. Alek's a teddy bear," I say. But my eyes are glued to the shiny-shiny. I wonder what it looks like out of the box, under the hood, how it handles. "Still, why *pay* a fence? Maybe there's a curse on it, like the Hope Diamond."

"You think?"

"Maybe Sergei will kill whoever delivers it—you know, to seal up the trail behind him."

"Dude, shut up!" Ant says, but he's laughing.

That's when I snatch it. It slips out smooth, but feels rough in my hands. Heavier than it looks.

"Wade!" Ant screams. "For God's sake!"

"I'm not gonna hurt it," I say, but I'm not even looking at him. I'm too busy making the sparkly car *vroom!* through the air. It maneuvers hairpin turns and executes daring loop-de-loops. I make brake-squealing and engine-revving sounds. I run the diamond-encrusted wheels against my arm, careful to make it leap over my bruises.

"Give it," Ant says, like he's my annoyed younger brother. "Please, Wade! Give it now!"

I look at him. I look at the car. I sigh and hand it over.

"It's not every day you get to play with a toy car worth over a hundred grand. Live a little."

"No. This goes back in the box and neither of us is going to touch it until we get it to Sergei. Okay?"

I give him a vague wave of my hand.

He's about to put it back in its cozy little box when his eyes go wide.

"Shit!" he says. "You broke it!"

He's right. I did. One of the wheels is gone. Oops.

CHAPTER 4

In the dream, it's not a squirrel that's in my way,
it's Anthony. The Frankenstein mobsters order
him to deliver a toy car for them. The car is so
cool, covered in diamonds, like little atomic particles, I have to play with it. *Vroom, vroom,* like a
two-year-old. *Vroom, vroom,* who cares about
Frankenstein mobsters? *Vroom*—I break it. Just
like Anthony may have broken the only way
to save the world. Ha. Wish I could break
Prometheus like that, just snap the thing in two,
instead of always trying to do the damn right
thing, like shaking myself back into the world,
turning to Anthony, and saying . . .

"We *have* to tell Finley."

"Are you *crazy*?" Anthony howls. "Are you out of your
freaking mind? No, no, no, no, no!"

I'm still a little dizzy and he's bouncing in his seat so
much it's hard to keep my eyes on the road.

"Look. Maybe there's nothing wrong. Or maybe it's a little thing we can fix in two seconds, but we have to find out."

"You heard him," he says. "They *want* us to be wrong. They won't let us run our sim again. We'll lose everything! The scholarship . . . the strawberries . . ."

We're alongside a big park and playground near Rivendale Elementary. There's a stop sign ahead and no one behind me, so I slow to a crawl and look at him steadily. "It's not just about us, Anthony, it's about—"

"Oh, shut up! Just shut up about the freaking world, already, will you?"

He shakes like a particle about to explode, slips off the belt, opens the door, and leaps out.

"Screw you *and* the world, Wade," he says as he stumbles. He rights himself and runs off into the field toward the playground, a big four-year-old.

Now I'm hyperventilating. Great. Perfect.

I stop, turn on the hazards, shut his door, and hop out after him. On top of everything else, I shiver at the thought of leaving my car in the road, but no one's in sight. I run after Anthony, glancing back at the car so often I nearly trip.

"Wait! Will you *wait* a minute?"

My car gets farther and farther away, but Anthony storms along, antlers wagging, until he reaches the playground. Two kids rock on the seesaw. When they see him, all crazed and fuming, they take off screaming, "Ahhhh!"

He ignores them, just circles the seesaw, grabbing his head, holding his antlers down.

A garbage truck pulls up in the lane opposite my car,

blocking the street. Of course another car pulls up behind mine and can't get around. Wonderful.

I catch up with him, trying to control my breathing. "If there *is* a mistake, won't it be worse for us when they find it?"

He moans, then sits on the seesaw. "What if they don't?"

Glancing back at the blocked car, wondering when it will start honking, I shake my head. "It's like you said yourself, Anthony. They'll go through our code with a fine-tooth comb, looking for mistakes. If there's a problem, they'll find it."

"You don't know that. They didn't even realize there was a problem to begin with, did they? And . . . and . . . there may be nothing wrong with our code! That's two possibilities, Wade," he says. He holds up two stubby fingers. "Two possibilities to your one! The odds are in *my* favor."

Honk!

There it is. The honking. Another car pulls in behind the first. Damn. Why doesn't the garbage truck move?

Pulse quickening, I sit on the opposite side of the seesaw. "How's this? We go back and just ask to look at the laptop for a minute. Tell him it has dirty pictures of Denby you stole or something, and you have to delete them. We'll boot the sim and check it. No mistake, we can leave. Okay?"

When I mention Denby, his face shivers. I don't know why. Random anxiety? He thinks a minute, then looks up at me. "What if there *is* a problem?"

Honk! Honk! Honk! Honk!

There are four cars behind mine now. All honking.

Honk! Honk! Honk! Honk!

I can't take it anymore. I turn to the street and scream, *"Will you shut up?"*

But they don't.

Anthony eyes me. My face feels flushed. I wobble, but I don't fall down. I can only imagine what I look like.

Anthony's head twists sideways, sending his antlers down along one cheek. "Geez, you look like you're going into a coma. Fine. We'll try it your way."

As we trot back, I'm apologizing long before the waiting cars can hear me. "Sorry! Sorry!"

A mother with a saucer-eyed toddler in a safety seat behind her gives me the finger. Even the sanitation workers on the truck give us a dirty look.

"Don't blame me," Anthony tells them. "I'm not driving."

I pull out. The electric motor hums as we move along.

Anthony's all glum again. "Sorry I freaked. This is your call."

"Do you have your meds?"

"Yeah."

"Take one."

"Then I won't have enough for Schapiro's exam tomorrow."

"Take one. I don't want any more butt jokes when we go back in there."

He does.

"Do you . . . really want me to say I've got nudes of Denby on there?"

"No. Do you?" I kid.

"Don't be ridiculous. That's silly. Of course not. No way."

He's babbling, so I ignore him. I go back through the meeting in my mind, parsing the details as I drive. It's like doing a crossword puzzle. Kind of calms me down. Red-head at the desk, conference room, strawberries, we have to be patient . . .

As we reach the Marriott, I have a new idea. "Finley's got a conference call, right? We watch him from the window. Once he's on the phone, we go in and say we forgot something. Car keys. Wallet. Maybe he'll be distracted enough for one of us to grab your laptop. Maybe he'll even leave to keep the call private. We'll check the code and sneak it back later. Okay?"

"I guess."

He's so freaking glum, it's killing me. As we pass the valet parking, I nod toward it and look at Anthony, thinking it might cheer him up.

He just shakes his head. "We may have to make a fast getaway."

I force a laugh, thinking he's joking. I have to think that or else I'll get nervous again. Have to keep moving, power my way through this. I drive along past the windows facing the lot: the conference room was six doors past a gym. A row of treadmills, visible even through the tinted glass, makes the gym easy to spot. Two windows per room would put our conference room at twelve windows past the gym.

Well, I was close. Twelve and thirteen are dark, but at window fourteen, the lights are on and somebody's home. A silhouette wanders by, talking to the air. Could be Finley, probably on a Bluetooth, having his conference call. Yeah, that's him.

There's a shortage of spaces, so I park on the far side of the building.

Anthony shakes his head. "Bad for the getaway."

Maybe he wasn't kidding. Or he's putting on a good show, trying to make up for dissolving into an embarrassing puddle of selfishness. If so, he's doing a good job. Once we're in the lobby, while I'm fumbling with the right phrasing to use on the redheaded clerk, he trots right up to her, cool as a cucumber. He even shakes his head to dangle his antlers, something he does when he's trying to look cute.

"Forgot my wallet in there," he says. "Okay if we head back for a second?"

She hesitates. "Are you guys *with* Prometheus?"

"We will be. Maybe I can get you a tour."

Ha. The meds must be kicking in.

She smiles. "Mr. Finley did say to put you guys through immediately . . ."

We take that as a yes and book down the hall. So far, so good, but when we reach the big wooden doors leading to the conference room, I stop.

"Do we knock or just walk in? Walking in, rude. Knocking, he might meet us at the door and not let us in," I say.

Anthony shakes his head. "We're in big trouble if *I'm* the calm one."

He knocks and opens the door at the same time.

"Better this way. We owe them, they owe us . . ." Finley is saying as we enter. He eyes us, points to his ear, mouths "board," and waves us back out. "Uh-huh, yeah."

I'm about to go, but Anthony holds his ground. Finley's brow furrows and he mouths, "What's up?"

Anthony pulls my wallet from my back pocket. He points to it, points to himself, motions toward the room, and shrugs.

Finley nods, mouths "private," then strides out the door and down the hall.

We're alone. Anthony's laptop is on the table.

"I can't believe we're getting away with this," I say. I look at Anthony, who's already turning on his laptop. "How can you be so calm?"

"I'm pretending it's a game."

"But it's not."

"Shut up. I'm pretending. You should pretend, too," Anthony says. His eyes dance across the screen.

"Shouldn't *I* do that?" I say, nodding toward his laptop.

"I can handle it," he says.

I have to be sure. I take a few steps closer. "Different set of eyes? You *did* make the mistake in the first place."

"I can handle it!" he growls. He looks at me. "Maybe you should head into the hall and keep an eye on him. Give me a signal if you see him coming."

"You mean hoot like an owl? I really think *I* should—"

"Trust me, Wade! Please, for once, just *trust* me!"

He gets up and starts pushing me toward the door.

"Look, if there's something on your laptop you don't want me to see, I swear the only thing I'll look at is the program."

"Go!"

He practically shoves me out, and then closes the door behind me. All of a sudden, he's in there with the most important program in my life, maybe in the world, and I'm stuck out here. Not good. I wish I could call Denby, but I don't want to make any noise. Besides which, she'd just tell me to trust him, too. At least I'd like it more when she said it. But I do trust Anthony. Can't trust your best friend, who can you trust?

I hear footsteps. Just someone coming out of the gym. My palms feel wet and sticky. Gotta focus. Details. Where'd

Finley go, anyway? Can't keep an eye on him if I don't know where he is. Someplace private, someplace close. Stairwell?

There's one nearby. I creep over to the door and peer through the little window to see if anyone's on the other side. All I can see are stairs. Quietly, I turn the handle and push. Finley's voice comes wafting through the crack.

"Kid's a nervous wreck thinking the world's going to vanish any second, you know? I can't tell him you're not planning to remove the shielding until some maintenance procedures scheduled for seven years from now. He'll run off to the press screaming the sky is falling, and we'll be screwed all over again."

Seven *years*? I'm ready to call the press *now*. I tell myself to calm down, that they're just talking. Finley understands the danger. He'll talk them into it.

"That's why you have to listen to me . . ."

There. See? He's a good guy. He'll tell them to . . .

"And just *lie* to these kids."

Wait. What?

"They're already willing to keep quiet for the sake of the town. Give them the scholarships, pat them on the back, then privately assure them the work's being done now. We're not talking about a couple of young Stephen Hawkings. One makes butt jokes and can't even keep track of his wallet. I'll make sure their code's buried. I've got their laptop and the only other copy's on the school main-frame, which we happen to own. Even if there's another backup, the code proves nothing without the run-through results. Do it my way, the problem's eventually fixed and everyone's happy."

Not everyone. I'm vibrating so fast now I have to let it out. Unfortunately, after the long night, the fight with Anthony, and now this, I pick the wrong way: screaming.

"Eventually? *Eventually?*"

My voice echoes through the stairwell.

There's silence for a second. Then, "Bob? Can I call you back?"

Shadows shift on the stairs above. I push the door closed and bolt back into the conference room.

Anthony looks up as I come in. "What?"

I nearly throw myself across the table, grab his laptop, and get one word out: "Run!"

He doesn't ask why, he just follows me out into the hallway. Laptop in hand, I pump my feet as fast as I can. Anthony's behind me, but not too far. If I wasn't hyperventilating before, I am now. I feel like my chest is going to burst. Things spin around me like the inside of a particle collider, but I manage to keep heading forward.

"Stop them! They've stolen my laptop!" Finley shouts.

Stolen. The word almost knocks me down. Being a lame-ass guitar player with a friend in debt to the mob doesn't seem so bad all of a sudden.

A wide intersection looms ahead of me. The entrance will be to the right. Ahead, down another long hall, is an emergency exit. Which way? Where did I park? Rather than slow to make the turn, I pick up speed, planning to try for the emergency exit. As I reach the intersection, I see two blurs of gray to my right.

"Hey!" one blur shouts.

Commanding tone. Uniform. Security. After me.

"Stop!"

Oh, I *do* want to stop. I *do* want to obey the rules. I keep going, more from momentum than will. I don't hear Anthony anymore, so I risk a look. Crap. The guards have him. His antlers wave up over his head as they pull him back. Finley's rushing up behind them.

My arm around the laptop, my legs continue moving until my body meets up with the emergency exit—hard. My head snaps back, but my elbow finds the bar and opens the door. I stumble into the lot, and make it to my car. I get in, slouch down, and wait.

Security guards come out soon after, but not Finley. Far off down the lot, the white taillights of a Volkswagen glow as it backs out of its space. The guards run toward it. They must think it's me.

I start my hybrid, grateful for the quiet electric motor. Shivering like it's the dead of winter, I pull out, and make my way to a rear exit. I drive down the main drag, staying *exactly* at the speed limit for about ten miles.

Made it. I'm not sure where I am, but I'm free, at least for now. Not Anthony, though. He's back there with Finley, probably telling him all about the mistake, how there was nothing wrong with Prometheus to begin with. But there is, I know there is. I'll need proof, one way or the other, fast. If I'm wrong, I can stop, turn myself in. If I'm right, then what? Tell the press? The Wilson Group will find out and try to shut down the collider permanently, and it's so long, Rivendale.

What a piece of work I am. What would my father think of all his sacrifices if he could see me now? Or Denby? Or Mom?

CHAPTER 5
CHAPTER 5

Dunno what Po puts in his coffee, but next time I'm getting decaf. Ant's mouth is moving, but I don't hear him. Images crash against my head like waves, and I'm sucked into an ocean of dreams. Hunchback-Ant begs me to keep quiet about his mistake, but, no, Super-Wade must do the right thing, speak the truth, fix the problem! We march back to Particle Dude, but he's busy on the phone, talking about how he's going to bury our data forever—Oh, no! Particle Dude is evil! I grab the precious program and run, only now poor Hunchback-Ant gets caught. Sheesh. If he's going to be in trouble in a dream and in real life, I may as well wake up. So I do.

It takes me a bit to refocus on the toy car. It looks like a little diamond turtle, stuck on its back, one wheel gone. If turtles had wheels.

"Oh, it'll be okay," I say.

"How? How will it be okay?" Ant looks up, all sad and confused. "Help," he says.

Even now he's not accusing me. It's like he thinks of me as the rain or the wind. He'll never understand me. Denby almost had it when she said I like to break things. Actually, I like to see what's *left* when things are broken. I figure that's the only stuff that counts, given that everything else eventually dies. Ant doesn't get that.

"I'll never even find the wheel! It's totally black, and tiny!" He looks around, eyes and antennae darting. He's overloaded, ready to blow. I've seen it before, like the one time I tried to show him a guitar chord.

Ignoring him for both our sakes, I dive into the eternal now and scan the asphalt; I see cracks, white stone, gum wrapper. I see metal, red and silver smooth. A soda can, crunched and on its side. Soda pools by the crack, only its surface isn't smooth. It has a little bump. I pick up the bump and hold it between my thumb and forefinger. Ta-da.

"That's a rock," says Mr. Negative. See? If I said, "Hey, I hear they just cured cancer!" he'll be like, "Yeah? What about all the people who are already dead?"

I roll it a bit, let the diamonds glisten against the black gold. *"Vroom!"*

He squints, smiles. "You're amazing, Wade. How do you do that?"

"Clean living, my boy. Let's try to put it back on, shall we?" I say. Ack. I almost sound like Super-Wade from my dream. I *hate* being the mature one.

He takes out the car, handling it like it's a radioactive isotope. He's about to hand it over when he remembers how he got here in the first place.

"Uh . . . maybe I should do it?"

"Knock yourself out."

Car in one hand, wheel in the other, he tries to push them together. I lean in to offer advice, but Ant pulls away. Seconds later, he quits.

"The little gold axle snapped. It's got to be welded or something," he says.

"Just put the car and the wheel back in the case and hand it over to Sergei. When *he* pulls it out and the wheel falls off, I'll say, 'Oooo, you broke it!' "

He looks at me, narrows his eyes. "You think that'll work?"

I shrug. "If these guys were really smart, would they be stealing?"

He nods. He opens the case, places the wheel inside, puts the car on top of it, and closes it. "What time is it?"

I look at my bare wrist as if I have a watch. "Dunno."

"I'm supposed to meet Sergei on Gudman at *exactly* three. Can we catch a cab?"

Remembering my driver, I shake my head. "Bus. Trust me."

We walk to the nearest stop and board a smelly dinosaur. Ant pays my fare and I hum occasionally to try to cheer him up. I hate to do it, but I actually offer advice.

"You're thinking too much," I tell him. "Worrying."

"A little."

"Don't," I say. "Makes your antennae bounce."

"Sorry," he says.

I almost feel like telling him how to carry himself, but I want to make sure I can go back to ignoring him once this is over, so I clam up for the rest of the ride.

How do I explain Gudman Avenue? Near The Rat, everything's worn, but it sort of functions. People are unemployed, but looking for work. It's the place you visit when you want to see how the other half lives in relative safety. Actually, in the case of Rivendale, it's more like the other three-quarters. The Rat's iffy, but Gudman's *definite*. Everything's broken, windows, doors, traffic lights. Cars sit up on crates like beached miniwhales. Even the people, flopping in alleys, lying under newspapers, look . . . well, broken. Most of the building numbers are missing, too, which makes Ant rev his abundant worry muscles.

"Crap. How're we going to find this place?"

"Behold the wonder that is me." I point at the only door with a brand-new BMW parked in front of it. The block-wide building looks like an old luxury apartment complex from the days before a nuclear war. The door is a big gray steel thing, not quite the right size for the space, with a thick frayed rope instead of a handle.

As we walk up, Ant sees enough of an outline where the numbers must've hung to tell him this is the place. But there's no keeping him from fretting. He swallows so hard I hear him. Case and envelope under one arm, he pulls the rope, and we step into a bare, windowless room. No windows, no doors, just sloppy white walls. Other than dust, crumbled plaster, and torn cardboard on the floor, it's empty. When the door swings shut, it gets kind of dark, except for the circle of sunlight from the doorknob hole.

"Fess up, Ant-man. Sergei's imaginary, right?"

Ant shrugs. "Maybe we're early. He said exactly three."

"Nuts," I say, kicking cardboard. "I hate being early. Then you have to stand around trying to figure out what to talk about."

He looks at me, amazed. "How do you do it?"

"Do what?"

"Not care. You get up in front of crowds and make up songs. You get your girl pissed every night, but always get her back. You even catch more pennies off your elbow than I do. Now we're meeting a paranoid fence with a broken jeweled car and you're still totally cool. How do you do it?"

I think about telling him how easy it is not to care after something hugely bad happens in your life, like your mother dying, how it can make you numb for the longest time, even leaves you with a deep well of numb you can dip into anytime, but I don't feel like bonding. So I say, "Some rise to indifference, some acquire indifference, some have indifference thrust upon them."

"You're not going to tell me, are you?"

"Nope. You'd just hurt yourself."

A kicked piece of cardboard slides along the floor. It turns out the room isn't *completely* empty. There was a cell phone sitting under that cardboard. A big digital clock on it counts the seconds.

"There you go again. You just kicked a piece of cardboard and—"

"Ant, what time were we supposed to meet him?" I ask, nodding toward the clock. It ticks down: 2:59:57, 2:59:58.

"A bomb!" he shrieks as he dives for the door. I grab his collar.

2:59:59, 3:00:00.

The room fills with the dulcet sounds of a "Mamma Mia" ring tone.

"Don't answer!" Ant cries.

I pick up the phone. "This Sergmeister? The Sergo-meter? The Sergster?"

"Please put your friend on."

The voice isn't harsh. If anything, he sounds as scared as Ant. Funny. Why?

I hold it out to Ant. "You."

Ant gives up another one of those loud swallows and takes it. "H-h-hello?"

It's interesting how much people communicate with their bodies when they talk on the phone, as if the other person can see them. As Ant says, "A friend" in response to some question obviously about me, his shoulders shrug. As he says, "Yeah, I got it," obviously talking about the toy, he hugs the black case. Then he looks at the walls and says, "Tape?"

He'll never stare at one spot long enough to notice anything, so I start looking, even though I'm not sure for what. Well, one sheet of drywall is not like the others. It's newer, and the joint tape, the stuff that covers the gaps between sheets, is half-hanging. I tap Ant and point.

"Got it," Ant says. He flips the phone shut. "We're supposed to pull the two pieces of tape off."

Ant takes the left, I take the right, and we pull. The strips come off easy. The drywall sheet falls like a card in Denby's house. Too-bright daylight floods the dark room. It's almost like a spiritual thing. As I wince, I say to Ant, "Really makes you think—if you walk in the light of God, does that make it hard for God to read?"

He doesn't answer. Either he doesn't get it or he's too busy staring at the fat-ass window we've uncovered. So Sergei *is* paranoid, like Alek said. Kind of creative, too. Beyond the window, there's an open square space in the center of the building. On the opposite side is another window. Ant points to it.

"We go through that and up to the fourth floor."

I smile and pat his back. "And you thought this wouldn't be fun!"

We climb over and across, then make our way up some white stone steps with a carved metal railing that may have been important once, but isn't anymore. It's all cracked and rotting like the rest of this place. I whistle. Ant shushes me. With almost everything boarded up, even he can't tell where we're supposed to go. When we reach the only door on the fourth floor, I give it a shave-and-a-haircut knock.

The door opens a crack and a bodybuilder in a T-shirt fills the space. He looks normal enough, except for one scar across his right cheek and another on his abdomen, so thick it's visible through the skintight shirt. Definitely not the guy on the phone. Not Sergei. After eyeing me and my stinky rainbow robe, he's ready to close the door again, but Ant holds up the case.

"The money?" Not-Sergei says.

An⁺ hands over the envelope. Not-Sergei peeks inside, then lets us in. At the end of a long hall there's an open area like a living room, with tall narrow windows covered in blinds. Sharp slivers of light crisscross the space like lasers. Sergei sits in a big cushy chair next to a little table behind the beams. At least, I assume it's him. He'd take the best chair for himself, right?

If it is, Sergei is one weird-looking dude. Young, but prematurely decomposing. What there is of his black hair is clumped in stringy strands, kept moist by a sheen of sweat covering his skull and his skin. Guy looks like a melting candle. And his eyes are big suckers, Ping-Pong-ball wide and sort of popping from his skull.

"Sergolini, can you dim those peepers a bit? It's bright in here," I say.

"I have a thyroid condition!" he barks, showing two long rows of tiny teeth. "And Lyme disease and chronic fatigue!" Instead of a period, his sentences end in wet, sickly coughs. "I can't help how I look, and I don't think I should have to explain it to you!"

The laughs keep coming. He grabs a tissue from the table beside him, spits into it, then puts the tissue in one of many plastic bags, also on the table, which he tosses into a wastebasket. Then he grabs a bottle of hand sanitizer, squirts some into his hands, and starts working them.

"This place is full of poison," he says. "Don't insult me again. And don't take another step closer. Don't they do laundry on your planet? What kind of lowlifes did Alek send? Figures only an idiot would take this job."

Aside from the tissues and the hand sanitizer, there's

something else on the table, looking heavy, metal, and black. A gun.

"Sorry," I say.

"Damn right you're sorry. Should be more like your friend here: afraid. Fear keeps people alive." He stares at Ant, who, I'm just now noticing, is practically shivering. "You sure he didn't follow you?"

"He?" Ant asks. "He who?"

"Klot," Sergei says. "Didn't Alek tell you?"

Looks like the name goes off like a bomb in Ant's head.

"A-A-Alek s-s-stole this from *K-K-Klot*?" Ant says.

I try to catch his eyes, but it's hopeless. "Easy, Ant. It's no biggie. You're with me, remember?"

I've never met Klot, but, really, how bad can he be? I mean, everyone thought Death was tough, but he was a puppy. If Klot used to be an artist, he must have a sensitive side. Why, I could probably bum a cig-gie off him.

"Of course he didn't tell you. You wouldn't be here if he did. Christ, *I* should have my head examined for being here," Sergei says with a weak laugh. "Why do you think he's paying me the cash up front? You think I put up fake walls and hang out in abandoned apart-ments for fun? Klot, frakking Klot! He and Smelser stole this right out of the museum. Can you imagine that? Like frakking ghosts. They say he used to be a sculptor, but a job like this? *That's* art. And what kind of brain-dead idiot steals Klot's biggest score? He's gotta be furious. I'm only in this because I owe that jerk's father a big favor."

I try to lighten the mood before Ant has a heart attack. "Come on, Serge, you loved making that fake wall, didn't you? It was pretty cool."

"It's not meant to be cool! It's meant to keep me safe!" Sergei blinks his creepy eyes toward the case. "Let's get this over with. That it?"

Ant nods and starts to hand the case over. It rattles in his hands.

"No, no!" Sergei says. "There's a bottle of disinfectant and some paper towels in the bureau. Put the case on it and wipe it down. Completely."

Ant complies, whimpering the whole time. When he's finished, Sergei pulls himself up and shuffles toward it, slowly, like it's painful to move. When he opens the case, the slanted light from the blinds hits the diamonds, spraying his sweaty skin with sparkles. He gives off this little giggle, like the sparkles tickle.

"*I* had a Hot Wheels that looked just like this. When Dad came home from work at the morgue, he'd sit with me and we'd play with it, y'know. If not for Klot, I'd buy this myself."

"Why don't you?" I say. "Klot's clueless. Bet you could hide it real good."

He looks at me, then back at the car. "I could. It's a good clean case. Nice vacuum inside. I could keep it clean in here forever."

I look at Ant, trying to get him to realize that Sergei doesn't seem interested in picking up the car. Given his fear of touching things, he probably never will, so no one'll ever know it's broken. Magic-Wade has pulled it off again. Once we get out of here and I tell Ant I told you so, my work's done.

But a loud bang from somewhere outside the door, down the hallway, says different.

Sergei throws his head up, like a vampire caught in sunlight. Not-Sergei comes storming toward us, shouting, "Klot!"

"Take it!" Sergei says, shoving the case at Ant. "I can't let him find me with it!"

"And I can?" Ant whines, backing away.

Sergei grabs the gun and waves it at Ant. Ant starts to cry. Geez.

"Shut up! Take it!"

Ant picks it up. Then things go from weird to surreal. Sergei's muscular pal, Not-Sergei, wraps his arms around his boss and lifts him off his feet like a child. Sergei squirms and whines. "No! Let go of me, Ben! You don't have your gloves on!"

"Sorry, boss. No time!"

With Sergei still whining, Ben starts backing up, faster and faster, until he's actually *running* backward, building up steam until he slams into a wall.

Smash! Thin plaster cracks against his back. Another fake. Ben winces, but holds on to Sergei and keeps pushing. The "wall" collapses around them. They fold into the hole like two toys, Ben a hard plastic action figure, Sergei a creepy cloth doll. Together they vanish into the dark space beyond.

"That was better than drugs," I say.

Ant doesn't think so. He's too busy sobbing. Little streams run down his cheeks like the sweat on Sergei's face. Maybe I could talk him down if there was time, but there isn't. If Klot shows and Ant's all weepy, things could go bad fast. Bullies hate weepers.

Footsteps pound in the outside hall. Time to do the Trickster thing.

"Hey, Ant, been a long day, huh? You're in no shape to face this, are you?"

"No."

I crack my knuckles. "Sergei's gone. Why don't you get your butt through that hole in the wall and skedaddle? I'll take the case and we can meet up later."

There's a banging at the front door. Fortunately, Ben locked it.

Ant whimpers. "Sergei said I had to keep the car."

I could tell him I doubt Sergei's going anywhere near that car now that it has Klot-cooties, but Ant's too terrified to listen. Instead, I say, "Fine."

I take the car and the wheel out of the case and plunk them in one of Sergei's sterile plastic bags.

"Take the car, give me the case. I can use it to distract them."

"You'd do that for me?" he says between sobs. "You *are* my best friend."

I grunt. When he dives through the hole and disappears, I feel like a weight's gone. Now it's me and my muse, and we aim to amuse. Let the games begin.

The door hinges shake loose. I slam the case shut, grab it, and run, not through the hole—that would make too much sense—but toward the front door. When it explodes open, I slip into the hollow between it and the wall so it hides me completely.

Two big-ass dudes stride on in, like they're stepping out of a nightmare. One walks tall, perfect posture, dressed in a policeman's uniform. The other has a great big head. Officer Smelser and Klot. It's like seeing cartoon villains in real life. If it's a cartoon they want, they've come to the right place.

They enter the living room. Before they can spot the escape hole, I step out and do one of those really loud whistles by sticking two fingers under my tongue and blowing. I love that I can do that. They turn.

"*Yoo-hoo!*" I say, doing my best Bugs Bunny. Then I hightail it out the door.

At the stairs it feels like my feet never touch the ground, like I fly from top to bottom. I allow myself a smug grin, then race for the next floor. I don't hear anyone behind me, but I keep going, down, down, imagining I'll eventually hit a level full of fire and brimstone with the devil there, down at the center of the Earth.

Doesn't happen. The stairs end in a fire door. Basement. Good. Maybe I can cross under the building and find another exit. If the door's not locked, I figure I'm free, unless there's a brick wall behind it. I grab the knob and pull. It swings open easily. Hail . . . Uh-oh. Not a wall, even better.

It's Klot and Smelser! Maybe they watch cartoons, too, or read comic books.

Comic books. Definitely comic books. Klot has on a leather overcoat so full of flaps and pockets, it must've used up a whole cow. Speaking of cows, up close his big head looks absolutely bovine. He's the cow-head master supreme.

"Y'like art, kid?" he says. "Think you know it when you see it?"

He talks in a low, gravelly voice. He probably got it from smoking, but I like to think it's because it's hard for a cow to talk.

I shrug. "Some art can be very *moo*-ving."

"Tough life, being an artist. Full of disappointment. Little appreciation. I know. They say the best art comes from pain. So when I recognize a real piece of work, real pain, real love, I take a lot of trouble to do something about it. Recently, I went through a lot of trouble to get a certain one-to-sixty-four-scale diamond-encrusted model car. Came in a case just like that one. Know anything about it?"

Straight-backed Smelser pulls the case from my hands. He walks so perfectly as he takes it aside, I find myself wanting to balance a plate on his head. He opens it and finds it empty.

"Guy's a real trickster," the officer says, handing the empty case to Klot.

"Where is it?" Klot says, holding the open case toward me.

"Where's what?"

"The car."

"Maybe it was towed for a *moo*-ving violation?" I laugh. "Sorry, sorry," I say. "But, seriously, you ever look in a mirror?"

I'm not worried. I pull songs out of my butt. I catch twenty-one pennies off my elbow. I survive wall falls, make pals with Death. Po's wrong about me and the kidney. "So, this car, was it worth a lot of *moo*-la?"

I don't see it coming. I just feel a weight slam the side of my head. I stumble sideways, into a wall. It takes me a few beats to realize what happened. Klot hit my head with the case, very hard.

Ears ringing, I press my palms against cheap stucco to keep from falling. An a-*moo*-sing comeback springs to my lips but doesn't make it out. Klot slams me again. This time I go down to my knees. The ringing is joined by a swelling sensation around my numb ear. Klot and Officer Smelser are all blurry, but I think Klot's getting ready to swing the case again.

I make a T shape with my hands, the universal sign for "time-out."

"Wait!" I say, surprised by how weak my voice sounds.

Klot doesn't wait. He disregards my universal sign and slams me with the case again, this time in the back of my head. I put my hands in front of me just in time to stop my face from hitting the linoleum floor.

A voice in the base of my skull screams that I should get the hell out of here. I tend to agree. Running is fun, right? I lunge forward on all fours, hoping to get to my feet.

Klot laughs. Weird laugh. Not because it's gravelly or cowlike, but because of what I hear behind it. Alek never wanted to hurt anyone, but would if he had to. Freaky-deaky Sergei would only hurt you to protect himself. Klot's different. Should've realized it when he smacked me for the third time, but I needed the laugh to tip me off: he wasn't insulted by the cow jokes. He's hurting me because he *enjoys* it. Which means I'm probably not going to be able to ask him for a pen or a cigarette, let alone another hundred.

Okay, no biggie. World's full of places to hide and I've done that before. I'm about to make it to my feet, when something clamps around my ankle and pulls. Someone grabbed my foot. Smelser? This time I don't get my hands out. My face hits the floor. My nose feels broken. Officer Smelser flips me onto my back. I want to resist, but I'm like a baby in a crib.

Klot tosses the case, then puts that big scary cow face right into mine.

"You think this is a game?" he says.

"You think everything's a game," Denby had said. She was right, but if there was ever a moment I should lie, it's now. The voice in the back of my head says exactly that. It says, "Say no! Say no! Tell him it's not a game!" But that's not Trickster. That's not me. So I give him my most smug smile and say, "Yeah."

Klot grins, not in a way that makes me feel closer to him. "Great. I love games. There's an art to the best of them. Art and pain. Let's see what you've got."

From one of his many pockets, he pulls a pair of clippers. It's about six inches long, thick and sharp, the kind you use for tough, small branches. "I'm going to cut off the top of your left pinkie and then you're going to tell me where my car is. Sound fun?"

He's kidding, right? Must be kidding. "Whatev," I say.

"Ready? One . . ."

He moves forward with the clippers. I want to call his bluff, but instinct pulls my hand away.

"Uh-oh! Someone's cheating!"

He nods at Officer Smelser, who kneels on my

forearm with all his weight, making it feel like the bone will snap. He holds my thumb and three fingers against the floor, leaving the pinkie dangling free.

He's *not* kidding, is he? He's going to cut off my finger.

Adrenaline rushes me, taking over my body, my brain, filling it with a whole new kind of energy, the kind Ant walks around with all the time. Fear. Fear so thick, I taste it in my mouth. It even takes over my words.

"Why don't I just *tell* you where the car is and we can skip the rest? I mean, you want the car, right? Have you seen it? It's really, really cool! Let me tell you, please!"

Klot looks like he's thinking about it, but he's not.

"Nah, I like it better my way. It's more artful, I think. Glad you're staying awake for this, by the way. It's no fun for me at all if you don't stay awake."

"It's with Ant! Anthony! My . . . friend. He lives with his mother on Clyde and Bruckner! Don't know the number. Two-story house. Aluminum siding, brown awning. I'll take you to him! He's got it! Really!"

Klot's head hovers over me. He shakes it like a disappointed god, his eyes so far apart they can't possibly work together. "Your *friend*? You betray a friend just like that? Didn't like you before, kid. Now, you make me sick."

"What's the world coming to?" Officer Smelser says.

"He's not exactly my friend! More of a hanger-on . . . ," I say. It doesn't help.

"You self-centered freak. I *was* bluffing. I wasn't going to cut your finger off," Klot says. "But now, now that I've seen you for what you are, well . . ."

"Wait!"

I scream. I really, really scream. He puts the clippers around the top joint of my pinkie. There's a sudden, sharp pressure and a popping sound, like a frankfurter exploding in a microwave.

I look. The tip of my finger is gone.

CHAPTER 5

CHAPTER 5

Just when it seems my crass, chaotic dreams *must* be better than real life, it turns out they're not. I'm still being chased. A freakish mobster named Klot is after me, coming for the toy car. I hide it with Anthony, but Klot finds me. "Where's my toy? Tell me or I'll snip off a finger!" Smug and stupid and totally unafraid, I say something *very, very wrong*, only I don't know what it is I said, and—snip— my pinkie rolls on the floor. The mobster is thrilled I didn't pass out. "No fun for me if you don't stay awake." I want to explain, no, I *did* pass out, I do it all the time, but before I can . . .

I'm awake. Sort of. Takes a while before I stop trying to remember what dumb-ass thing I said to Klot, even longer to realize I still have all my fingers. Not sure how I got here, but it's dark and I'm parked on a side street with a great view of the forested hills outside Rivendale. I'm not sure how long I was out, probably hours. That happens sometimes, especially after a panic attack. Prometheus is beyond the hills, right in the open. Inside it, even now, particles are smashing one another. Any one, at any time, could . . .

Or not. I still have to check the code and the battery on Anthony's laptop is dead. Even if I find an outlet, that thing's slow. The school mainframe would be faster. Schapiro works late sometimes, why not head there? Just thinking about the lab relaxes me. It's a sanctuary, a place I helped build, a place where everything makes some sense.

Used to be anyway. The moment I see RHS my heart feels like it's decided to crawl out of my chest and manage life on its own. Can't say I blame it. Three Prometheus security cars, a police cruiser, and a black sedan are parked out front. Two men in gray security uniforms stand nearby, one with oddly perfect posture. Once again, I've got Finley's words in my head: "The only other copy's on the school mainframe, which we happen to own."

Son of a bitch! I kill my lights and park. Don't want to carry the laptop, in case I'm spotted, so I leave it under my seat and sneak up to the lab window. I crouch behind a low row of bushes, out of sight, but close enough to the gray guards to confirm the obvious.

"This is Smelser," one says into his radio. "Tell Finley they're just about done. No problems. Just an irate math teacher. Nothing we couldn't handle."

Finley. Was it only a few hours ago I wanted to be like him?

Window bars obscure my view of the lab, but I see Mr.

Schapiro inside, blinking like crazy and looking "irate" and helpless as five guys in suits are very busy, likely erasing all my hard work from the last three months. I slump against the wall and rap the back of my head against the cool brick, not knowing what to do.

Minutes later, Schapiro's reedy voice, tightened to a near-whine, echoes in the school entrance: "I'll have every newspaper here in an hour, you understand me?"

If they do, they don't seem to care. They just head for their cars.

I'm just wild about Harry . . .

What? My freaking cell phone? Great. It's playing some ancient Eubíe Blake song. I usually keep my phone on vibrate, but Denby likes to embarrass me by loading that crappy thing whenever I'm not looking. Just what I needed. I jam my shaking thumb onto the volume.

. . . and Harry's wild about me!

Smelser, the guard who mentioned Finley, stares at my hiding spot for the longest time.

"I've got all your names!" Schapiro screams. His face red, he waves his small fist and blinks furiously at them. Smelser chuckles and joins the others. Once the last car is gone, Schapiro's shoulders slump in defeat.

I stand and cough. I'm not clearing my throat to get his attention, I just cough. It's a nervous thing. He's startled for a second, then smiles sadly.

"I take it the meeting with Dr. Finley didn't go well?" he asks.

"Not so much, no."

"They left the coffee machine. Want to come in and talk?"

I nod and he leads me in. It's a good thing I couldn't see clearly through the window, or I would have screamed at the damage: overturned desks, shredded papers, a dark hollow in the mainframe, like a wound, where the drive bays used to be, frayed wires, cracked circuit boards. This place was supposed to be the beginning of everything for me; now it looks like the end. I practically fall into a chair.

"They promised to replace everything, as if that made it all right." He pours us each a cup of coffee, thick and black. Given my nerves, coffee's the last thing I need. I take it and sip. It sears my tongue, but at least it's a distraction.

"Wade, I'm so sorry. I feel like I let you down."

"You? How?"

"I may not have totally agreed with my . . . with the Wilson Group, but I never trusted Prometheus either. I know how people get when their livelihoods are at stake. Merciless, stupid. I should've warned you. You did some incredible work—"

I cut him off. "That's the *really* stupid part. Anthony thinks he made a mistake. I'm not even sure the sim was right."

He twists his head to the side as I explain the rest, then sits back, purses his lips, drinks some coffee, and blinks. "So you're telling me you've still got the code, and that maybe there isn't any mistake. How long would it take to find out?"

"On the mainframe, minutes. On Anthony's rig? How much coffee you got?"

"Go get that laptop and I'll put up a fresh pot."

While I boot Starbuck's rig, I briefly think of looking for

whatever it is he was so afraid I'd find, but that hardly seems important. I load the code and scan the section he was supposed to fix.

I've read through it so many times the numbers and commands fly by, but I force myself to slow down and pay as much attention as humanly possible. I go through three times just to be sure. Then Mr. Schapiro goes through it twice more. But there's nothing. It's perfect. I should feel pleased, vindicated, but instead there's just a bubbling deep in my gut. This means that not only is there really a one-in-ten-thousand chance the world could end, but without the data from the run-through, there's no way to prove it.

"Okay," Schapiro says.

"Okay? Okay, what? Okay, we're screwed?"

The long lines of fluorescent bulbs in the lab's ceiling are reflected in his rimless glasses as he stops blinking. "Wade, I'm going to talk to you now not as a teacher, but as a friend, and a concerned citizen. If you repeat what I'm about to tell you, I'll lose my job."

"I won't repeat it."

"What if I told you I could put you in touch with someone who'd be able to get you access to Prometheus so you could rerun your code and get a copy of the results?"

"Please. Who could do that?"

"Someone from . . . the Wilson Group."

"Oh. Uh . . . Mr. Schapiro, I know you used to be a member and were married to someone from the group, but . . ."

He laughs. "Not someone. My ex is Judith Wilson."

"What? *The* Judith Wilson? She's, like, totally insane! What's she going to do, teleport me into Prometheus from her orbiting starship? She's . . . Oh. Uh, sorry."

He starts blinking again. "No, that's okay. One of the reasons we split up is because of her extreme . . . well, because we disagreed about things, especially legal strategies. Sometimes I think Prometheus would have been shut down permanently if we'd stayed together, but this job came up, I met you, and I decided to try to change the world in a different way. No matter where you go, there you are, I guess."

"But . . . she's the one who asked for the shielding in the first place. She will want to close Prometheus permanently. Everyone will lose their jobs!"

"I didn't say there was no downside. But what's the downside of keeping things as they are? Look, Judith doesn't have a starship, but she does have a friend, working inside Prometheus, who may be able to get you access to their computers."

"Legally?"

"No."

My knees wobble. He pats me on the shoulder.

"These are your calculations. It's up to you. Other than Judith, I don't know what I can suggest."

"I have to . . . have to . . ."

"Think about it?"

"No. Hyperventilate."

He smiles, thinking I'm kidding, then looks worried as he realizes I'm not. Among the mess, he finds a paper bag for me to breathe into.

Once I calm down, I say, "I have to call my father and Denby."

"No, Wade. Listen, a cell phone can be tracked and they'll be . . ." He stops, catches himself. "And I sound like

Judith. Another reason we split. Call whoever you want. I'll wait here."

I step into the hallway. It's late, but Dad probably figures I'm out celebrating. What can I tell him? That I'm considering doing something that could get me arrested and that, if it works, will make his business dry up? And by the way maybe we should move to the moon for seven years in case the Earth becomes a blob of antimatter?

I call Denby first. She picks up on the first ring.

"Hey, how'd you like your new ring tone? Hope I didn't embarrass you—much."

"No, not much, but it almost gave my hiding spot away to a bunch of thugs!" I want to say, but she keeps talking.

"It's a little late for the double dinner date, but Anthony said he'd take a rain check. He's trying to reach you. Where are you?"

"You talked to Anthony? Is he okay?"

"He sounds great. Why wouldn't he be okay?"

"Why would he sound *great*?"

"I don't know. What's going on?"

"Denby, sorry, I gotta go."

"But—"

Heh-heh, you said butt.

Anthony. Damn it. I check the log. Yep, he was the one who called while I was hiding. I hit his number on speed dial. Possibilities dance in my head, none good. Especially when he picks up and sounds . . . psyched.

"Ahab!"

"What's going on? Did you tell Finley you thought there might be a mistake?"

"No, what would I do that for? He wanted to compromise, so I conjured my inner Wade and pretended to be all ethically twisted up, then let him talk me into a deal. They're going to do the maintenance in *three* years instead of seven *and* we've still got our scholarships! I'm taking a tour tomorrow, but, if you ask nicely, maybe I can pull some strings with Dr. John and get you invited along. *If* you're cool with the plan."

"I am *not* cool with the plan! I checked the program; there *is* no mistake!"

"Oh. Even so, three years is more than twice as good as seven, so I don't know what you're so pissed about. Wade . . . did you look at my e-mails?"

"Will you forget about that? This isn't middle school. I don't care what's on your laptop! I don't know where to begin to tell you what's wrong with making deals with Finley. Do you know they just ransacked the lab?"

"He said they'd replace everything."

"You *knew*? You call him and tell him the deal's off!"

"No. I'm grateful for all you've done, but this whole end-of-the-world thing is your issue and I'm canceling my subscription. It's just math to me."

"What? I'm the one who brought you on board with this. I'm the one who told you about your ADHD!"

"I know, I know. Wade, I'm doing this for you, in a way. Your anxiety screws you up more than my ADHD. Just return the laptop, which is mine, by the way, and everything will be fine. Finley says that since they own the Prometheus code, technically your program's theirs, too. I don't want to testify against you, but I'm not giving up that scholarship, either. I'm not."

I flip the phone shut and nearly hurl it across the hall. A brand-new emotion finally pushes all the fear right out of me: rage. I storm back into the lab, kicking open the door as I go.

"Please call your ex-wife, Mr. Schapiro. I'd like to talk to her."

He blinks and starts hitting keys on Anthony's laptop. "I'll see if she's online."

A little while later, after an awkward conversation between Mr. S. and his ex, I find myself staring at the round head, white hair, and twinkling blue eyes of Judith Wilson. Through the webcam image, even though I know we both believe we're discussing the fate of the planet, I get the sense of someone terribly calm. Though she's in her fifties, I can understand why Mr. S. was attracted to her. She seems surprisingly intelligent.

"You think I'm a fool, don't you, Wade?" she says. Her eyes sparkle like there are little toy-car diamonds in them.

No point in lying. "Yes."

"Fools try to change the world to match their desires. Wise men try to change themselves to match the world. Therefore all progress is made by fools."

I smile in spite of myself.

"My ex-husband tells me you're concerned that I'll try to shut down the collider permanently if the shielding is removed."

"I just don't think your theory about a parallel universe being opened up makes any sense. The shielding caused the real problem in the first place."

"Well, you are a bright young fellow, aren't you? How about a compromise? If you deliver the proof, I'll agree to have the shielding placed *outside* the ring. That would brings the odds of a strangelet being produced back to a billion to one. What would you say to that?"

I think about it. I nod. "I'd say we have a deal."

She smiles, even wider. "Wonderful. That was easy. And now, the hard part."

CHAPTER 6

CHAPTER 6

At least in dreams I'm not sickening. With
Hunchback-Ant captive, I, Super-Wade, fix the
program and hook up with groovy subversives
who plan to sneak me into the heart of
Prometheus so I can run it on their computer,
foil the plans of Particle Dude, get the truth out,
and save the world. Woo-hoo! Almost seems
fun until a wave comes and dumps me back in
the real world. *No!* If I wake up, I'll have my . . .

Pinkie gone.

Klot smiles. Did he really do it because I betrayed
Ant or was that his idea of art?

I feel sick, dizzy. It's hard to believe this is me. It's
like part of me is watching myself saying, who's *that*
poor pathetic sap?

Someone touches my wounded finger, sending nee-
dles of agony through my hand and up into my forearm.

It's the corrupt-yet-posture-perfect Officer Smelser, wrapping a handkerchief around the stub. Like a doctor, he presses it against my chest and says, "Hold that tight."

Trembling, I do. Why so kind? Maybe he was a good cop in another life.

The tip of my pinkie sits on the linoleum floor in a little circle of blood that looks like melted cherry ices. Klot picks it up and rolls it between his thumb and index finger. He tosses it to Smelser, who puts it in another handkerchief and stuffs it in my shirt pocket.

"Know what? Don't tell me where the car is," he says.

"I already did. Ant . . ."

Klot flicks a business card and a few quarters at my face. "Whatev. I like playing with you. I find you inspiring. Get it and call me. If the car's not in my hands by tomorrow, more fingers. Between you and Anthony, that's twenty. Maybe I'll keep 'em, make a sculpture."

Officer Smelser says, "There's an emergency room two blocks south. Maybe they can sew that back on for you. I wouldn't wait too long."

They stand. They walk off. As everything swims around me I hear them banter.

"Idiot. Dressed like a bagman. Imagine that beautiful jewel in that joker's grubby hands."

"Maybe he's got one of those mental challenges that gives him an attitude problem. My niece is on medication for that sort of thing."

"Nah. I know a clown when I see one. Thinks he's immortal. Thinks nothing's worthwhile. I'm surprised he's survived this long."

. . .

I don't remember how I got to the ER. The pinkie tip's back on, supposedly, but I can't see it. A thick bandage, dark brown with dried blood, covers the finger.

"How do I know it's there?" I ask the doc. "It doesn't even hurt."

"Oh, it'll hurt," he says. He's overworked, tired, but trying to stay human. He scribbles on a pad, hands me a scrip for Vicodin. "That's what these are for. Come back in ten days. If we take off the bandage and there's no pinkie, just write 'cancel' on the bill. By the way, do you still want to stick to that story about how you lost it catching pennies off your elbow? I gave you a tetanus booster, in case the uh . . . *pennies* were rusty, but there may be something else we need to know."

If I tell him, he'll tell the police. What good would that do? Officer Smelser would show up to take my statement, and probably my thumb.

"It's like I said. Pennies."

Sure, *now* I can lie. Why not to Klot?

"Right," Doc says, shaking his head. "You're one lucky guy."

"How do you figure?"

"Well, first, you got here quickly, right before you passed out. Second, a nurse saw the blood on your pocket and found the finger. Third, that's the first finger I ever sewed on and, far as I can tell, it came out pretty good."

"First time?"

"I did it once in med school, but that was on a corpse. Come to think of it, it fell off afterward. But hey, considering how many people come in with bullet wounds, stab wounds, or heart attacks, you're a lottery winner."

He's funny, like me. Only he fixes things. Things— hell, people.

He looks down at his clipboard. "Hey! No income, no insurance, no charge. The man's a winner again!" He points to a chair with a neatly folded robe and boxers. "Your . . . *clothes* are there. They were washed."

"You didn't have to do that," I say.

"Yes, we did. You can keep the hospital scrubs, too. The nurse will have a few more questions."

After I refuse a visit to social services and a dozen other programs, I'm released with nowhere to go but to hell in a handbasket. I walk about a block from the hospital perimeter, out of the glare of the streetlights, sit on the curb, and put my head between my knees. I half-expect to start dreaming again, but I don't. Wonder if what's going on there could possibly be worse than *this*.

No dream, but I'm filled with horrible thoughts: I think about getting the car from Ant before he can give it to Sergei, beating him senseless if I have to, just to get it. I think about handing it to Klot, even blaming Ant for breaking it if he notices—and I've got a feeling he will. I think about Ant sobbing like a baby as Klot and Smelser drag him off.

"Serves you right for being evil in my dream!" I say to no one.

Got to get that car. I need Ant now more than he ever needed me.

There's a pay phone across the street. I could call Information for his number, but I don't even know my best bud's last name. I'm only sorry I remembered the street when I was talking to Klot. Po'd know, but The Rat's the first place Alek would look for me, and I have no idea how he'll take all this. At the least he'd want his money back and Sergei did not seem open to refunds.

Denby. She'd know Ant's cell. Her name I know, even the address. Are we still speaking? Maybe. She was pissed about the money. Imagine how she'll feel about my giving Klot Ant's name. Well, I don't have to mention that. Plus, if I get Klot the car, I'm really *saving* Ant, right? Right. Tell me another story, Mommy. I'm starting to feel as comic booky as my dreams.

I reach the pay phone and plop my quarters in the slot. The polite mechanical voice comes up with a number and connects. A few seconds later, Denby answers, sounding so worried she must have started worrying before she even picked up the phone.

"Wade? You're *calling* me? My God, what happened? Are you dying?"

"No. But I need Ant's phone number."

"Sure. I'll get it."

At that moment, I realize I put Klot's quarters in the phone and that's all I have. "Den, scratch that. Can you . . . call him and get him to meet me?"

"Okay. Where?"

Now she gets picky. "I don't know! Uh . . . Gatwick's Guitars. He walked me there once and bought me some strings. Tell him to meet me out front, stat."

"Are you okay?" I feel her concern, all warm and bubbly, even through the phone. Usually I can't stand it. Right now, it's good.

"Let's just say I don't want to look back because something may be gaining on me. It's . . . I'll be fine. Just call Ant, okay?"

"You know I'm here if you need me, right? You know where I live."

I sigh and say, "Yeah. I do. That's why I called."

Even after I hang up she stays with me. I know she's doing exactly what I asked. I know she's worried, thinking. Denby thinks too much, right?

A quick walk east brings the barred doors and windows of Gatwick's Guitars into sight. They're closed for the night, so I hang to the side, gritting my teeth at a sudden, stabbing pinkie-pain. The anesthetic's wearing off. Oh, goody.

Before long, a familiar hoodie and chinos rise from reality's blur. When a dreadlock slips and dangles I know for sure. It's Ant.

What do I say? How do I act? Can't let him see me desperate. He'll freak like it's the apocalypse. Got to get myself together, give myself a pep talk. Yay, me! I am *so* cool! I'm the Clown-king's main man! I tug the subtle threads that connect all things! I'm here and now, not now and then! I dance atop the thin brick wall in my robe of many colors!

No, wait. Fell off that wall. Damn.

Too late, he's here. Oh, I'll be fine. He worships me. I saved his sorry butt back at Sergei's apartment and he doesn't know what came next. I'll get the car for Klot, then figure some other way Ant can pay off Alek. Alek will probably be thrilled the car's gone. I pick up my carefree persona and slap it on my head like that duck from Denby's bad joke.

"Ant-man. What's up with your bad self?"

His face is grim. White. Worse than when Sergei waved the gun at him. He raises his eyes toward me. They're not darting left and right as usual. He's enjoying one of those brief moments of deep focus, like his hyperactivity has been forcibly drained. His antennae shake like wobbling lips as he talks, and neither of us likes what he says.

"K-K-Klot and Smelser were at my house. They said *y-y-you* gave them my name and address, Wade. That true?"

He *knows*. I feel the carefree duck try to slip off my head and fly south for the winter. Got to think, got to say something witty, like "Oh, that, it's no biggie!" Only better. Only I can't. I can't.

"Were you there when they showed up?" I ask, trying not to stammer myself.

"Mom was. When I got home, she was sitting on the floor in the kitchen, sobbing, surrounded by broken dishes. Her best china. I thought Klot did it, but she said it was her. After they left, she smashed them herself, because she was so upset. I told her everything, Wade, about you helping me, about the money, about Alek, about the car. She thinks it's her fault because she didn't raise me well enough."

"At least she's not blaming you. That's a plus."

His brow furrows. "My name! Did you give it to them?"

I've never heard him angry before.

"No! Did you . . . uh . . . give them the car? I mean, it's all over now, r-r-right?"

The stammering gives me away. Ant looks me up and

down. His expression changes. He knows I'm lying. "I wasn't there. I *couldn't* give them the car. Good thing, too—since it's broken."

One of his antennae points toward my bandage. "What happened to your finger?"

"Cut myself shaving."

"No, Wade. No." There's a new tone in his voice. Contempt. He's trying it on for size, to see how it suits him. "What happened to your finger?"

"Someone cut it, okay? No big deal. Klot cut it . . ."

He narrows his eyes even further. His dreadlock antennae straighten.

". . . off. Klot cut the tip off, okay? But the doc sewed it back on. It's fine! And I've got a prescription for Vicodin! See?" Grinning, I hold up the crumpled paper. "Want some?"

"You *did* do it. You *did* tell them I had the car!"

"No . . . yes. A little. Just your first name, and the streets, but that's all I knew. I wasn't going to abandon you or anything. I have a cunning and ingenious plan that'll take care of everything."

He lifts his head like I hit him. "Like you took care of your debt to Alek by taking my money?"

"Hey, I won that fair and square!"

"Did you? Or did you *know* how to catch those coins? My mother thinks you cheated."

"What are you talking about? I've never done that before in my life."

"Just be honest, Wade. Tell me."

"I *am* being honest!"

He pulls a sterile plastic bag from his pocket and dangles it. It's the car. My lifeline.

"Tell me. Tell me you hustled me and I'll give you the car."

It sparkles through the plastic. The broken wheel is wedged in the folds, separate from the body. Like my pinkie was.

"I need that toy car, Ant. We can work the rest out."

"You need it? Then say it, Wade. Say you cheated me."

"Okay, fine! I *cheated*. I always cheat. That's all I do! I can catch *thirty* frakking pennies if I feel like it. Believe what you want, I *need* that car!"

I scream the last sentence so loud my throat hurts. The sound echoes up and down the block. Ant tosses the bag to me. I snatch at it with my left hand, but drop it. The pinkie throbs. I go to the floor, scooping it up, making sure it's not scratched or . . .

He shakes his head. "You're over, man."

"Right. Once I get this to Klot I'll clear you with Alek, I swear. So it's broken. I can figure that out, too. I can . . ."

He flips open his phone and presses some numbers.

"What're you doing? Now's not a good time to call—"

"Alek? Anthony. You got the money, right? No, I haven't got the car, but I know who does. Keep me out, and I'll tell you who has it so you can get word to Klot. Deal?"

"Ant?"

"Wade's got the car. He's in front of Gatwick's Guitars. You're going to tell Klot he was the one who stole it in the first place? Fine. No, no hard feelings."

He flips the phone shut. We look at each other.

"My mom emptied her savings to pay Alek. She worked eight years, overtime in Walmart and it's all gone because of you."

"Not because of me. She didn't have to—"

"Yes, she *did*. She didn't want to take any chances, because she loves me! I used to think it was so great you don't care about anything, but—"

"Ant, Klot will be after me. What am I going to do?"

"Whatev," he says. "Whatev."

Then he walks off.

I lean against the wall, a hollow feeling in my hollow gut. I look around, up and down the street, up into the sky. Nothing but directions everywhere, wisps of air, smells, sights, sounds, any one of which might lead me someplace wonderful, on some great adventure. But for the first time, even though the world is wide open all around me, I have no place to go.

I kind of wish that Prometheus accelerator were still running just so it *could* destroy the world. Now would be good.

CHAPTER 6

No rest in dreams. My pinkie's bandaged in an ER
that's as sterile as a monkey cage. Klot's out there
somewhere in the dark, hiding behind the stars,
ready to take more fingers if I don't find his toy.
Here, Anthony is pissed at me. Can you believe it?
He's pissed at *me*, over whatever I said to Klot. My
pal gives me the toy car, then dumps me, leaves
me to wait for the finger-man to find.

My head bobs back and forth. I open my eyes. Mr. Schapiro
is shaking me with one hand. He's got a cup of coffee in
the other.

Right. It's morning. I'm at his house. On his couch. Part
of the deal. Judith Wilson said I shouldn't call or go
home—it'll be the first place they'll look for me. And Mr.
Schapiro's place? Looks like Judith's getting some heavy-
duty alimony. It's a cramped one-bedroom over a seedy
diner in the only gross section of Rivendale. Funny how

the collider that could end the world also ended his marriage.

"You sleep deep," he says, as I struggle up to a sitting position. "Here. The good stuff."

I'm still twitchy from the "bad" stuff, but I take the cup and sip. Tasty. I nod approval. If this is his only source of nourishment, I'm beginning to understand why he blinks so much. I'm starting to blink faster, too. Beats fainting.

There's a manila envelope in his hands. "Judith sent this by courier."

Inside is a building map, a badge, and a clear bag with a thick plastic oval inside. It's sleek, like an iPod, and just about as big.

"Is that a terabyte flash drive?" I say.

"*Two* terabytes."

An hour later I'm on a propane-powered bus packed with commuting Prometheus maintenance workers. I'm wearing overalls and a fake employee badge that should be good enough to get me into the building. Thanks to Mr. Schapiro's "good stuff" I'm not only fretting like crazy, I'm also blinking so fast everything has a kind of strobe effect to it.

I sit in the back, trying not to look suspicious as I hold a cloth bag with Anthony's laptop and the flash drive, now loaded up with the sim. I'm supposed to load the code, use Anthony's webcam to stream a video of the proceedings, then e-mail the data results back to Judith. If I try to stream or send e-mail through Prometheus, they could track and block it. Not to mention figure out where I am.

If I didn't already feel stuck in a bad end-of-the-world movie, when the bus reaches the peak of the hills outside

Rivendale, I get a sudden, breathtaking view of Prometheus. Talk about Ahab and the white whale. It's so huge my brain's ability to do much of anything stops. The actual ring where the collisions take place is underground, but there's an enormous mound of brown dirt right above it. A thirty-mile circle of dirt.

A smaller circle (Smaller? Maybe only three miles in circumference?) intersects the large one and there's a tall, white building in the center of that. The building's angles are sharp, its construction a series of rectangles, so it looks kind of like a giant house of cards. There are parking lots on either side and, at one end, a huge man-made pool, with a bronze sculpture of a stylized atom in the middle.

I've loved that sculpture ever since I saw photos of the installation. Almost makes me sorry I abandoned my own art: my music. It's abstract, smooth and round, twenty feet tall. Wish I could remember the artist's name. Some local who made it big. But big is relative. Next to the ring, the colossal statue looks like an ant.

We drive through a security gate and up to the building entrance. As the bus doors hiss open and I stand to exit, I feel totally numb. Good. Numb is good. No feelings, no passing out. I follow the workers. Doing good, heading inside. No brain, no pain.

Until I slam into a transparent door. Ow! The guy in front of me didn't hold it open, and you can barely see the damn thing. Ow, ow, ow! Holding my throbbing nose, try-ing not to draw any attention to myself, I stumble into a vast lobby that looks almost as if it's still outside. It's not just the door. Everything's made of some type of clear material, like glass, so there's sky visible all around. Even the different levels are see-through. On the bright side, the simple shapes make it easy to match what I'm seeing with what was on the map in Judith's envelope. I'm supposed to head down now.

The elevators are, thankfully, a little less twenty-third century. By the time we reach the basement and the wide access corridor that everyone uses to move quickly between sections, the color and construction are as bland as at Rivendale High, if slightly better lit. I was expecting a power hum, like from an electrical plant, but it's only the same old fluorescent buzz.

At the intersection of B25 and C12 I pretend to tie my shoelaces, and let my "fellow workers" get ahead. They don't seem to mind that they've never seen me. Judith said the lower-paying jobs have a high turnover rate, so there's always someone new. Once the group rounds a corner, I try to head the opposite way but immediately trip on my laces and crash to the cement. Great. My laces really were untied. I was so nervous I didn't notice.

Perfect. No one has to catch me. I'll probably kill myself just trying to get to the computers. There should be a stair-well here, where I'm supposed to meet my "inside" contact, but where the hell is it? The side of the corridor looks like one big wall, heading off for a mile. If I can't find it . . .

Phew. There. My eyes are still a little teary from slam-ming my nose, so I didn't notice it until I was almost on top of it. The gray door's designed to blend into the gray wall, making it harder to spot.

I step inside and trip on my shoelaces again. At least this time no one's watching. I get up, brush myself off, and wait at the bottom of the stairs. And wait. And wait. Finally a door opens somewhere above and footsteps clack downward. A slim shadow appears through the railing, so I kneel, planning to pretend to tie my shoelaces again, in case it's not my contact. Only since my shoelaces are untied, I decide to really tie them. Tightly.

Pretending to tie my laces was also in Judith's instructions. She had a lot of those. Despite her lively demeanor, I can see where her paranoia might have driven Mr. Schapiro crazy. Right now, though, I find it comforting. She also made it clear that Prometheus isn't a military base or a secret installation. They give public tours. Security's good, but not insane. The most important thing is to relax and act normal. Act normal. Ever have a doctor tell you to breathe normally? How do you do that? Last time a doctor asked me to do that, I got so worked up from trying to figure out how, my blood pressure shot up. Act normal. Ha.

Whoever it is stops right in front of me and, frankly, she has really nice legs. Only, I'm not done with my laces just yet and I wind up working on them until she coughs impatiently. I look up into the sharp, pretty face of a brunette woman. I realize at once we have something in common: anxiety. She looks so tense she seems ready to burst into flame. I want to say something, but Judith's instructions were "not a word."

I give her my badge, she holds out another manila envelope. It shakes so much, I catch a breeze off it. Goody — we're both amateurs. When I take the envelope, she skitters back up the stairs. Her nerves do not help mine. Not at all.

I wait until she's out of sight before I strip off the overalls, revealing a now-crumpled shirt, tie, and dark pants. Of course I have to untie my damn laces again before I can get the overalls all the way off. Turns out I'm much more Maxwell Smart than James Bond.

Then I try to straighten the shirt and close the top button. Mr. Schapiro's smaller than me, so his shirt is tight, suffocating even, but I manage. I roll the overalls into a ball, stuff them in the bottom of a garbage can, take the new fake ID out of the envelope, and return to the access corridor. So far so good. I think I'm about halfway through my instructions. Shoelaces? Check.

Now I have to find a hallway called E7 and follow it north to an intersection with a thinner white hallway that leads to the Special Computer Section. Everything's clearly labeled, as if designed by, well, scientists, so it's easy to make my way. Turns out E7 is a main artery for traffic. Beeping vehicles that look like golf carts carry white-shirted executives and scientists. LCD monitors hang every twenty yards, showing the latest Prometheus news.

I feel exposed, choking a little from the tight collar, but tell myself it's easier to hide in a crowd. In fact, I repeat it over and over: "It's easier to hide in a crowd. It's easier to hide in a crowd." All that handy numbness I experienced on the way in? Wearing off now. Could be the nose, the collar, all the tripping, could be my nervous contact, could be me, but fear trickles from my brain into my body, faster and faster.

Of course disaster strikes. Two of the three passengers in one of those beeping carts look familiar. A dreadlock dangles like an antler from one of their heads. Anthony. Seated across from him? Finley. This must be Anthony's tour. Great. Perfect. I wish Judith had given instructions for this. Me? I stand there like a petrified squirrel.

Finley's back is to me, but Anthony sees me. His eyes light up and a grin spreads across his face. For a second he looks like he's going to wave and say, "Ahab! What's up with your bad self?" I'm terrified he'll actually do it. I can tell by the crazed gleam in his eyes he's definitely off his meds again.

But I stare him down somberly, and his grin freezes. I can almost see his brain catching up with the situation. Slowly, the smile vanishes. The question is, will he turn me in? He's made it clear he doesn't believe in this silly end-of-the-world stuff. Will he keep quiet for friendship's sake? Yesterday I trusted him completely. Today? Oh hell, he's still Anthony. He'll keep quiet. He's got to. Without the Ritalin, in a few seconds he may just forget to tell anyone.

Even so, I move, racing against time and my own growing fright.

The farther north I go, the less traffic there is. When I finally turn off E7 into the narrower, white hallway, I'm alone. I tell myself that if Anthony had said something, there'd be alarms by now. I tell myself that, but my heart's slamming against my ribs like a boxer beating a punching bag. Slick sweat gathers on the side of my face.

Oh God, what am I doing here?

Saving the world, remember?

Okay, I'm in the white hall. Almost there. Judith said I was home free if I got to the computer terminals. The main systems are upstairs. This room is a backup, what they call a redundant system. No one ever comes here, except for maintenance.

I make it to the door and swipe the ID card's magnetic stripe through the electronic lock. Nothing happens. Is this the right place? The card has some sweat on it from my hand. I wipe it off and swipe again. The indicator turns green. The lock clicks back.

I step in and get my power hum, a low, deep vibration that I hear in my ears and feel through my feet. The room is long and narrow, a bank of computer terminals on either side of a central island. Circular lights hang low over each station, suspended from nearly invisible wires. The floor is gray linoleum, reflecting back the circles of light. It's also empty, just like Judith said, and, I might add, pretty cool-looking.

One of the monitors is active, and it isn't showing a simulation. I can tell from the readouts it's displaying the *actual* workings of Prometheus, live. Wow. The images are slowed down, of course, to make the nanosecond interactions visible. Particles explode and vanish. No light green strangelets yet. Hey, if one shows up in the next hour, I'll be among the first to know. Oddly enough, I find that soothing.

I pick a terminal that can't be seen from the door and sit in a surprisingly comfortable chair. I type the log-in and password Judith gave me. The screen lights up. I'm in.

The rest should be insanely easy. I just have to set up the laptop webcam feed, connect the flash drive to the terminal port, and press the button on the flash drive — everything else is automated. The sim will run and even if they catch me and I can't e-mail the data, Judith will have the video feed as proof. She and Mr. Schapiro will contact the press. I'm not usually very sensitive to romance, but they seemed a little happy about working together again.

Easy, right? But my hands shake as I pull out the plastic bag with the flash drive. I need both hands to pop out the USB plug and hold it steady enough to connect. Now for the webcam. I pull Anthony's laptop out of the cloth bag and start it up. As it boots, to calm myself, I watch that other monitor, taking comfort in knowing that the world isn't ending yet.

I feel even better as I'm able to get the video feed going. At least I think I'm feeling better until I point the webcam at the terminal and glimpse my face on the feed. Do I really look *that* scared? Denby's right. I take things *way* too seriously. But now is not the time to stop.

Before I hit the button on the flash drive, I get the e-mail ready. The program opens and shows me Anthony's draft folder. Geez, he keeps it full. What's he got in there? Love letters? Was *that* what all the fuss was about? They're all to the same address. So that's why he didn't want to date any of Denby's friends. He's got someone special on his mind. Wonder who he's stalking.

They're all to . . . *Denby?*

My inner voice stutters, "Uh-uh-uh . . ." The fate of the world vanishes. I scroll through his writing, catch a sentence here and there:

He can't be thinking about you half as much as I do . . .
We laugh. You just make him tense.
Fear isn't love.
He'd trash the whole town for the sake of his paranoia.
You feel sorry for him? Is that it? Feeling sorry isn't love.
Just think about it. Once. Just once.

I don't see any answers. Of course not, Denby couldn't have written back. Could she? Could *this* be why she hasn't answered about our engagement? No, she wouldn't keep it from me . . . unless he's right and she feels sorry for me. Unless she was waiting until the project was over? Yesterday I wouldn't have thought Finley was a liar. Last night I wouldn't have thought Anthony could turn on me. Even so, until just now I wouldn't have thought him capable of this.

Denby! I want to call and ask her, but Judith said no calls.

I can't . . . I can't . . . I can't think about this right now. I have to press the button!

He'd trash the whole town for the sake of his paranoia.

Would I? Oh God, what if he's right? What if the code *is* still wrong? I'll . . . I'll page through quickly, it's fast on the flash drive. An extra minute, that's all, just a minute to focus on something else and get all this doubt, all those *e-mails* out of my mind. What if . . .

Focus! I do, and something catches my eye immediately, something basic, something simple, something that couldn't possibly have been missed, the equivalent of spelling "the" as "teh" in a newspaper headline. A huge, obvious mistake. Not in Anthony's code, in *mine*. Mine! Is *that* the mistake he sort of remembered, but couldn't?

He was right. He was right about me, too. I'm paranoid. Crazy. Worse than Judith Wilson. My God, I'm working with her now, aren't I?

It is there, isn't it? I'm not hallucinating, am I? No, I see it. It's not a dream. It's simple to fix, but my fingers shake too much. The pounding in my chest morphs into choking. My neck swells against the tight collar. I'm strangling. I loosen the tie, fumble with the top shirt button and wind up yanking it off in frustration. It rolls across the floor. Cooler air hits my neck, but only makes things worse.

He'd trash the whole town for the sake of his paranoia.

How can I be sure it's my *only* mistake? How do I know there aren't more?

Fear isn't love.

My field of vision shrinks, gets hazy at the edges. I look at the active terminal, see little dots of color indicating the particles inside Prometheus. No light green. Not yet. Then why does it feel like the world is ending?

A harsh, sharp sound whines in my ears. Three loud blasts that repeat. An alarm. Could just be a fire drill, but it's the last straw for my shattered nerves. I can't do this without knowing for sure. I grab the flash drive and the plastic bag, pocket them, and run.

When I make it back to the white corridor I see my name and face plastered on the hanging LCD monitor and realize three horrible truths all at once:

1. The alarm is for me.
2. Anthony's betrayed me in more ways than one.
3. *I've failed. I've failed to save the world.*

Sorry, world. Sorry, Dad. Sorry, Denby.

CHAPTER 7

Bravely, Super-Wade sneaks into Prometheus,
where a hot brunette provides a fake ID and dis-
guises me as someone who works for a living.
Hunchback-Ant, the guy I backstabbed in reality,
spots me, only here *he's* as evil as Particle Dude.
When he screams, everyone chases me, but I
make it to the computer and whip out a James
Bond iPod-like flashy drive. It's so cool I wish I
had one in real life. All I gotta do is push a button
and save the world! But . . . but . . . something
freaks me out. What? I don't know, but I go from
Bond to emo in ten seconds. I start to faint.
Where's Denby when I need her? Oh, yeah . . .

I stand at her door in my bathrobe, boxers, and new hospital scrubs. At least they were washed. Light dribbles
onto the floor from under the door. Inside I hear music
and girls. They're laughing in that special giggly way

boys give up on in their teens. Beneath my feet, the floor rumbles from the freezers in a deli below. I could stay here forever, wedged between the giggles and the hum, but my pinkie hurts so bad.

Bracing myself against the throbbing, I knock with my good hand. Nothing. I knock harder. Shadows move behind the peephole.

A muffled voice sounds, "Who is it?" Not the voice I expect. Too hoarse. Older.

I'm too close to the peephole. I step back so whoever it is can get a good gander at me. I think of myself as looking cute and harmless. They disagree.

"Ew. Go away or I'm calling the police."

"Denby," I say. "I'm a friend of Denby's."

The eye vanishes. A few seconds later, another eye appears. It's blue, younger, more familiar. The door rattles and creaks open. The music gets louder, but no one's giggling anymore. Denby's face drops when she sees me.

"Jesus, Wade, you look awful. Anthony find you?"

"Yeah. Denby, can I . . . can I crash here?"

I don't think the question surprises her as much as my tone of voice. She scans me up and down, the same way Ant did, glances back inside, then at me again.

"You just . . . wait there," she says.

She goes inside. There's talk. It gets kind of loud. Someone, probably Denby, is smart enough to raise the volume on the music, so I don't have to hear what a bad idea they think letting me in is. The voices grow resigned, then quiet. The music is lowered. Denby opens the door and nods for me to enter.

I walk in to the stares of two girls I've never met, but who've obviously heard of me. One looks like a librarian, glasses and her hair tied in a bun. The other's a dancer, in a black leotard, glaring at me as she stretches her leg muscles. I manage a weak smile and a wave of my hand, too late realizing it's the one with the bandage. The dancer hisses, like "Oooo, that must hurt." The librarian's all about the data.

"How'd that happen?"

"A mobster thought I stole his diamond-studded Hot Wheels car, so he cut off the tip of my pinkie to prove a point."

"Nice," the librarian says. Her tone tells me I scare her and had best be gone soon.

"He's kidding!" Denby says. "He's always saying things like that, trying to be funny. It doesn't always work. You're kidding, right, Wade?"

I shrug. Can't lie, can't tell the truth.

Denby grabs me by the arm and pulls. As we exit, I see the dancer and the librarian eye each other knowingly. I'm sure they've told her a million times she shouldn't have anything to do with me. Probably the one thing all three of us agree on.

Since she split from home, Denby's shared this place but, like I said, I've made a point of never being here, not wanting to give the wrong impression, like if I came in, I might stay. It's nice. Peaceful. No sharp edges. There are lit candles all over, casting grand wobbly shadows. The mattress on the floor is arranged like a couch, with long thick pillows to lean back against. There's a dresser, some posters, and a quilt hung on the wall like a decoration.

She leads me to the mattress and gently pushes me down. I feel myself relax into it and almost fall asleep right then and there. But Denby lies next to me, puts her head on a pillow, and asks with her eyes what the hell's going on.

Struggling to keep the duck off my head, the one with my crazy carefree persona, I tell her. I don't elaborate. I just watch those blue eyes the whole time, little candle flames flickering in them. I see her concern, her worry. I see her opinion of me confirmed but, even after the worst of it, I see her still caring. She believes me, but I show her the toy car anyway.

"And now Klot thinks you're the one who stole it from him?"

"I'm sure Alek and his dad will do their best to convince him."

"Oh, Wade. Something finally caught up with you, huh? I'm so sorry."

"I guess the question is, now what? I show up with the car, Klot will probably just kill me, which may be better than losing more fingers."

She shivers. "I don't know! This is so crazy, I have no idea. Maybe find someone who does? Someone smarter. I'd ask a teacher. Do you know *anyone* who could at least give you some advice?"

I shake my head no.

"Family?"

Again, no.

"I know your mom died, but you never told me about your dad."

That's Denby, filling in the blanks, moving in that

invisible furniture again, like in her Rumi poem. No reason not to say. "He was a recovering alchy, fifteen years sober. When mom died, he tried to hold it together, pay the mortgage. We had a little house by the bay. But without her part-time income, he could barely keep it. When I said I was quitting school to be a singer, he had a shit-fit. Told me if I did, to find my own place. So I did."

"And you never went back to see him?"

"Once. He was gone. House for sale. Guess he bagged it. Probably in an alley somewhere with a bottle in his hand."

Denby's eyes get all wet.

"What about Po?" she asks.

"Po? What about him?"

"Maybe he'll have some idea what to do."

"Oh, he'll know exactly what to do. He'll laugh his head off at me."

"So let him."

"Then he'll kick me out."

"He won't. He loves you. You remind him of his uncle."

"The idiot who lost his kidney?"

"Yeah, but don't you see the way he gets all misty whenever he talks about him? Besides, why do you think he puts you up?"

"Because my music keeps him in business?"

She shrugs. "Barely. He didn't open a coffee shop in that part of Rivendale because he was planning to make money. He did it for the same reason you sing, because he loves it. He's been around a lot. He's perfect. Get some sleep and go talk to him in the morning."

I bristle. I want to grab my duck, shove it back on my head, and leave. But my options are limited. "Maybe you're right."

She twists her head, surprised. "You've never said that before."

"Really? Then I take it back," I say with a wicked grin.

She pushes me down with a little slap to my chest, then kisses me. I grab her warm arms, tug her closer, keeping our lips together all the while. She's so warm. It's all so peaceful. I feel the candlelight flickering against us, even with my eyes closed.

I hold her tighter, press my hands along her back, let my fingers touch the colors of her tattoo. I think about getting a little closer physically. Denby never wanted to go too far without that commitment thing; now I'm thinking that since I might die any day this might be a good time, but . . . it feels kind of slimy. I hesitate. She pulls away, kisses me on the forehead, and says, "Sleep."

She's right. I'm almost unconscious as it is. Before I catch the next wave to dreamland, I take the precious plastic bag with the car and the wheel and put it on a small nightstand, next to a dark brown candle, round and curly. In the flickering light it takes me a second to recognize that the candle has a face.

It's a bust of Pan, the Greek satyr, one of the original tricksters. I remember Denby showing it to me at The Rat. She said she planned to pretend it was a gift from me, since I never bought anything for her. It's a good candle. I have great taste in non-gifts.

She curls up into me. I turn from Pan, fall asleep, and dream.

No Super-Wade. Just me, just dreaming I am where I am, quiet and sad on the mattress. There is one difference, big one, kind of hard to miss, really; there's a giant head hovering over me, even bigger than a cow's. It's not real or fake, it's both, half in my mind, half in the room, looking familiar, like it's been here as long as the air and I'm the upstart newcomer. It grins, waving its fire red hair, making lines in its thick white skin, showing cracks in its teeth like black rivers, burning me with the mad gleam in its bloodshot eyes. It's him, the guy Po always said would turn on me. Trickster, and he's eyeing me like he's hungry, famished for a good joke. I'm it. Why me? Because I used to not care, but can't anymore. He chuckles like he's watching a chicken dinner try to fly. Then he laughs his horrible laugh. Molten hot, it rips chunks from my edges, blows holes in my gut, shreds every piece of me-meat, like wet dirt, till I'm all gone, not even a punch line anymore.

I wake. Denby's snoring peacefully. The candles are out. The beginnings of morning leak through the windows. Drowsy, I turn to candle-Pan. His face is half-melted. He looks the way I felt in the dream, but the crazy eyes and hungry grin are still there, perfect and pointed. The dripping wax around his eyes makes it seem as if he *is* looking at something, down and to the right.

What's so damn funny, Clown-king? What are you looking at?

The plastic bag. Only . . . what? The car's not in it, or the wheel. They're gone! I bolt up, fast enough to make Denby mumble. I look closer. There's some kind of computer part inside. It's sleek plastic, so cool I remember wishing it were real.

I *know* that flash drive. It's from my dream. From my frakking dream! It's the one with the program that'll save the world. I must be asleep, or half-asleep, or a tenth asleep—enough asleep to allow me to believe that that thing is here.

I pick it up, squeeze it, roll it through the bag. Feels real. So do I.

I'm just wild about Harry! And Harry's wild about me!

What the hell is that? Denby's cell phone? Where'd she get the crappy ring tone? She stretches and answers it in a mumble. Her eyes are closed, so she doesn't see my panicked face. On the other end, someone screams, as loud as Trickster's laugh, but much, much sadder.

"I'm sorry . . . could you . . . what?" Denby starts off trying to calm whoever she's talking to but winds up getting upset herself. "No! No!"

I'm still trying to get this all to be a dream, but she shoves the phone against my ear and I hear the pained screecher call my name: "*Wade* did this! That selfish monster!"

I look at Denby and furrow my brow to say, "Who is this?"

She mouths, "Ant's mother."

"Who . . . who did what?" I manage.

"They *took* him! They said *Wade* would know what it was about. I can't even get the police to—"

"Took him? Who took him?"

She describes a clean-cut police officer and a man with a very big head, then asks, full of venom, "Who *is* this?"

I'd like to answer, but I don't know. I don't know who I am anymore. The duck is gone. Blew off in a storm. And Ant? I don't even have the car that might have saved him, just a piece of a dream I barely remember and a life I wish I could forget.

CHAPTER 7

I don't dream. I just stop being.

When I come to, I'm not cuffed or in jail, I'm outside, nose-down in grass and dirt. A breeze plays on my back, almost like Denby tickling me. It cools the sweat my borrowed shirt is soaked in. I should be thrilled, but I'm not. I roll to get the grass out of my mouth. I'm on a sloped hill, a hundred yards from a side exit to the building. Above me the forest begins. And it turns out I didn't get here by myself. The woman who gave me the ID badge is also here, looking down at me with a mix of fear, disgust, and concern.

"I thought you were dead," she says.

"No, I'm fine, I think. Thanks."

She's tense, just like she was in the stairwell, afraid to make eye contact. She holds out her shaking manicured hand. "Give me back the ID."

I yank the ID from my pocket. She snatches it, spins, and trots down the hill.

"Wait!" I just want to thank her, apologize for screwing up.

"Don't talk to me! Don't even *look* at me." She runs like something's chasing her.

Taking the hint, I hobble up into the woods and find a big oak to hide behind. When I dare a peek, I see, below, a dozen gray-suited security guards rushing through the parking lot. A few search car to car, others put their hands to their foreheads and scan the woods.

When they stop looking, I head uphill. I'm not sure where to go or why. It would be crazy to go back inside and try again, and I'm not that kind of crazy. I can't even trust myself to check the code again. So what else? I can't call or head home — Prometheus will be looking for me. At least I don't have another panic attack. I'm even too tired for that.

It takes hours but I reach the strip mall at the outskirts of town, exhausted and dehydrated. I'm afraid my face will be plastered on all the TV screens in the window of the local Best Buy, but there's nothing. What next? No more directions from Judith. I'm on my own. Mr. Schapiro drove me to his place last night, so my car's still a few blocks from school. Good a place to go as any.

I manage the last few miles and get in. When I feel the wheel in my hand, I realize there *is* someplace I have to go, something I have to deal with, some*one*, before the world ends: Denby.

Her house is about ten minutes away. As I drive, the only related news I hear on the local radio station is about a false alarm at the collider. *False*, huh? What could that mean? Maybe they think I ran the sim and they don't want the press or the locals looking for me. Maybe they want me for themselves. Ha! I've never been *less* of a threat to them.

As I get closer to Denby's, a black SUV pulls behind me and seems to follow. Some big Slavic guy is at the wheel, trying to look tough. His personalized plates say ALEK18. Probably nothing, but paranoia seems like my last friend, so I slow down until he passes me, then park and walk the last half mile.

When I get to her street, instead of staying on the sidewalk I clamber along the backyards toward her parents' nice colonial. I'm two houses away when it dawns on me that some guy tramping through people's yards isn't exactly incognito. I'm full of mistakes today. Too late to fix any.

Great. Now a woman's staring at me from her kitchen window. I smile and wave, hoping she'll recognize me as Denby's boyfriend. She waves back, but keeps watching. I'm about to abandon the backyards when I see a limo parked across the street. It's a different make from the sedans at the high school, or the SUV, but it's the same black.

Perfect. Can't run. Can't go in the front door. I sidle closer to Denby's, like a crab, trying to stay out of view of both the kitchen-woman and the street. What if her parents spot me first? They like me well enough, but her mom's been staring at me cross-eyed since I gave her daughter that engagement ring. Right now, frankly, Anthony has the brighter future.

The first floor seems empty, but I see a wonderfully familiar shadow in the second-floor hall. It's her, listening to her iPod, swaying her hips and moving her lips to a song I can't hear. Probably "I'm Just Wild About Harry." Heh.

A trestle alongside the house leads to the roof of their sunroom. From there I can get to the hall window. Why not? Wouldn't be the worst thing I've done today. So I climb. The wood creaks, and I'm sure I kill a rose or two. The roof is more slanted than it looks, but I still get my hands to the second-floor window ledge.

Only, it's my feet I should have watched out for. They slide from under me. My knees crash into the aluminum siding, crunching it. I nearly lose my grip, but hang on by the tips of my fingers.

Even through her earbuds Denby hears the crash. She yanks open the window. The expression on her face belongs in the dictionary, next to the word "surprise."

"Wade! What—" she says loudly.

"Shh!" I say, half from pain, half from fear someone in the limo will hear. She pulls her buds out and I'm happy to hear *I'm just wild about Harry!* Nice to be right about something.

Still clinging to the ledge, I whisper, "Are they here?"

"Is *who* here?" she whispers back.

"Prometheus. Black car out front."

"The limo? Cheryl Cannon's going to France with the senior class. Her parents didn't want her taking the bus to the airport."

"Oh," I say. "Never mind. Could you help me in, please?"

She pulls at my forearms and I scramble in.

"Why didn't you use the door? Don't get me wrong. You don't surprise me often, you know. Not until lately, anyway."

I wipe my pants, rub my knees, then rise. I am so happy to see her, for a second I manage to forget how badly I've screwed up and why I'm here.

"Where have you been? Your dad's worried sick. Between him and Anthony I feel like I'm your social secretary."

"Denby, I know I'm an anxious jerk, I never relax, I'm no fun, and I'm probably a lot of other lousy things I don't even know about, but are you seeing Anthony behind my back?"

"Okay, now you're getting a little *too* surprising."

"Are you?"

"No! What a ridiculous—"

"Did he send you any e-mails about . . . his feelings? And what a lousy boyfriend I am?"

"What? Hey, it's not like anyone has to *tell* me what a lousy boyfriend you are. What kind of feelings are you . . ."

She looks at me a moment. The meaning behind my words catches up with her and her mind adds two and two. That definition-of-surprise look creeps up on her face again. "Oh. *Oh!* No. *No!* No way. He *has* been looking at me funny lately, but I thought he was just lonely. Wow, awkward, huh?"

"A little," I say, but really I'm too busy exhaling to get to awkward yet.

She looks at me, righteous and annoyed. "You didn't think *I'd* do anything like that, did you? With your friend? With anyone? I mean, you want to marry someone you can't even trust?"

I put my hands on her shoulders and rub her arms, not for her so much, but for me. "I'm sorry. It's been a long day, and it turns out I can't trust my best friend *or* myself."

She strokes the side of my face. "Wade, tell me what's going on before I kill you. I *will* kill you, you know, and that would be very sad because I *am* terribly fond of you."

I look around, out the window. "Is *anyone* here?"

She hesitates, probably about to demand I answer her first, but she's taken in enough of my haggard appearance to give me some slack. "Mom's with her sister in Bay Ridge, Dad's in Chicago until Monday. Chet and Bobby are at college. I'm alone. So talk."

"Can I have some water first? Please?"

"Sure. Why not? Would you like to see a menu?"

On the way to the kitchen, I start my convoluted story, pausing only long enough to see Cheryl Cannon climb into the backseat of the limo as the driver loads her bags.

Denby takes me by the hand and sits me at their breakfast nook. For a second I have a little fantasy, like we're already married and this is our house (a trifle smaller than I'd imagined). Only, instead of a theoretical physics professor or a mathematician, I'm a total screwup. When I'm done, I repeat my last sentence three times: "I don't know what to do. I don't know what to do. I don't know what to do."

She shrugs and smiles. "I'm sorry for all you're going through, but it's nice to hear you say that for a change. What do you want me to do?"

"Nothing. I just wanted to see you and find out about Anthony before the world ends or I get whisked off to some secret detention camp for wayward programmers."

"That's not going to happen," she says, squeezing my fingers, feeling them shake. "Geez, you poor thing. You need some rest, a bath. Go home, ask your dad for help."

"I can't. I can't even call him."

"That's crazy paranoid. Just leave your precious flash drive with me if you're so worried."

I twist my head side to side, rolling my eyes as I struggle to get out the words.

Denby looks hurt. "You still don't trust me, or do you think *all* my ideas are stupid?"

"No, no. I'm making faces at myself. I don't want to go home because I don't want to tell my father. I'm afraid he'll . . . Look, I haven't told anyone this, ever."

She softens, waits.

"You know he's a recovering alcoholic. He was two years sober when he met my mother. What you don't know is that after I was born he took a job he hated, to pay the bills, lots of pressure. When I was six months old he had a slip, a lost weekend. A lost two months, really. He . . . abandoned us. Mom freaked. She had the house on the market and was in touch with a divorce lawyer when he turned up and begged for one last chance. She gave it to him, and he pulled himself together. Went to regular meetings, got that job at Prometheus, made peace with himself, been sober ever since."

"And then she died."

"Yeah. It hurt me so much, but he was crushed, like an invalid. In AA they say you never really recover, you're always recover*ing*. People slip and start drinking anytime. It was only a little while after Mom died that Prometheus was temporarily shut down by the lawsuit and he was laid off. He once said the only thing that stopped him from drinking then was that *I* was doing so well. If I could pull myself together, he owed it to me and Mom's memory to do the same. Ever since, I feel like if I screw up I'll take him with me."

There are tears in her eyes. "I still think you should

talk to him. It's his turn to be the strong one. Maybe he'll surprise you."

His turn. What if he doesn't take it? I bristle. I settle down. I bristle again. "I should let him know I'm alive. But I can't go home. They *will* be looking for me. I can catch him tomorrow morning, I guess. He always stops at the Java Hut to sneak some real coffee. Thinks I don't know, but he leaves the receipts all over the place."

"Sounds like a plan."

"Can I . . . can I stay here tonight?"

"Of course," she says. She leans forward to kiss me. I lean forward, too. Our lips meet. We kiss for a while, but then I feel something stiff in my pocket. The flash drive.

I pull out of the kiss. "Denby?"

"Yes?" she says dreamily.

"Do you have a decent computer?"

She gives me a look of mild annoyance, then sees me take out the bag with the drive.

"Way to ruin a mood, Einstein. Right, right. End of the world. Come on."

She leads me upstairs. The house is all clean, straight lines, level family photos centered on the walls, until we get to her room. There, the light changes from white to auburn, the sun filtered by sheer cloths tacked over the windows. Her mattress is piled with stuffed toys. The cheap bust of Plato I gave her sits alone on her night table like a treasure, but her laptop sits on the floor in the middle of the room, half-covered with dirty laundry. I could never live in this kind of mess, but I always love seeing it here. It's totally Denby.

She kicks the clothes off the rig and opens her palm toward it. "Have at it."

So I do. I feel stupid for doubting her, for letting Anthony's e-mails get to me, but knowing she's still with me lets me stay calm enough to focus. I spend the next few hours going through my code again, correcting my stupid mistake, finding one more, checking it, proofing it, over and over as if I can somehow see what the results would be like if I ran it again. It's good. It makes me feel like I'm doing something useful, something I'm capable of. It makes me feel like myself.

Denby, being herself, is more interested in ordering pizza and forcing me to eat a slice. Once I do, she leaves me until I'm finally, finally finished.

When I am, I tell her, "I don't know what running it in the simulator will do, but at least now I know it's right."

"Great. Can we please go to sleep?"

I look at her. "Even if the world could end anytime?"

"Especially. I want to be rested for it."

I look at her like she's crazy. She punches me in the shoulder.

"If you're on a roller coaster to hell, Plato, you may as well stick your hands up in the air and try to enjoy the ride."

"For you? I'll . . . try."

She shakes her head. "Not for me. Not for your dad. Not for the world. For *you*."

I shrug. "That, too."

It's only then I notice how dark it is outside, only then I glance at the clock and realize it's past midnight.

"Wow. Sorry. Want me to go to the guest bedroom?"

"No," she says. "Roller-coaster time."

She yanks me to the mattress and kisses me. I fumble to put the flash drive back in the bag and next to the bust of

Plato. I turn back and kiss her for a while. I know it doesn't make objective sense, but time feels like it stops. I imagine that even the particles in Prometheus are taking a break, and all I'm doing is trying to find the line where Denby ends and I begin, just so I can lose it again.

Eventually we fall asleep.

Dreams come, but they're different. It's not another world. I am where I am, in Denby's room. Plato's head floats above us, looking down at me with white marble eyes. He seems disappointed, like I missed something. What? I followed every detail as best I could. There's nothing left I can think of. I'm done now. Done. *Nothing? Done? There's still you, isn't there?* His dead eyes tear into me, analyzing my every thought, feeling, memory. Once he figures something out about me, it *vanishes*. Once a part of me is known, it's no longer needed. It's just dirt, and Plato hates the dirt of life because it's not perfect. So he shreds me with understanding until I'm nothing but a particle, fading after a nanosecond, a strangelet that never touches the vacuum's end.

I wake, panting.

Denby snores peacefully. Morning light, turned deep auburn by the drapes, makes the room's edges glow. I turn to the bust of Plato. He glows, too, but still seems disappointed. Then I look at the plastic bag at his side. It doesn't look right.

The drive . . . it's gone!

Gone? Wrapped inside, instead, is the most ridiculous thing I've ever seen: a toy car covered in diamonds. One of the wheels is off. It's broken. I *know* this stupid toy. I know the broken wheel. It's from my dream.

I tell myself I'm asleep, or half-asleep, or a tenth asleep—whatever fraction of sleep will let me believe this thing isn't here, that this thing, which should only exist in some psychedelic corner of my mind, hasn't crawled out into the world.

I pick it up. I squeeze it. By any way I can measure real, it's real. I'm not dreaming. My time with Denby feels more like a dream than this. But that, that was just the calm before the storm. The hurricane is here.

My head spins, faster than it did when I ran from Finley, faster than when I read Anthony's letters, faster than when I found my mistake. It spins so fast I feel like I've careened out of my body and am falling into nothing. I fall out of my mind, out of my heart, out of everything, as if even the idea of a bottom is impossible, and falling is all there is.

CHAPTER 8

"Going to say something?" Po doesn't bother looking up. Was he expecting me? Does he already know about Ant? The Rat doesn't open for hours, but he's here, rubbing the coffee bar with a big, wet rag that has so many stains it adds more dirt than it picks up. The sopping blue cloth looks like a weird little ocean wave rolling around the pockmarked wood.

"Denby tell you I was coming?"

Now he stops, looks at me. "No. Did you hurt that girl?"

"No!" I try to sound offended, but I'm too shell-shocked.

"Because if you did . . ."

I take a few steps in from the door. "You're not making this any easier."

"Am I supposed to? And what the hell is *this* anyway?"

I sit at the bar. "Po, I'm screwed."

He shakes his head. "You were screwed when you were born."

"No, Po. More recently."

"How bad?"

"Bad enough I want to talk to *you* about it." I hold up my bandaged pinkie.

He tosses the rag into the sink, then levels his eyes at me. He's got a bunch of colors in there—flecks of green, brown, bits of red capillary, and a wee bit of yellow in the corners.

"So talk."

I do, but it's a lot tougher than talking to Denby. This feels like a job interview. All the while, he's like a statue. I don't even get a rise when I say stuff is falling out of my dreams. I toss the bag with the flashy drive right onto the counter, like it's the Loch Ness monster. Still nothing. Then I realize it doesn't prove a thing.

"Po, I'm not even treading water. I'm sinking. Can you help me figure out what to do?"

He comes to life, but slowly. The lines on his face move like little snails, squirming into what I think is a grimace. "Let me show you something, Clown-boy."

He turns and starts pulling his shirt out of the back of his pants.

"Po, man! I bare my soul and you're going to give me crap about your uncle's kidney again? I make myself open and you give me a joke?"

As I say it, it dawns on me how often I've been on the flip side of that.

But Po doesn't look like he's joking. "Let me show you something," he says again.

He pulls up his shirt, exposing his lower back. The skin's thin, white, the bumps from his spine even whiter. There's also a long reddish scar above where his kidney should be. This week has been full of surprises, and I guess it isn't done yet.

"It wasn't your uncle."

"No."

"That's why you think you know me? Because you think we're alike?"

He nods. "Most of you, anyway. The only thing I could never figure is why you stick to one woman. I could never do that. I had lots of girls. The only one I couldn't get was the one who got me. I was always showing off in front of her, taking whatever chances I could to get her attention. Finally, she invites me to a hotel. We have drinks, we kiss, just once. I pass out and wake up with my kidney gone."

He winces like the scar still hurts, or maybe it's just the memory that hurts. "Wound went septic. Lost forty pounds, nearly died. My uncle paid my hospital bills and I spent the next six years working it off on his pig farm. You know pigs? I hate pigs. Too smart. They know they're going to be turned into bacon, and they don't like it."

He leans forward and whispers conspiratorially. "The thing that took me years to figure out is that it wasn't the girl that did it to me. She could've been anyone."

I think I know where he's going. "It was your*self*, right? Your own self-destructive—"

"No, no, no, you idiot! Well, yes, but no, too." His

eyes get wide, like he's opening them all the way for the first time in years. "It was Trickster! He did it. Once you invite him in, he comes. Then he's you and not you, in your head and out of it at the same time. The bastard sits in between, making everything and everyone look like a joke to you and making you look like a joke to everyone."

Whoa. Ever since he started bringing that gun down to the basement to protect himself from the rat, I knew he was superstitious, but I never realized how deep it went.

"Po, do you mean, you know . . . metaphorically?"

"Sure. What's a metaphor?"

I get a flash of that hungry face from my dream, and shiver. Another flash: a plaque in my mother's workshop, VOCATUS ATQUE NON VOCATUS DEUS ADERIT. "Summoned or not, the god will be present." A final flash, from Dad's AA days, a photocopy on the bulletin board, an anagram for sober: SON OF A BITCH, EVERYTHING'S REAL.

Everything, I guess, included Trickster, and I sure had done my best to summon him.

"Okay, say I believe you. Why not? Stuff's falling out of my dreams. Trickster's as good an explanation as any. But what do I do? How do I get rid of him?"

He makes a face. "I don't know. Wait, I do know. You almost die. You work on a pig farm for six years. You stop being like him. You stop being an asshole."

"I can't just do that. I've been working at it for years. Where would I start?"

"You got where you are by respecting nothing, so you get back by showing respect. Hated my uncle, resented him because I owed him. I was so stupid I would have died rather than owe him, but I obeyed him. I showed him respect. So, you, you pick something and start being respectful toward it."

"And that will help me with Klot?"

"It might. Probably not, but at least you won't die an asshole. You got any better ideas, Clown-boy?"

"No. Respectful? Like what?"

"I don't know. You pick!"

"Ant's not talking to me, and Denby—"

"Keep that poor girl out of it! Bad enough she cares about you. What about parents? You love your parents?"

I bob my head. "My mom. She's easier to love than Dad. She's dead."

"Ever been to her grave?"

I look at him. "No. Not since the funeral."

"Right. So, all this? Klot, dream bag, broken toy? Stop it. Forget it. It's only important if you think *you're* important, and you've got to start understanding that you ain't. It'll be here when you get back and, if it's not, you'll have to live with it."

"Even Ant? What if they—"

"The sooner they find you, the sooner he's dead. Go visit your mom. It's the last place they'd look for you anyway. Have a nice long talk. Show respect."

I have no idea why this should make any sense, but it does. "Okay," I say.

"So go! Go now!"

I look down at my bathrobe and scrubs. "I . . . I should change."

"No shit, Sherlock. That's the idea."

I mount the stairs, on the way up to my room, when Po calls, "Hey!"

He nods at the plastic bag I left on the counter, the flashy drive inside. "Take that out of here. It's Trickster's business, and I only got one kidney left."

CHAPTER 8

I go through all the explanations for where the toy car came from—whether they're possible or not, even Judith's theory about an inter-dimensional rift, which this thing might have somehow fallen through. Of all the options, my own complete insanity seems the most likely. I have fainting spells, why not schizophrenia with hallucinations? When I told myself I had to let go of things more often, I didn't figure on this.

But once the room stops spinning, I feel so *normal*. Shouldn't I feel different? Wouldn't a psychotic break be more uncomfortable? Something?

I don't tell Denby. I just pocket the toy car and look worried. Sleepy, she figures I'm freaking out about everything else, and repeats in a slurring drawl that I should go talk to my father.

Sure, tell Dad: "Hey, Dad, as long as I'm psycho, how about the two of us get a bottle of the cheap stuff and keep drinking until everything goes away? I'm up for it!"

No. There's got to be an answer. I just have to find it. And I do have to see Dad. I can't keep him in the dark anymore. If I show him the toy car and he doesn't see anything, he should be the one to take me to the psychiatric hospital.

As I drive toward Java Hut I briefly think I should have disguised myself or borrowed Denby's car but, really, at this point, this *is* a roller coaster to hell, so what the hey? My vague stab at letting go is rewarded by an utterly normal trip. No sedans, no security cars, no suspicious helicopters. Not so much as a daredevil squirrel. Why would there be? Finley must know I blew it by now. If I'd run the sim, there'd be a record on the terminal, and he's had plenty of time to check.

Java Hut, a brick-and-mortar establishment and the most popular coffee place in town, invades my field of vision. Hell, it's the *only* coffee place in town. There was some dive for a while in the seedy section of Rivendale, The Mouse? But it closed after a year. Java Hut's upscale, courtesy of Prometheus, which secured the loan that got the business started. Good investment. The morning crowd's so big, I have to wait for a spot. I'm afraid I'll miss Dad until I see his cranky old Honda, and snag the space next to it.

Espresso is bad for his blood pressure, but so's being miserable, so I adopted a don't-ask-don't-tell policy. Coffee won't kill you as fast as booze, and he likes to have a bit of a private life. My being here, scoping the long line for his familiar close-cropped head, breaks a boundary. Sorry, Dad, but I've crossed a lot of those lately, especially if you count the whole dream/reality thing.

I'm inside less than ten seconds when a familiar hand

grabs my shoulder. I know who it is before I see his face. Instantly, I relax and feel at home, safe, even if it is an illusion.

"Prodigal son!" Dad says, grinning. "You couldn't call?"

"Prodigal dad," I say, with great somberness. "I could not. I need to talk to you."

He nods, still mostly pleased to see me. "I was going crazy wondering where you were. It's not like you to have a good time. I'm next in line. Want anything?"

"Chamomile tea."

He makes a face, like I'm missing the whole point of Java Hut, so I add, "I've had a lot of coffee lately." To prove it, I show him my hand. My fingers shake.

"Whoa," he says, and goes to order the tea.

We're soon at a table in the back, me smelling my tea, him sipping his espresso.

"You're not hassling me about my blood pressure. This must be serious. What's up?"

The words stick in my throat. "It's hard."

"You kill someone?"

I look down.

"What? You *did* kill someone?"

"No! It's just that it's pretty bad, and . . ." I hem. I haw. I finally spit it out. "I'm worried you'll start drinking again."

He sighs. "I've told you before, I can't promise I'll never drink again. I can only promise to try. But being your father is one of the things that makes me try. That means I want to be able to help when you're in trouble, whatever it is. I barely do anything for you anymore, you're eighteen, but at least I can listen."

So I talk. I tell him about my fainting spells, about Finley, about breaking into Prometheus, about Anthony's e-mails to Denby. I even tell him all my recent weird dreams. I tell him everything, except about the diamond toy in my pocket. I'm enjoying feeling like his kid so much I don't want to get to the part where it's time to haul me off to the loony bin.

He listens, waiting until I'm through. When I am, he leans back and says, " 'Brief as the lightning in the collied night . . . so quick bright things come to confusion.' "

The quote makes me smile. "Right. Mom said that whenever she gave up on a project."

"Yeah. Shakespeare, I think. Wade, wow. Just as you think you win, your hopes get destroyed and you get gutted by your best friend. No wonder you're having panic attacks," he says. He leans over and grabs my wrist. "Just means you're human, like the rest of us poor slobs."

"But I'm *always* almost passing out. Sure, this time it's the end of the world, but it's always *something*. First time it was a math test."

"It could be biological, too."

"Mom used to faint?"

"No, me."

"You?"

"Don't know if you noticed, but I'm not exactly a rock, emotionally. It started after high school. I'd graduated top of my class and was accepted to Yale. For me, life was politics, so that summer I became involved in a local election. My guy was a reformer, a saint who could do no wrong. I canvassed, I called. Person by person, I was going to convince everyone to vote for him."

"And?"

"We were still way behind in the polls, but then I heard

a rumor that our opponent was accepting bribes. If I could prove it, we'd win. I went berserk trying. I stalked him. I took secret photos of him. I stole his trash. I even tried to break into his house. I could not, would not let it go. Days before the election, I had chest pains, hyperventilating, the works. Then we lost. That weekend, I went to a bar and, for the first time, I started drinking to feel better."

"That's hard to imagine."

"That I could faint?"

"No, that you were ever eighteen."

"Ha!" He swats his hand toward the side of my head, but I duck. "See that? You *do* have a sense of humor buried in there somewhere."

"But how do you *not* take it too seriously if you're the only one who can prove the world might end?"

He shrugs. "How could *I* not take it too seriously when I was the only one trying to stop some corrupt asshole from being elected? Or when I had a six-month-old baby and a job I hated? I grew up worried about a nuclear war between the United States and the Soviet Union. Now we've got global warming. But if you stop living because you're so afraid, you forget why anything's worth saving in the first place. You *have* to. Some things in life aren't just out of our control, they're out of *any* control. They're ridiculous, absurd. Part of you knows that. That's why you keep dreaming you're a jokester. You have to let go."

"Dad, the dream I had? The one about the diamond-encrusted toy car?"

"Exactly. You're dreaming about a *toy*. That's how the stress comes out. You have to take it easy, be kind to yourself. Try to—"

I pull the car out and put it on the table between us.

"Holy shit!" he screams. "Is that for real?"

Guess he sees it. He backs away from the table, his calm falling away like a mask.

"It's . . . it's . . ."

His hands shake. People stare.

"Dad, calm down. Please."

He looks around, sees all the eyes on him, then sits again fast.

"Where the *hell* did that come from?" he whispers.

"Probably the same place the flash drive went. Meaning, I have no idea."

He picks it up, holds it in the air between us. A few people are still staring, so he hands it back to me. "Put it away."

I shove it in my pocket.

"I'll ask one more time. Where'd it come from?"

"As far as I can tell, it's from my dream."

He stares at me, scans my face for the longest time, looks *at* my eyes, then tries to look *behind* them. After a while he gives up. He knows he either has to accept that I'm telling the truth, or accept the fact that he can't tell if I'm lying or crazy.

"Some things in life are just ridiculous, huh?" I say.

"I didn't mean *that* ridiculous. Either you're screwing with me, someone's screwing with you, or the gods are screwing with everyone. I . . . I don't think it's you."

"So what should I do?"

He holds his palms up and exhales. "When things get crazy, I try to follow the AA program, the Twelve Steps. We don't usually deal with things falling out of dreams, but the

DTs can get just as crappy, so I guess it still applies. It's all I've got to offer, anyway. The first step is to admit that you're powerless over something and your life has become unmanageable. In my case, alcohol, in your case . . . stuff falling out of your dreams, I guess. So, stop trying to fight it. Accept it."

"Accept it? How."

He exhales again. "Whenever I need to be reminded of something important that I was totally powerless over, I go talk to your mother. Puts me in my place, and once I'm in my place, it's a comfort to remember her."

He means I should visit her grave. It's been a sore spot between us for years.

"You haven't been there since the funeral. You've never seen the headstone."

"She's not there! She's gone. It's a stupid, gaudy ritual."

"Wade, sometimes stupid, gaudy rituals are all we have."

CHAPTER 9

The cemetery was never far. More than a few times I'd be bumming around and recognize a street or a landmark that made me think, "Oh, Mom's buried near here somewhere. I should go." But then I couldn't find it, like it was invisible, and the urge faded. Of course I didn't ask directions. I always figured that wherever I wound up was where I should be. Funny, if you *do* look at a map or ask directions, turns out that'll get you places, too.

About three miles from The Rat, behind a row of big old apartment buildings that border the park and the nicer part of town, there are some rolling hills you might take for a golf course. From a distance, the hills look littered with golf balls, white, evenly spaced, all in lines, until you get close enough to realize they're headstones. Game over.

I stand at the front gate, not remembering exactly where Mom is. I think about summoning my muse, but go to the office instead. The woman there, in her fifties,

in a clean thrift-store dress and coiffed hair, ignores me.
I guess she doesn't like the way I look, even though I'm
wearing my best jeans, T-shirt, and wrinkled overshirt.

Finally, I say, "Can you help me, please?" and give
her my mother's name. There's some kind of maintenance money due, so along with the grave number,
she hands me a bill. Normally, I'd crumple and chuck it,
but I'm supposed to be respectful now, right? Grudg-
ingly, she tells me how to find my mom's grave.

By the time I'm back outside, I can't remember what
she said, so I figure it out by following the signs, count-
ing the numbers. 247B, like an apartment.

Shouldn't I be feeling something, something different from usual? I don't, not even as I get closer, not
even as I find the right row and trudge along the headstones. Some have photos of warmly smiling people
etched into the stone, others have fresh flowers. Some
have dates telling me that whoever's buried there died
as a child.

Then I see the pink marble my father picked out in
those surreal days right after she passed. I still don't feel
anything, just the memory of where that deep well of
numbness came from, and the weird buzz in my head.
Looking at the stone isn't like seeing something real,
it's more like staring at a photo a million years old. A
dream. Less real than the flashy drive in Sergei's germ-
free plastic bag.

I came here to show respect, to think, but I don't feel
like I can do either. I try. I stand on the grass in front of
her name and shut my eyes. I rub the flash drive through
the plastic bag, feel its strange coolness. In the closed-eye

dark it *all* feels distant, like none of it—The Rat, Ant, Alek, Klot, Po—has anything to do with me. It's all way over there somewhere, and me, I'm right here. I begin and end here . . . don't I?

I sense it even before I open my eyes. I'm not alone. Someone's standing at the end of the row. His hair is clean. His clothes are new. He's got some kind of jacket on over a black T-shirt and light brown pants that make him look like a nerdy clothing-store clerk. He looks like one of those ants who *want* to live in Denby's house of cards.

I don't like him, not at all, which is unusual since I don't think about most people long enough to like or dislike them. But I *know* him. Don't know how, but I do. My heart leaps. For a second, I think it's Dad. But it's not. No. This guy's way too young. From the way he's looking at me, I can tell he's thinking the same thing. He can't stand me, either, but he knows me. He's my age. My height, my hair color, my eyes . . . my . . . ?

Then I see it. There's a bag in his hands. Through the clear plastic, diamonds sparkle, diamonds in the shape of a toy. The car. *The car!*

All my nagging half memories fall together and club me in the face. Once upon a time in my sticky comic-book dreams, I looked in a mirror, and he was what I saw. This guy. Super-Wade. The fainter. He's from my dream, like the flashy drive. The thing in my hand is *his* James Bond flashy drive.

He looks at me, totally blown away, like he's realizing the same thing at the same time. We know who we are. We're us. We're me. We're Wade.

He walks forward, eyes dancing over my face, my body. His brow doesn't furrow, it ripples. He's thinking hard. A real thinker. Like Denby. Like I used to be.

"Geez," I say to him, "do you have to think so much? I can smell the wood burning in your brain from over here."

"Did Prometheus open up a space/time rift when it made that first strangelet? Was Judith Wilson right? Do we have parallel lives?" he asks. "Do our dreams access another dimension?"

"Like I know what you're talking about," I say, unable to avoid a little nose-laugh. "Maybe it's more like that butterfly thing."

He scrunches his face. "You mean Chuang Tsu? The man who dreams he's a butterfly, then wakes up never knowing if he's a man dreaming he's a butterfly or a butterfly dreaming he's a man?"

"Bingo."

"But how is that possible? *Both* our lives can't be real, can they?"

"I don't know, man. I didn't do it. Trickster's business. Does it matter?"

"Trickster's what? That a rock group? Of course it matters. *Everything* matters!"

"Whatev." There are other things I'd rather be talking about. Besides, I came here to be respectful, and Mr. Science is making it tough.

"Whatever? Are you kidding me? Your whole life's a mess! You quit school, you don't have a job. You can't commit to Denby. And you said *something* so stupid it made a mobster cut off your finger!"

So he dreams me, too. And he's getting personal. Maybe I'll take that crap from Denby, but I don't have to take it from me.

"Yeah? At least I didn't faint before I could press a button! What did you see that scared the crap out of you anyway, big shot? A mouse that wasn't connected to a PC? At least I'm not trying to force my girlfriend to marry me because I'm scared she'll run off."

"Shut up! And my life is none of your business. And . . . and . . . *you* abandoned Dad."

"He abandoned *me*, asshole." It dawns on me I'm talking about stuff from his life I shouldn't even know about. But the more I talk, the more I remember. "And you think your way is better? Yanking him to all those meetings, forcing him to go to work, managing his paychecks, talking him out of trying to get laid so he can work overtime instead? You treat him more like a pet than a man! Christ, he *should* run away! And your friends? Hunchback-Ant sold you out—"

"Anthony. His name is Anthony."

"Fine. Anthony. Hunchback-*Anthony* sold you out to Particle Dude! You've got his and Denby's life planned out for the next ten years. What do they call that in fancy psychological talk?"

"Enabling?"

"No. Control freak. You're a damn control freak. You treat everyone you know like shit."

"So do you!"

"Freak!"

"Loser!

We get quiet. We look away. We look back.

I point to the bag. "You've got my car."

"Yes."

"And you know I've got your computer thingy, right?"

"Flash drive. You think . . . you think it means we were *supposed* to meet?"

I shrug. "No. I'm just saying, just pointing out the obvious. But, yeah, maybe. Maybe we were supposed to meet. Here."

We look at the stone. We read her name.

The anger melts. It's just not important. Not here.

"You remember what she said before she died, right? What she asked?"

"Oh yeah."

My mother used to sing, strong and loud, crazy and proud, but her last words came in a whisper. We recite them, taking turns. When I stop, he continues.

"Life is short, Wade. Too short and too precious to waste on being afraid, too short not to risk it all and go for what you really want. Too short not to ever *decide*."

"So promise me just one thing—that you'll find out what you really want to do, in your heart of hearts and, no matter what it is, you'll do it."

I know he has the same picture in his mind as I do. She's lying in the hospital bed, facing her favorite window and the bay. The tide was in when she spoke, but going out. When the water left, so did she.

But she wanted me, us, to decide.

We look at each other and talk to ourselves. It doesn't matter who says what.

"Part of us wanted to work hard to make the world a

better place, and the other part wanted to quit school and become a singer."

"And when it came right down to it, we were more like her than she realized. We just couldn't choose between the two."

CHAPTER 9

It takes time to reassure Dad that I'll call him if I need him. Then I have to spend more time convincing him he shouldn't take the day off and sit by the phone in case I do. It's a tough fight, but after I swear a blood oath that I won't hesitate to interrupt him, and remind him of everything he just told me about "letting go," he agrees.

As his cranky Honda vanishes from the parking lot, so does my desire to visit the cemetery. Going to visit my mother's grave is a damn silly idea. It has nothing to do with anything, nothing to do with strangelets or Anthony or dizzy spells. But I promised Dad I'd go, and, pound for pound, it isn't any sillier than any other idea I have. It's certainly not as silly as this diamond car in my pocket.

Trying *not* to imagine the world ending at any second, I drop by the house first, to shower and put on some clean clothes. I put my cracked laptop on the kitchen counter. Just to delay leaving a little longer, I tinker with it a bit, tell myself I might still be able to boot it, get the code out of it. But I don't get anywhere, so I plug it in to charge and give up.

Rivendale Cemetery isn't far. I even know exactly where Mom's plot is. The week she died, Dad put a map of the graveyard on our bulletin board and used a red pen to X the spot. Details.

So far, he's right about this clearing my mind. The awkwardness of the trek pushes my other worries to the back of my head, but I'm not happy about it. I am glad my memory holds true. Even on the one-lane road that winds through the cemetery, I don't wonder where to park. When I get out to mount the monument-dotted hill, I'm only sorry I didn't stop farther away. I could've used a longer, slower walk.

They're not kidding when they say graveyards are peaceful and quiet. The air is crisp and the cemetery big enough to give it that kind of special silence usually only found on days blanketed with thick snow, when it feels as if both the world and me are alone in my head.

I trudge toward plot 247B, thinking, as I get closer, that I should be feeling something, *anything*, but I don't, not even as I pass among the headstones. Some of the graves have photos of the departed. Dad wanted to get one of those, but I stopped him, thinking it was tacky. Maybe I was wrong. There's something special about the faces.

As I pass a gnarled old oak, the pink quarried-marble Dad picked stands out like a flower in a field of white, black, and gray. Nice choice. It looks good against the grass, the sky. Doesn't seem as harsh as the others. Doesn't seem as dead.

Getting closer, I find myself looking forward to reading

her name, the dates, closing my eyes to think, or better yet, stop thinking. I take out the bag with the diamond toy in it. Don't know why I brought it with me. Maybe to show her.

Only, someone's already there.

Who?

He stands right on her grave, like it's his place, not mine.

Our eyes meet. My God, what a piece of work. What a mess. He looks like a street person, only he's as young as I am. Maybe he's a crack addict. His hair's a rat's nest, his skin gray, like it hasn't seen the sun in years. He's thin, too, enough for his cheeks to be sallow, which makes his eyes seem bigger, stick out slightly. And there's this strange, wild glint to them, an animal sparkle. No, not an animal. More like . . . a clown.

Though his face has no particular expression just now, the lines conspire to make it look like he's sneering, not at me but at everything, the entire world, like it's some big joke, and he's the only one who gets it. Don't get me started on his clothes. Torn jeans, stained T-shirt under a drab olive overshirt. Exactly the sort of person I hate, a parasite, a hedonist, not caring about anything except what feels good. No worries. *Hakuna matata.* Ha.

While I scan him, he scans me, eyes narrowing as he sizes me up. I get the feeling his opinion of me is at least as low as mine is of him. I doubt we know each other. How could we? But . . . I *do.* Don't know how or why, but I know him. Seems like he's thinking the same thing. We know each other. From where? School? There are more than a few losers at Rivendale High. He's my age. My height, has my hair color, my eyes, and, if you put a few pounds on it, my . . . face?

There's a plastic bag in his hands. In it, I see the flash

drive. My brow was furrowed but, seeing that, my face and mind go blank. He's staring at the plastic bag in my hand—the car—with the same void expression.

Then I remember. I wish I didn't, but I do. Once in my dreams, in the filthy bathroom of that coffee dive, I looked in a mirror. I was so horrified by what I saw I forgot it, until now. That's where I know him from. It was him. I was him. This wreck. He's like the diamond-studded car. He's from my dream. In the dream, he's me.

He knows it, too. Figured it out the same moment I did.

I step closer, my brow crunching so tightly I feel it pulse. He burns me with the wild light in his crazy eyes. He grins. Like everything else, he thinks this is funny.

How could this happen? Am I insane? What kind of insanity is this?

"Geez," he says, in a lazy but accusatory way, "do you have to think so much? I can smell the wood burning in your brain from over here."

I think out loud: "Did Prometheus open up a space/time rift when it made that first strangelet? Was Judith Wilson right? Do we have parallel lives? Do our dreams access another dimension?"

"Like I know what you're talking about," he says, with an insulting little laugh. "Maybe it's more like that butterfly thing."

Butterfly thing? What is he . . . "You mean Chuang Tsu? The man who dreams he's a butterfly, then wakes up never knowing if he's a man dreaming he's a butterfly or a butterfly dreaming he's a man?"

"Bingo."

"But how is that possible? *Both* our lives can't be real, can they?"

"I don't know, man. I didn't do it. Trickster's business. Does it matter?"

I don't believe this guy. "Trickster's what? That a rock group? Of course it matters. *Everything* matters!"

"Whatev," he says.

"Whatever? Are you kidding me?" He is really pissing me off. Details of the dreams flood me. "Your whole life's a mess! You quit school, you don't have a job. You can't commit to Denby. And you said *something* so stupid it made a mobster cut off your finger!"

"Yeah? At least I didn't faint before I could press a button! What did you see that scared the crap out of you anyway, big shot? A mouse that wasn't connected to a PC? At least I'm not trying to force my girlfriend to marry me because I'm scared she'll run off."

He knows. He knows me, too. "Shut up! And my life is none of your business. And . . . and . . . *you* abandoned Dad."

The sneer vanishes. "He abandoned *me*, asshole. And you think your way is better? Yanking him to all those meetings, forcing him to go to work, managing his paychecks, talking him out of trying to get laid so he can work overtime instead? You treat him more like a pet than a man! Christ, he *should* run away! And your friends? Hunchback-Ant sold you out—"

"Anthony. His name is Anthony."

"Fine. Anthony. Hunchback-*Anthony* sold you out to Particle Dude! You've got his and Denby's lives planned out for the next ten years. What do they call that in fancy psychological talk?"

"Enabling?"

"No. Control freak. You're a damn control freak. You treat everyone you know like shit."

"So do you!"

"Freak!"

"Loser!"

We go quiet for a long time. We look at each other like it hurts just to see. We turn away for a break, then look back.

He breaks the silence, pointing to the bag. "You've got my car."

"Yes."

"And you know I've got your computer thingy, right?"

"Flash drive. You think . . . you think it means we were *supposed* to meet?"

He shrugs. It's annoying the way he shrugs. "No. I'm just saying, just pointing out the obvious. But, yeah, maybe. Maybe we were supposed to meet. Here."

We look at the stone. We read her name. It spite of all the strangeness, the quiet calms us.

"You remember what she said before she died, right? What she asked?"

"Oh yeah."

We recite it, word for word, breath for breath, taking turns. We don't skip a beat.

He begins. "Life is short, Wade. Too short and too precious to waste on being afraid, too short not to risk it all and go for what you really want. Too short not to ever *decide*."

When he stops, I continue. "So promise me just one thing—that you'll find out what you really want to do, in your heart of hearts and, no matter what it is, you'll do it."

As we speak I know he has the same picture of her in his head I do, lying in the hospital bed we brought home so she could spend her last days with us. We'd hoped it might be a week, but it was only two days, as if she could finally relax at home, let go.

Let go.

She lay facing her favorite window. It overlooked the little bay out back. A land bridge, made of piled stones, came and went with the tide. The tide was in, but going out. When the water left that last time, so did she.

But she wanted me, us, to decide.

We look at each other and talk to ourselves. It doesn't matter who says what.

"Part of us wanted to work hard to make the world a better place, and the other part wanted to quit school and become a singer."

"And when it came right down to it, we were more like her than she realized. We just couldn't choose between the two."

CHAPTER 10

CHAPTER 10

We try to swap bags, but when they touch, reality shudders and skips a beat. All of a sudden I'm alone. Maybe I always was. Maybe the whole thing was just a whacked Very Special Christmas TV Show, a drug-induced spiritual journey, or a goddamned, god-awful nightmare. Maybe Po slipped me something. I really don't trust his coffee anymore.

I look at my hands. No, I still have the flashy drive. And there's more, much more: I'm not in my own worn, comfy clothes anymore. I'm in pressed tan pants, jacket, and black T-shirt. Everything's clean, stiff, and itching. I put my hand in my hair. My fingers pass through. It's combed. My pinkie? Perfect. No bandage.

I'm not me anymore, I'm *him*. Super-Wade, only that's too cool a name. The Other Guy.

Is this Trickster's business, too?

I look up at a giant clown head that isn't there and scream, *"What do you want with me?"*

Nothing. Not a giggle, not a smirk. At least I still think like me. At least I think I do. Crap. I don't even *want* to think about any of this.

I stumble out of the graveyard, take a very long, dizzy walk Ratward, looking for home, but Po's hand-painted rodent sign is gone. There isn't even a clean spot where it hung. It looks more like it was never there. No, no, no. Enough already.

I run to the door. Boarded up. I look in through cracked windows—the insides are empty, gutted. I try to circle the building, but Alley-Oops is blocked by a huge Dumpster I've never seen before. Even the trash in the alley looks different.

This is like that sappy black-and-white movie Mom made me watch at Christmas, *It's a Wonderful Life*—only more like *It's a . . . Hey, This Totally Sucks!*

"Got a dollar?"

I leap, but relax when I finally see something familiar. It's Brosius, looking paler than usual but at least it's him. You'd think he'd know better than to try to borrow money from me, but I'm glad to see him.

"No, Bro. Where's Po?"

His stoner face scrunches like it's a major effort to get his brain to work. "Oh, wow. The old guy who owned the coffeehouse? Went out of business two years ago. Sure you don't have a buck?"

Out of business? I never thought of it *as* a business. What's up with that?

In the alley, past the Dumpster, I spot a cardboard hut full of rags and newspapers, all arranged like a big nest, a Brosius nest. Alongside, there's a little pile of broken glass vials. Crack. And here I thought he was only into weed.

"Brosius, when did you get all whack?"

He doesn't hear me. He's still about the buck. "Mind if I check your pockets?"

"What're you, trying to mug me? *Me*? Please. Open up those slitty eyeballs. Do I *look* like I have money?"

"Yeah. You do."

Wait. He's right. I do look like I have money. Does that mean I do? That'd be a kick. I shove my hand into my pocket and discover something better. Car keys. Whoa. Was the blue electric future car real, too? Well, well, well. I'll have to check this out. Things may not be so sucky after all.

Once I buy Bro and myself a hot meal at the diner across the street (with a freaking *credit card*! And my signature *matched*!), I head back to the cemetery alone, a man with a mission: to find the Other Guy's wheels. Why not? Always wanted a car. Always wanted a pet monkey, too, but that's beside the point.

When I try the key in a few blue cars, it doesn't work. All I get are some nervous stares. Fortunately, before I wind up arrested, I remember the *electric* part. There's only one blue hybrid around. Neatly parked, so familiar, it glows. And what do you know? The key fits. And if the key fits, I say, drive it.

Sliding behind the wheel feels like I'm having a daydream about being exactly where I am, a kind of constant déjà vu. Yeah, this is the dream world, all right, only it doesn't seem as crazy or comic booky as I remember it. What was it Po said about Trickster making the world look ridiculous? Probably twice as true of dreams.

I start the puppy up and cruise. As I move along, more déjà-details float to mind, like how the car has both a gas and an electric motor. To test it, I put the pedal down to make the gas engine kick in, then slow down so the electric motor takes over. Cool!

Clothes aside, maybe this isn't so bad. Maybe this is even great. My old life wasn't working out very well anyway, right? And now, no broken toy car, no Psycho Klot, and I've never been happier flexing my pinkie. If I remember correctly, Hunchback-Ant's evil, but you can't have everything, right? At least he's alive. And Denby's running from my marriage proposal.

So what's the worst? That stupid Super-Wade fantasy about Prometheus destroying the world? Like I care. The collider was shut down in my world without me lifting a finger. Respectful or not, it can't possibly be my problem.

I zip along, free as a bird, sunlight beaming through the windshield, cool breeze blowing from the windows. A left here, a right there, following my whimsies without recrimination. Feels like old times, until Po's words come back and kill the buzz—if this *is* Trickster's business and, really, it kind of has to be, he could show up and squash me any minute now. So what am I supposed to do? What is there to respect?

I slow down. Another turn and things get *too* familiar. The street's tree lined and wide. Kids flood out of a school bus, so many different colors to their clothes they look like a living laundry pile. Beyond the backyard plots there's a small bay with a land bridge made of stone, only above water when the tide's out. I'm home. This is where I lived before I quit school. With Mom. And Dad. Now I *know* Trickster's messing with me.

My chest gets kind of tight, but I creep down the block anyway. I see the house and tremble. No for-sale sign. In the dream, the Other Guy still lives here with . . . Dad.

I should pull a U-turn and floor it, but I don't. Not because I'm trying to be "respectful" either. I'm in a trance, like when I was stuck watching Denby build her card house. I can't leave.

I park in the driveway, slip my key in the front door, step inside, and turn off the burglar alarm as if I've been doing it every day for years. How do I even know the code?

It's like I'm stepping into church wearing my stinky bathrobe. Normally that wouldn't bother me, but . . . could Dad be here? Not deadbeat-drunk Dad, the Other Guy's clean and sober version. Love to see that. Wouldn't I? Respect? Respect.

"Dad?"

Can't believe how shaky my voice sounds. Damn.

"Dad?" a little louder.

No answer. I make my way past Mom's old work-shop, still untouched, still full of her projects, and head into the kitchen. So here I am, smack in the middle of the life I left behind. I feel as if I betrayed it, same as I betrayed Ant. Every sight is a pang. Looking at the coffee machine hurts. Seeing the junk mail hurts. Okay, not everything. There's a broken laptop on the counter I don't recognize and that doesn't hurt, but next to it is a picture of me, Dad, and Denby at some kind of picnic, all smiling like we mean it. That stings like a son of a bitch.

And last but not least, there's a Post-it on the fridge, a note in handwriting I know so well it bores into my head like a whispered voice:

Took a break to see if you were home. No such luck. Heading back. Sorry I can't help more, but I want you to know I believe in you. I know you'll find a way. Love, Dad

I look up into a familiar mirror on the wall. One of Mom's projects, made from an old window frame but never painted. That's me? No way. Not a zit on my skin or a hair out of place. I growl, muss my hair, and yank open the jacket so hard I tear a button. It skitters against the tiles. I look around for some old spaghetti to sit in.

This is wrong. I want to go back. Even with Psycho Klot waiting to lop my digits, I want to go back. That's the life I should be respecting, the one I should try to make better. I don't belong here. This isn't home. Not me. Not home. Not Dad. Not Denby. Not even Ant.

Crap. Ant, the cheery puppy who thought I was the greatest until he got a clue. He's kidnapped, his life in danger. How do I help him if I can't get there from here? The Other Guy still has the toy car, even.

Wait.

I'm here, so *he's* there, stumbling around my life, realizing he knows it from his dreams. And what would he do? Would Other Guy just leave Ant to Klot? Nah. Not OG! He's all anal and disciplined and principled and into fixing things, like the world and people. *He'll* try to help Ant. Of course he will. Hell, he'll probably be better at it than I was. He'd have to be.

Is that it? The reason for the big switcheroo? So we could help each other's lives? Maybe it's not just a joke, maybe it's what they call a blessing in disguise. Am I here to get all James Bond and break into Prometheus for him?

I pull out the plastic bag and stare at the flashy drive, nice and smooth, with one button. It looked easy enough in the dream. He just had to connect it to some computer and press that button.

Oh . . . hell, I've got nothing else to do, right?

What do I remember? Particle Dude was supposed to make OG's data public, only he turned out to be evil. Public, eh? I take another look at that smashed-up laptop. It's split down the middle, but it's got a built-in webcam and a mobile Internet connection (hey, I know a *little* about computers, I just don't like to talk about it). But does it work? Someone was charging it. I jam the button. Nothing. I bang it against the counter a few times—*Wham! Wham!*—it boots. Sometimes things just want to be hit.

I toss the laptop in a cloth shopping bag (what a bunch of politically correct freaks!) along with the flashy drive, and hop into my Ratmobile ready to fight truth, justice, and Whatever Else Gets in My Way.

Then I sit in the driveway, trying to figure out how to work the GPS, but there's too many buttons. Screw it.

Even I know the accelerator was built just outside town. I head north, up into the big forested hills that surround Rivendale. And what do you know? It turns out you can't miss a particle collider if you try.

At the crest of the hill, I see it. Talk about dreamscapes. There's a huge O carved into the ground, twenty or thirty *miles* long, like someone's playing tic-tac-toe with God. There's also a main building that's probably huge, but from here it looks like a white zit.

As I drive downhill the circle vanishes, but the white building rises up and bears down on me. I feel like an ant in Denby's card house. The biggest tacky thing here in tackyland isn't the building, though, it's a huge pool to the right with the ugliest bronze statue you've ever seen in your life sitting in the middle. I think it's supposed to be an atom, but it looks like a bronze giant threw up. Not just ugly, this thing is *oogly*.

Out of nowhere, I get a deep mischievous urge to break that oogly statue. But that wouldn't be respectful, would it? My days of being the guy the duck has stuck on his ass are over, aren't they?

I come up on the parking lot entrance: a gatehouse and two guards dressed in gray security uniforms. A nice white-haired Gray stands beside the gate ready to check IDs. A younger Gray, looking bored, flops around in the gatehouse. I figure he probably has two buttons in there with him—one to open the gate, the other to contact fellow Grays. Maybe there's a third that releases food pellets.

Hm. Time for some dream-think. If OG already broke in, they'll know my/his face, the car, and probably how many bowel movements he's/I've had. Only an asshole would try hitting the front gate. But . . . how the heck do you break into a particle accelerator *without* being an asshole?

That mischievous urge rises again, whispering its wacky answers: "Wade, what if I'm here because being a jerk is what you can do that O-guy can't? Would one last fling with Trickster be so bad if it was for a good cause? It'd be like breakup sex."

Well, I know what Po would say but, hell, he doesn't even have a coffee shop in this world. You out there, Clown-king? I did want to be back in the zone. Sure, I didn't figure on it being the *Twilight Zone,* but still. So, metaphorically speaking, I grab the duck and shove it on my head. It's a little tight, but it still fits.

Ahem. As I was saying, if going in through the front gate doesn't make any sense, that's just what I'll do.

I pull up bold as you please. A green Subaru's ahead of me, so I idle and watch. The driver flashes his wallet at Old Gray, who nods his official Gray approval to Young Gray, who presses a button. The gate rises, the Subaru drives in. No reason I can't do the same.

I pull up and raise a smug eyebrow at Old Gray that says, "These are not the droids you're looking for . . ." I flash OG's library card. Seems for a sec he's buying it, but he ruins it all by looking closely.

"Wait here, please."

Old Gray steps back to talk to Bored Gray. It's okay. It's all going according to plan. I just don't know what the plan is yet. As they whisper Gray to each other, I put the hybrid in reverse and back out.

"Wait!" Old Gray says.

I nod. I smile. I keep going.

"Wait!" he says again, raising his hands. Bored Gray stands. About ten yards from the gate, I stop and shout, "Sorry!"

Old Gray looks suspicious. I catch his eyes, smile at him again, and slam my foot on the pedal. I barely hear the electric motor, but the car jerks forward good as any six-cylinder. Old Gray jumps. Bored Gray, not so bored anymore, presses one of his buttons.

My car—hee-hee—*Other Guy's* car, slams the wooden gate. I'm disappointed it doesn't crack like in an action flick. Instead, the gate tilts up and over the car, scraping the hood and leaving deep, horrible scratches in the nice blue finish. When it hits the windshield it finally bends. It doesn't snap even then, just sort of splinters.

And here I am in the parking lot. Any decent spaces? Nope, but the party's just starting. A tan and black security car fishtails around a corner and heads at me. On my left, I see another, so I swerve toward the building entrance and the little road connecting one parking lot to another.

I zip along, the building on my left. On my right the manicured grass slopes gently up until it hits the wooded hills. From the other lot, a third security car comes barreling straight at me. Past him, I see the big pool and the oogly statue. I have come to hate that statue more than Denby's card house.

The car heading for me picks up speed. Wants to play chicken? Works for me. The distance between us melts like ice on Po's grill. I know, because sometimes I sneak into the kitchen just to melt ice cubes there.

Seconds before impact and the Gray driver doesn't blink. All of a sudden I realize why—he must be thinking we're not going fast enough for the crash to be deadly. It'll just total the cars and send the air bags flying. I'll be pinned and even if he's knocked out, his fellow Grays will have me. Nice try, Mr. Gray, but my deck has an extra joker. At the last instant I swerve, bounce over a sidewalk, and get me a piece of that grassy slope.

It's steeper than it looked. Between the rumbling, the bumping, and everything tilting left, it feels like the car will roll, but it doesn't. I sail past the security car, head down, and slam back onto the road. Ha! Good thing I don't have my own car in my regular life. I'd probably be dead by now.

Tires squeal behind me. Through the rearview mirror I see the two cars from the other lot trying to get around the third.

Past a row of about thirty executive parking spaces there are only three things ahead of me: a small embankment, that great big pool, and that oogly statue.

The statue calls to me. It's saying, "Break me, Wade! Break me!"

That'd be crazy even for me, though, right? I can still swerve, continue the merry chase, but is this a last date or what? I think Pan. Charlie Chaplin. SpongeBob SquarePants. I look in the rearview mirror again, not at the cars chasing me, but at my eyes, hoping to see just a bit of that madman glint, one last time.

It's there, baby.

I grin. I floor it. I do forty, push fifty. I hit the curb in front of the pool. The hybrid goes sailing up and over the embankment and into the air. As the deep, placid waters of the pool flash before me, I spot a bronze plaque at the statue's base with the artist's name. A giant K is all I can make out. K for Klown-king?

Other thoughts fill my head, like how my last fling with the Clown-king may turn out to be my last thing, *period*.

And, apropos of nothing, I wonder how Other Guy's doing in *my* world.

CHAPTER 10

When we try to hand off the bags, there's a jolt. Not a shock, or a physical thing, not even a sudden shift in vision, more like a gap in a film, a break in consciousness, but so quick, so unexpected, it leaves me rattled. He's gone. At least as far as I can see. I'm alone.

The bag. Damn. It's still got the toy car in it. No flash drive. So was he a dream? This is not the calm humility I pictured for my quest here. I don't know what to let go of or what to hold on to. I take some deep breaths to relax, but something awful, something rank fills my throat and lungs. What is that terrible smell?

Oh. It's me. Denby always tells me I wash too much, but this feels as if I haven't showered in months.

I already don't like where this is going, and now it gets much worse. As I slowly look down at myself, hair dangles in front of my eyes, too long to be my own. It's *his*, his hair. The clothes, responsible for half the stench, they're his, too. My hair itches like crazy. When I move to scratch, a feeling like electricity races along my pinkie, followed by a pain so deep it makes me nauseous. There's a bandage on the finger, loose, filthy, barely clinging.

Oh my God, I'm *him*!

Tears flood my eyes, from confusion, from fear. I look down at the stone and notice the date. Today, exactly three years ago. It doesn't begin to explain any of this; I don't think anything can. It only makes a kind of senseless sense.

I stagger back to where I parked, but my car's gone. Was it stolen? No. I'm him, and he doesn't have a car. I think about heading home, but he doesn't have a home. I check my pockets for my cell or my wallet or my keys or my money, but he doesn't have any of that either. I don't even want to think about Dad, or his version of my father. And the monster, Klot, is he real, too, out there waiting for me?

Scattered dream images rush me like memories, some old, some new. None give me any answers. Klot is real. I see his face as clearly as a nightmare induced by too much pizza. He wants the car I've got in this bag, only it's broken, and I can't give him a broken toy. What can I do? Where do I go? Mr. Schapiro's? Maybe he's home. Back in that crappy godforsaken neighborhood. A good three miles away. Great. Perfect.

I think of trying to hitch, but *I* wouldn't pick me up, so I walk. My finger throbs more and more, as if it's getting infected. It needs a new bandage, some antibiotic ointment. HE, the other me, is too stupid to take care of his own wounds.

The poorer part of Rivendale starts a little sooner than

I remember. There's a walk-in clinic before the real waste-land begins, so I head in. The smell inside is worse than me, and there's a crowd of coughing people all waiting for a doctor. A woman with a baby in her arms is at the counter, complaining she's been here two hours. She hacks up a gob of phlegm that lands near my feet.

When I tell the receptionist what I want, she seems happy to have one less person on line and just hands me what I ask for. If I want to see a doctor, she suggests I come back tomorrow. I walk to the end of the waiting room and open a battered wood door marked as a unisex restroom.

The toilet's clogged. The sink seems clean enough, though, and the new bandages she gave me are wrapped and sterile. Trying not to inhale, look in a mirror, or touch anything, I gingerly remove the old bandage. The tip of my pinkie's a deep, nighttime purple, and there's a thick solid dark line circling the top joint ringed by pus. I have to wash it.

The hot doesn't work. As the tap spits freezing water on my pinkie, I swoon. The paper towels look like sand-paper, so I tear the cotton gauze for the new bandage in half and use that to dry the wound. I squirt on the contents of a little tube of antibacterial ointment and wrap the new bandage around. It tingles, burns, but in a few moments, the deeper pain eases.

At least I don't have to worry about gangrene getting me before Klot does. The thought of a real Klot terrifies me but, so far, no panic attack. Amazing, considering. I glance in the mirror and see, between cracked glass and dried drops of cheap hand soap, HIS face. HE doesn't have panic attacks, does HE? And this is HIS body, right? Well. Hooray for HIM.

I trudge out past the coughers, back to the street and a long walk through the wasteland. It seems worse somehow, like there's more unemployment, more poor. I worry the dealers or street people I pass will come after me, but they don't, because, hey, I look like I belong.

Finally, I see the diner below Mr. Schapiro's. But when I look up at the windows where his apartment should be, they're either broken or boarded up. Wow. How is that possible?

Maybe here Mr. S. is still with Judith? He did say he might have stayed with her if not for his new teaching job. Hm. I was the only one who came to help him with the lab. If I quit school, then no one would have shown up. Could he have quit because of that? And what else does that mean . . . ?

I rush into the diner. The place is all but empty. An angry short-order cook growls, "Where's my twenty bucks, Wade?"

I think I know him, vaguely, from the dreams. I touch my pockets, then remember they're empty. "I'm sorry. I'll pay you back as soon as I can."

"That's a new one. Usually you just run back out."

"Do you know . . . could you tell me if the Prometheus Particle Accelerator is running?"

"What is that, one of your stupid jokes? If it's running, you want me to catch it? That's a bad one even for you. You know that thing was shut down."

There's a British phrase Mom liked to use: "gobsmacked." It means utterly astonished. That's me. Gobsmacked. Right here, right now. Because I didn't show up, Schapiro must have gone back to Judith Wilson, helped with the lawsuit, and had the plant closed down permanently. No Prometheus, no strangelets. The world, this world, is safe *because* I quit. It's like that movie Mom made us watch at Christmas, *It's a Wonderful Life*, only backward—everyone's life isn't in danger *because* I quit!

Son of a bitch! I start laughing. The cook growls again, but I can't stop. I step back into the street, still hysterical. I laugh so hard, tears come to my eyes. It's funny. It really is. It's stupid, sad, pathetic, and funny.

As my guffaws slow down and I wipe my eyes, I see something across the street that wasn't there yesterday: a cheap hand-painted sign with a rodent drinking coffee. It's the place that shut down in my world, The Rat. It's HIS home, I know it. Talk about surreal. It's like visiting a movie set. *This is where Wade Jackson's bizarre fantasy life was originally shot . . .*

I can't take my eyes off it. The inside lights are low, but the front door's ajar, so I walk in, almost like I'm in a trance. In the center of a large open space, littered with tables and chairs of questionable stability, I see a wiry man with powerful muscles visible through his thin, wrinkled skin. He mops the same spot on the floor, over and over. What's his name? I think I know him, too, much better than I know the cook.

"Po," I say, remembering.

I'm just naming him, the way a three-year-old might point to a chair and say, "chair," but he picks up his head. "You visit your mom?"

"Uh . . . yes, I did."

"Good. What'd you decide to do with that thing?"

"Thing? You mean the car?" I pull out the bag, just to remind myself it's real. "This has nothing to do with me."

Po walks over and slaps me in the face. Really hard.
Wham!

"Ow!"

"Of *course* it has to do with you. It's in *your* hand, ain't
it? At least Trickster gave it back to you!"

"Geez!" I say, rubbing my face. "Ow! Back? What do
you . . ."

Right. He was probably expecting to see the flash drive.

Po has a point. It *is* in my hand now, with Klot looking
for it. That's probably why he hit me. He sure as hell doesn't
want Klot coming here.

So if I've got the car, HE must have the flash drive in
my world, with my problems—like Prometheus. I'm not
one for spiritual explanations, but could that be why we
switched? To solve each other's problems? Kind of makes
sense. I wouldn't want HIM performing surgery on me, but
HE *is* crazy enough to break into Prometheus again and
run the simulation without fainting. Crazy enough to try,
anyway.

Would HE do it? Would HE try to do the right thing by
me and, if so, should I try to do the right thing by HIM?
HE'd probably say why not? But what can I do for HIM?

Po's waiting, like a statue. "So?" he says. "What're you
going to do with it?"

Since Mom died, two words always pop into my mind
when I'm asked a question about some problem, whether
it's about ADHD or particle colliders: fix it. Can I fix the
car? At least I can take a look. I walk over to the dark,
uneven, pockmarked coffee bar, pull out a white napkin,
and empty the bag onto it.

What a ridiculous, ridiculous thing. A toy studded with

diamonds. Probably worth enough money to feed a small village for a decade. Something the angels could use to drive to their dance on the head of a pin. I roll the little wheel between my fingers, staring at it, front and back. Strange world, huh?

Po steps closer and looks over my shoulder.

"Screwed that up good, huh?"

I want to shush him, but he may hit me again, so I keep studying. The "axle" that held the wheel is a solid gold wire, not meant to be played with. Gold's not very strong, so it snapped. There's a bit still jutting from the body, another bit inside the wheel. Jewelers are always soldering silver, gold, and copper. What's the melting point of gold? Pretty low, I think. It's not the same as a circuit board, but the principles must be the same, right?

"Po," I say, "do you have a soldering iron I can borrow?"

"You can't solder," he says, waving me off.

"Matter of fact," I tell him with great confidence, "I can."

His face is stone. I can't tell if he's surprised.

"Come on," he says, hobbling toward a rear door.

I wrap up the pieces in the napkin, put it in a pocket I hope doesn't have holes, and follow. Though the room might be a kitchen, it's more a health inspector's nightmare — which figures, given this is a dream. Just to make it more surreal, Po pulls open a trapdoor in front of what I think is a stove, then disappears into its blackness.

I stand at the edge, waiting, until he growls, "Come on!" again.

Great. Perfect. The old wood of the narrow stairs creaks beneath my weight as darkness swallows my legs, arms, shoulders, and head. After ten steps, I hit a concrete floor so cold I feel it through my (*HIS!*) ratty sneakers. Above, the light from the kitchen's a perfect square. Not a single ray seems to enter the basement.

A *click*, and the dank space lights up. There's a single bare bulb dangling from a power cord hooked to the low ceiling. It's a big area, filled almost entirely with aging boxes and crates. Most are rotted, ready to spill their contents. There's a particularly big pile at the back wall, still mostly in shadow. It blocks three cement steps that lead to a storm door. Among them, something moves, making a little wake in the moldy cardboard, a wake about the size of a dog.

"It's the rat," Po says. "The one you wrote the song about."

"Right."

"Quiet!" Po howls at it. "I'll put a c-c-cap in your hairy ass!"

A cap? Oh, look, Po has a gun in his shaking hand. Great. Perfect. It's a little one, but I bet it works. He waves the barrel nervously toward the sound. When there's no further noise, he yanks open a creaky wooden drawer in a workbench. After sifting through some nails and screws, he withdraws what looks like the first soldering iron ever made, along with the roll of solder that came with it.

Rather than plastic, the power cord's shielded by cracked cloth. The nib, the point of the iron, is covered in ancient gunk. Po unravels the cord and plugs it into an outlet. The bulb dims as the iron sucks energy. He stretches the cord, rests the iron and solder on the workbench, then stands back like he's more afraid of it than of the rat. Smoke twirls from the nib.

"Make your magic."

Right. Even if I were willing to touch it, it's way too big, twice as thick as the wheel. The one back in school had a head like a needle. How'm I going to manage this? Easier to figure out how many angels can dance on the head of a . . . wait.

"Po, you have a pin or a needle? And maybe some steel wool?"

"What do I look like, a seamstress?"

"Nothing?" I say. I spot a mended tear on his shirt. "Then how did that get fixed?"

He grunts, says, "Don't tell anyone," and ferrets among some boxes until he produces a sewing kit.

"Steel wool's upstairs." Before he goes, he hands me the gun. "Just in case."

I shake my head. "I'm not shooting at it."

"No," he explains, "but if it comes for you, you can kill yourself."

He's kidding. I think I see him chuckling to himself as he climbs up the stairs. I *hope* he's kidding.

Seconds later, a wad of iron wool tumbles down the stairs. I rush over to scoop it up, not because I'm in a hurry, but because the rat might be watching. I use the wool to clean the gunk off the iron as best I can, being careful not to burn myself. Some of the crap is so thick, I try prying it off with a screwdriver I find lying next to a rusty hacksaw. I'm thinking of using the hacksaw on the remaining gunk when I realize that maybe this is gunk I can use.

I take a needle from the kit and wedge the thick end between the gunk and the iron. If I'm lucky, the gunk will hold the needle long enough to heat it. Now all I have to do is use the heat of the needle to soften the little piece of gold axle enough to get it to bind with the smidgen of gold left in the wheel.

That's *all*. Sheesh.

There's a small iron vise on the bench. I take the car out, lay the wheel on the table, wrap the car in the napkin for protection, and gently, gently, tighten the vise around it, the broken axle sticking up. It glints in the bulb's dim light, still the weirdest thing I've ever seen, except maybe myself in a mirror lately.

I feel eyes on me. I'm afraid it's the rat, but it's Po. He's fascinated.

"Please," I tell him, "just don't say *anything* for three minutes."

He nods and keeps watching, as if I'm a TV show.

Think. It's what I do, right? I have to admit, I enjoy this kind of work. It's like checking over the computer code. It calms me. Physics has always been easier to understand than people. Dad wanted me to let go of all this rational stuff, but hey, I'm only supposed to do that *after* I run out of options, yes?

So, details. I have to touch the needle to the axle long enough to make the tip melt a tiny, tiny bit, then jam the wheel on, perfectly centered, before it cools. If I'm terribly accurate and lucky, the gold will bind and the wheel will at least stay on. Too much heat and the axle will dribble away. If I miss when I jam the wheel on, or push too hard, it will squish the axle. What's that? Three ways to fail? On the lighter side, when I hold out my hand it's steady, not shaking. My raging mind has yet to wreck HIS nerves.

I hold the wheel between thumb and forefinger, so close to the edge of my skin, I drop it three times before I get it right. Then I practice lowering it onto the axle. Easier than I thought. First two out of three, I get it right, so I stop. Time to, as they say, just do it.

I pick up the hot iron and inch the needle toward the car. Even with HIS nervous system, I strain my hand to keep steady, which makes my pinkie hurt like hell. My position is wrong; I'm too high. I get down, put my knees on the concrete, rest my chin on the table, and get as close as I can to the car, which, unfortunately, is also close to the smoking iron. The chemical stink can't be good for my lungs.

"You're going to solder that thing to your face," Po says with a chuckle.

Rather than respond with something witty, I bring the iron in, touch the tip of the needle to the little nub of axle, and hold it there. All at once, Murphy's Law clicks into place. Everything that can go wrong does.

For starters, I feel scorching heat against my forehead. I'd forgotten how long HIS hair is. I'm afraid it'll catch fire. That's not even the biggest problem. White smoke puffs from the napkin. The paper is touching the side of the needle. If it bursts into flames, it'll melt the whole freaking car.

The tip of the axle shivers almost imperceptibly. It's ready, even if I'm not. Now or never. I lower the wheel into place and yank the iron back just as the napkin bursts into flame. I move so quickly, the needle, red hot, scrapes my forehead. I drop the iron, slap the side of my head, and blow out the napkin, all at once.

Oh yeah, and I fall down backward onto the concrete where I'm so focused on my forehead, I roll right onto my pinkie. I howl, hurting too much to wonder if the car survived. Po's on me in seconds, beating my head with a rolled-up newspaper, like I'm a disobedient dog.

"Hey!" I shout. "I'm burned, I'm not on fire!"

He swats me a few more times, I think just for the sheer pleasure of it.

My pinkie throbs. I feel a scratch on my forehead in the shape of a jagged line. Great. Wonderful. Now I look like a sloppy Harry Potter.

The car. The stupid toy. Have to see what I did to it. I put my right hand on the table and pull myself back to eye level with the vise.

Crap. Oh crap. A charcoal black piece of burnt napkin, wafer thin, covers half the car. If it seared the surface, it was all a waste. I flick at the paper with my good pinkie. It falls away like a dying leaf. Beneath it, nothing. Not a scratch. Whew. So far so good, but don't forget the details. I swallow, then give the wheel a little spin. It rolls, perfectly.

Well, what do you know? I fixed it. I've fixed the most stupid thing ever. Not the world, not my friends, but *that* I can fix. In spite of how ridiculous it is, a grin spreads across my face.

Po helps me to my feet, "accidentally" patting me on the back in the process.

"Now you just have to give it back to Klot and hope he doesn't kill you."

Though I'm burned and bruised, dream images flood my brain. I'm thinking clearer now, if not about *my* life, at least about HIS.

"No. It's not Klot's. He stole it. I'll set up some kind of sting for the police," I say.

"That fall give you amnesia? Klot owns the cops. He's got Officer Smelser working with him. And he's got Ant kidnapped."

This is more complicated than I thought. Anthony's kidnapped? I have to remember, he isn't my Anthony. And Smelser, wasn't that the name of the Prometheus security guard? Wonder how that happened. Must've been fired when the collider was shut down and managed to get on the police force.

"If he's a crooked cop, maybe I can get a recording of him helping Klot."

"How you going to do that, Sherlock?"

"Got a security system here? Maybe a webcam?"

Po grins, broad and friendly. "Webcam? Sure I've got a webcam!"

He turns his back to me and points to a spot slightly lower than his kidneys. "Right here . . . in my ass! You frakking clown, what do you think—"

He's cut off in mid-sentence.

"Relax. Won't make any difference now," a voice from my dreams says. It's the same voice, icy as death, that said, "No fun for me if you don't stay awake."

Klot found me. HIM. No, me. HE's far away from here. I'm the one Klot'll kill.

Two silhouettes are on the stairs, one with a monstrous head that nearly blocks all the light above it, the other trim, with perfect posture. They step into the edge of the bare-bulb light and even though he's dressed as a policeman instead of as a security guard, I recognize Smelser. I can't bring myself to look at Klot.

My borrowed calm? Gone. Twitching, I try to focus past Klot, out to the still-dark wall of the basement, the pile of boxes blocking the only other way out, the three stairs up to a storm door. One of the boxes shifts. The rat waits. I think, for me.

CHAPTER 11

Security cars lie helter-skelter at the pool's rim. Grays scratch their heads and stare at the blue electric future car at the bottom, on its back. The wheels and chassis muck the water's beautiful stillness. It sure is a zero-emissions vehicle now.

The oogly statue shivers, seems to whine, drawing their attention. I didn't quite hit it head-on with the car, but I nicked it pretty good.

Creak!

Yes! Better than I thought. The atom bends, splits, and tumbles into the pool. Got it! Damn, that feels good.

More Grays rush from the building. They're all just, "What the hell?" Other people tumble out like animals escaping a zoo, employees of all wages: Maintain-ants, Tie-guys, Tie-girls, No-ties, even folks in lab coats who look like Scien-ticks. They all must've heard me split the atom through the walls of their environmentally controlled offices.

The party-pooper Grays try to send everyone back inside. But no one budges. They want to watch. In best unruly mob tradition, they're fearful, but fascinated. And why not? It's hands-down the best thing I've *ever* broken.

Of course I'm still alive, gloating behind an oak. Once the car jumped the embankment and was no longer in view, I rolled out. Driverless, Electric Blue skimmed the statue while I scrambled for the trees.

My utterly cool move came not without cost. The flashy drive looks fine, but the already cracked laptop folded again. Now it looks more like a flapjack-laptop. Clock's ticking, too. One of the more athletic Grays has his shirt off and looks like he's going to dive down to the car. If he reaches it they'll realize I'm not wearing a seat belt.

Time to move. I do a little shimmy along the trees, then slip in among the gawking employees like I'm one of them. A fire door keeps opening and closing as even more people come to join the fun. That's my way in.

I'm almost through the door when a forty-something Tie-guy stops me.

"What happened out here?" he says, all bossy, like he's my supervisor.

I shake my head and speak in deferential tones. "Sir, someone drove a car right into the pool, sir! Someone *crazy*, sir!"

"Wow!" he says.

He nods. I nod. We keep moving, he going out, me going in.

The fire door leads to a stairwell, so I walk down and find myself in a huge access corridor. If it's not from the dream, it should be. Sure as hell doesn't belong in reality. It's like the space station from *WALL•E* down here, a mobbed indoor highway, everybody in a hurry to beat their feet and get wherever they think they're going. Some of the Tie-guys and -gals even have beeping golf carts. Too good to walk, I guess.

Moving through this robo-crowd is tougher than dancing on the Alley-Oops wall. I dodge carts, dance past rushing groups, and surreptitiously snap my fingers to the ticky-tacky percussive stylings of hard shoes on polished concrete. There are wall-mounted LCD TVs every thirty yards. My pretty picture is up on all of them, next to a live feed of the underwater car. Luckily, the running text says I'm still down there, and the emergency vehicles are on their way. That's great—more time—unless someone sees the photo, sees me here, and adds two and two. Bet there's one or two mathematicians in a particle collider.

Not too shabby, if I had the slightest idea what to do next.

A beeping cart answers that one for me by running over my right foot. Now I know exactly what to do: hop around in extreme pain. I end up bouncing backward into a stairwell, where I knock over a trash can and nearly fall. If Trickster's here, he may be trying to kill me. Or not.

Gotta love that synchronicity. A set of Maintain-ants overalls, bundled nice and neat, spill from the bottom of the trash. I know those clothes. They're Super-Wade's disguise. Cool. I slip 'em on and zip up. Not only do they provide a bit of cover, but they make me remember something else, a certain hot brunette with a fake ID. If the clothes are here, how far can she be?

I try to jog my memories and get flashes of her button nose and severe expression. On brain TV, or whatever you want to call the pictures in my head from OG's life, she didn't want to get too involved. She wanted to play (or as OG might say, "do the right thing"), but not fully commit. Girl after my own heart. Bet *I* could get her to help again.

My photo's all over, so if she's here, she knows I tried to get back in. If she was freaked the first time, this time she's probably sticking to her office, shivering and hoping I'm dead. With everyone else heading outside to the accident site to gape and gawk, that'll make her easier to find. "Easier" being a relative term in a giant building with hundreds of rooms.

Okay, so let's tip the odds. She had to have a high-level job if she's handing out fake IDs. An upper window office among the Tie-guys and -gals? I start climbing stairs. At first only No-ties and Scien-ticks pass on their way down but after a few floors the clothes get more expensive and it's a Tie-party, all executive types.

I pop out into a hall that might as well be on another planet. Is this a theme park or a place of business? It's spaceship slick with indoor trees in the center of every intersection. The doors are all curved like portholes, with small circular windows just above eye level. Most are open and the offices empty, except two. I creep up on the first, turn the handle, and push the door.

Whoa! Inside are two people going at it on top of this clean white desk, sending white paper and white office supplies flying. Judging from the clothes, one's a No-tie, the other a Scien-tick, but it's hard to tell who's who since their clothes are mostly on the floor. I guess they feel a draft from the open door, because they stop and look at me. I want to suggest they get a room, but they already have one.

"You didn't see anything!" the woman says.

"You don't talk, I won't tell!" I say. Her eyes narrow, like she's going to recognize me, so I close the door.

At the second closed door I decide to look through the little window first. There she is, the girl of my dreams, staring at her screen, white-knuckling it, teeth clenched. Her name's even on a plastic tag—Charlotte.

I guess from the more-sterile-than-a-eunuch decor, the neat paper piles, the family photos, and the poster of a cat "hanging in there," Charlotte's usually bored, and her rebellion was a fantasy, like my cabbie following that car. And if that last office is any indication, there's no dearth of sexual tension in this place. I decide to play it like a spy movie with an accent on the romance scenes.

I open the door, close it behind me, and conjure my inner James Bond.

She looks up and gasps. I give her a suave half smile.

"You're alive!" she says breathlessly.

"For now," I say.

I walk toward her, getting a little too close. She rises, looking like she can't decide if she wants to scream or kiss me.

"Get out of here," she whispers. "They'll find you."

Nice. I think we've seen the same movies.

"No. You have something I need."

I step forward, she steps back. "I . . . can't . . . ," she says. Her voice gets a little breathy, like that time Denby wanted me to stop kissing her neck, but really didn't.

"I think you can. I think you want to."

I bring my face closer to hers. Her breath quickens. Hoping Denby in both worlds will forgive me, I kiss her. For half a second, she kisses back, then pulls away.

"This is crazy," she says. "Crazy."

So nervous she can barely control her hands, she stumbles around to the other side of her desk and pulls on something taped to the underside. An ID card. She grabs a marker and writes something on the back. Probably her phone number. She looks me in the eye and presses it into my hands.

"Go," she says. "Just . . . go."

So I do. Next time, I'll try playing pirate. Harrr.

But go where? I head back down to the inner highway. It's a little quieter. Judging from the monitors, the crowd at my crime scene is standing room only, so I'm as alone as I'll ever be.

Somewhere down here is that computer OG needed to use the flashy drive on. I get flashes, memories, but they're not the same as directions. I wander, I try to smell it out, I try to call on the Clown-king for another favor, but the only thing I find is a candy-bar vending machine, and I haven't got any change.

I do manage to spot a you-are-here map. Only problem is, I have no idea what a super-special computer section would be called.

Son of a bitch! There it is, in glowing type: SPECIAL COMPUTER SECTION. Now *that's* a map.

A few more twists and turns and the concrete gives

way to all white, like the offices upstairs, only no trees, and everything's glowing from hidden lighting. A wall-mounted LCD tells me the tow trucks have arrived to pull the hybrid out. Time's a-wasting.

But here I am. I reach a flat white windowless door with no handle, just one of those electronic locks with a stripe reader. I slide the ID card Charlotte gave me and— *click*—it unlocks. Ha! Two rows of fancy computer terminals and cushy chairs greet me.

Only one screen's lit. It's showing all these little colorful dots bouncing around. Something tells me that's not the one to mess with, so I sit at a blank screen. Oooo! *Great* chair! Wonder if I can steal it. I pull out the ultra-white flashy drive, which matches everything in the place. I just have to connect it. But how? It's all smooth.

"Work!" I say to it. "Do your thing!"

Was worth a shot. I check for plugs. Nada. I shake it. I tap it against the table. Things are going nowhere fast, when all of a sudden a little arm pops out. Even I recognize a USB port.

I plug it into the terminal and the screen comes to life. Oops. Another dead end. It wants a log-in and password. Even if I remembered what OG used, the nasty Prometheans would have changed it by now. Is this the end of Wade Bond?

Nope. Not yet. I must be smarter than he looks (get it?) because I remember Charlotte wrote something on the back of the ID. And here I thought it was her phone number. I flip the card over. Log-in and password. So I'm not as cute as I thought? No, there's her number, right below the password. Still got it.

I type and the display lights up like a Christmas tree

on a very special episode of *iCarly*. Now, the knuckle-cracking, earthshaking, all-unnatural moment of truth. All I have to do is press the button on the flashy drive, right? The one OG couldn't deal with. The suspense is unbearable. To quote Oscar Wilde, I hope it lasts. So I stretch it out a bit.

Why *did* OG faint? Nothing around I can see. That other screen's beeping a bit, and there are a few light green dots bouncing around on it, but I don't see anything scary about that. That may be a little mystery I have to live with.

My finger hovers over the button. Soon, all OG's dreams will be fulfilled. I just have to . . .

Nah. There must be *something* else I can do first. This is too rich *not* to share with the world. How bad is that flapjack-laptop? I flip it open. Actually, it's more like I unfold it, and a few pieces of metal and plastic fall out. The On button looks crushed, but when I press down hard, the light comes up. Something whirs and hums, and it ain't me.

Cool. Now I can contact the folks at home about this exciting threat to their existence. I click me some keys and, lo and behold, my too-clean face appears on a little screen. I send the feed to a bunch of addresses, like See-NN, the Nudge Report, *The New York Whines*, YouTooTube, MyMyMySpace, and anything else I can think of. Soon as it looks like I'm connected, I do my thing.

"People of Earth, I am here in the smelly belly of the beast, about to show you all, live and in real time, why the Prometheus accelerator, that ayatollah of rock 'n' roll-ah, is a grave danger not only to you and to me, but to whoever sits next to you as well! I am a trained professional, so please do not try to save the Earth at home!"

Then I laugh like a mad scientist, which probably isn't appropriate, and slap that little bad-boy button on the flashy drive because I know it wants it bad.

I flip the laptop camera toward the terminal screen and keep talking.

"Okay, screen says it's running a sim program. Hey, maybe it's *The Sims 3 Particle Accelerator Add-On*! Now it's uh . . . loading . . . parameters from the flashy drive and . . . and . . . uh . . . well, *this* is totally dull, huh?"

Then something less dull happens. Damned if I know what, but it's pretty. Little particle dots run around and crash into one another, making lots of colors. After two seconds, it's totally boring again. I owe my audience something more, so I sing a little song, tapping out the beat on the desk.

> *Ain't got no idea just what is what*
> *But there's a big red and a tiny blue dot*
> *And they smack each other an awful lot*
> *Why can't they just be friends?*
>
> *Why's all this smacking going on, girl?*
> *Look at those green ones coming outta that swirl*
> *Are they the nasty dots that'll eat up your world?*
> *Why can't they just be friends?*

The light green dots get bigger and bigger and make one big light green dot, then they suck up all the other dots, and everything goes green.

That's it? That's saving the world? Yawn.

"Sorry, folks, guess that's all!" I say to the laptop. I give it a big kiss. *Smack!* "Watch for me in your e-mail and/or local prison!"

I pull the flashy drive from the terminal and put my video on a loop, so the outside world will continue to hear my dulcet tones. I connect the flashy drive to the laptop and press the button again. A bunch of text zips up the screen. The system looks like it's e-mailing for about twenty seconds, then nothing.

The only sounds are the power hum, myself singing, and the beeping light green dots on that other monitor. Hm. Now there's like six or seven of them bouncing around. Funny, they're the same light green as the dots that filled up my screen. What's up with that? Someone in the building must be watching it. I mean, they wouldn't *all* go outside, right?

Otherwise, quiet as a cemetery on a snowy day.

Until the door slams open like a frakking canon blast, and a Tie-guy with salt-and-pepper hair and a furious look 'pon his visage storms in, screaming, "You!"

And I'm like, "No, *you*!"

Then I recognize him. "Hey! Particle Dude! What's up with your bad self? And I do mean *bad*."

"Security's on its way. Don't move, and get away from that terminal."

"Well, which? You want me to stand still or get away from the terminal? You don't do this often, do you?"

He looks around, then heads for a terminal. *Not* the one I was using, but the beeping one with the light green dots on it. There are like ten dots now.

"Managed to start running your simulation again,

huh?" he says, shaking his head. He sits down at the keyboard and starts typing.

There's something creepy about those dots, so I try to tell him. "Dude . . ."

"Good thing I stopped you in time. You could've destroyed the reputation of this facility, this *town*, all for the sake of your paranoid little high school project."

"Dude . . ."

"Oh, I admit the math was right, but come on, Wade, we've been running for three years, another three would have been fine. The odds are still ten thousand to one."

"Dude . . ."

"I'm doing you a favor. Rivendale would've lynched you. Now you'll probably just get a few years."

I put two fingers beneath my tongue and blow one of those really shrill whistles to get his attention.

"Dude, okay, thanks, really, but you should know *that's* not the terminal I ran the whachamacallit on. I used this one behind me." I step aside to show him. "And, I finished. Done deal, which leaves me to kind of wonder, you know, what *you're* looking at."

"Huh?" he says. Pretty unimpressive for the main villain. Klot had better dialogue at least, plus he had that whole big-head thing.

He eyes the terminal behind me, and the cracked laptop with the webcam, then snaps his head back at the one he's sitting at, the one with all the light green dots.

"I'm no Particle Dude," I tell him, "but aren't those little light green thingies the dangerous eat-up-the-world kind?"

"There was a test run today, but they'd be monitoring . . . No. That's not possible . . . it must be . . ."

Now there's like fifteen, so you can't miss them. And PD? All his cool confidence gets sucked away like water down a toilet.

"My God, my God, my God . . ."

"Yeah, that's what I was thinking. Wow. The Other Guy . . . I mean, *I* was right! It's the end of the world. Go figure. So, can you shut it down while we're still alive?"

I'm happy to say it looks like he can. His fingers fly across the keys, the screen flashes. Freaky. I guess everyone else *did* leave. Good thing PD's here, or that might've been it for the whole ball of wax. Phew. And I mean, *Phew!*

But then PD's face gets whiter and whiter and all of a sudden, he stops.

"I can't . . . I can't . . ." he says.

"Can't? Can't what? You need me to spell something for you? Keep typing!" The little green dots are still there and now there are more. Do I have to sing the song again?

"I can't just shut it down. If I'm wrong, it's my job, my reputation. I have to tell the board. They have to decide . . ."

Then the idiot pulls out his cell phone.

"Whoa! No. Don't *have to* all over me. I think we're a little past that. Shut down first, ask questions later."

He ignores me and starts pressing buttons on his cell. Then he turns away from me for privacy. The screen gets greener and greener. Holy crap.

"Are you frakking nuts?"

I rush up and pull him backward in his chair.

"Get away from me!" he screams. And I realize he is, he is frakking nuts, not like Klot in a sadist kind of way, but in an executive-tunnel-vision kind of way where you can't see the forest fire for the tree. He ain't gonna help without permission.

I kick the chair. He and it go wheeling down the aisle. They crash and fall sideways, PD bumping his head hard on the floor.

I turn to the screen, stare at all the light green dots. There're so many bouncing all over, they remind me of Ant trying to focus on something. This is bad, really bad. About as bad as it can get, I think, without the whole idea of good, bad, and indifferent just vanishing. I scan the screen for an Off switch.

"Particle Dude! It's the end of the world!" I scream. "How do I stop it?"

He lies there and moans.

I turn back to the screen. My eyes dance over all the words at the sides of the picture until I spot something marked Emergency Shutdown. I click it. Then I click it again, for good measure. Then I click it over and over and over until I'm smashing the frakking mouse against the desk, making little mouse-bits fly everywhere.

All of a sudden, that low power hum that fills the room drops lower and lower and lower, then stops. The light green particles start to vanish. Ten . . . six . . . three . . . nothing. The screen goes blank.

I furrow my brow. "Hey, did I just save the world?"

Particle Dude doesn't answer. He's still moaning.

An alarm goes off. The lights start blinking. I can think about this later, or better yet, forget it. Time to go.

"You can mail me a thank-you note after your head clears, PD."

I dive for the door and rush through the empty white corridor. A quick glance at an ever-present LCD tells me the accelerator has indeed shut down. I also get a nice view of all the Grays screaming something like *Everybody out of the pool!* and racing back into the building, doubtless after little old me.

I run up a level and head for what I think is the opposite side of the building. All the lights are flashing, all kinds of alarms are blaring. On my way out, the only person I pass is a single Maintain-ants guy, the only man who stayed at his job. He stands by a fire exit, pushing a sloppy mop against the floor. He looks at me. I wave. He waves back. Then he goes back to his mopping. As I pass, I catch a glimpse of an old face of multiple ethnic origins. Po? Could it be? Nah.

I reach the exit, head up, out, and into the woods.

After ten minutes of running, I sit on a log and feel myself vibrate. I'm pretty sure I did save the world. His world anyway. Oh, I've probably messed up most of his life with the breaking-and-entering thing, and wrecked his entire car. Could be worse. Could be the other way around—most of his car and his entire life. But the world! Me? What a rush! OG helped, I guess. Maybe he's not so bad.

So, why am I still here? If I'm done, shouldn't I get beamed back home or something? Maybe at least a cab ride? Nope. I end up taking a long, long, long walk back to Rivendale, figuring I can at least pass Best Buy, tune in to a local news broadcast and hear about the price on my head. I mean, no way will PD admit what I did, right?

The walk is quiet, except for the occasional police car and fire engine rushing by on its way to Prometheus, but I'm increasingly tickled with myself. Being an asshole *does* have its uses, huh? By the time I reach the strip mall I'm totally cocky, like I really can do anything, like that old duck is getting stuck on my head again.

But as I make my way past the Party Store, something in the window grabs my eye. It's Halloween season, and there's this costumed mannequin wearing a mask. Never seen anything like it. It's Charlie Chaplin as a demon—all wild-eyed, with flowing red hair and horns, not grinning, leering. I feel like that face should be floating above me, ready to eat me. It's Trickster, reduced to a mask.

I look at my date for the evening, grin back at his grin. He is dangerous and beloved. He likes messing with me even more than I like messing with the world, which is why I guess we should break up. Do we have to, though?

"Thanks," I say. "That was a wild rush. I loved it. You're not so bad, are you?"

Had to open my mouth, right? As the last syllable leaves my lips, a Prometheus security car screeches onto the sidewalk right in front of me, nearly pinning me against the display window. Two Grays, hands on guns, leap out and tell me not to move. I don't.

"Wade Jackson?" a Gray with perfect posture asks.

"Uh . . . sort of."

The other Gray takes this as a yes and cuffs me.

"Aren't you boys out of your jurisdiction? What about my rights?"

"We spotted you in the woods, on Prometheus property, shot you while you were trying to get away," perfect-posture man says. He sounds familiar.

"Whoa, whoa, whoa!" I say. As he shoves me into the backseat, I get a good look at his face and freak. "Smelser?"

He's confused, eyeing me, trying to figure out how I'd know him. Then he gives up. "My cousin designed that statue, you little freak."

Smelser's a Gray? And he has family? I'd be amazed if I wasn't scared shitless. I guess in my world, when Prometheus shut down, he wound up on the police force. But how'd he hook up with Klot? He's kidding about shooting me in the woods, right? Then again, the last time I figured someone like him was kidding, it cost me a finger.

He gets on the car radio, smiling as he reports, "No, no police around. He's ours."

"Switch to your headset," a voice at the other end tells him.

He shrugs at his partner, slips on the 'phones, and that's the last time I see him smile. After he listens for a while, he looks downright unhappy.

"What?" Smelser says. In fact, he says it a bunch of times. He turns off the radio and lets loose a little moan, like he's been shot. A gut wound. "I am definitely on the wrong side of the law."

If only he knew.

Smelser turns to me, struggling with himself, exaggerating the politeness. "Dr. Finley asked me to tell you that he is *very* sorry, and on behalf of himself and *the world*, thank you. I'm also to offer you a ride home. So . . . would you care for a lift to your residence?"

Finley, huh? That must be Particle Dude.

"What?" his partner says, but Smelser raises a hand to silence him.

"Uh . . . no, thanks. I'll walk."

"Good," he says.

I hop out. The security car pulls away. The waters of chaos rush forward, the waters of chaos recede.

My heart's still slamming in my rib cage as I look back in the Party Store window. Trickster, the Clown-king, leers back at me in the form of cheap latex. I *asked* for that, didn't I? All of a sudden, breaking up isn't so hard to do. I run off, leaving the duck behind, and Trickster laughing on his own.

The old house isn't far, so that's where I go. The lights are on. I know Dad must be there, but that doesn't stop me this time. Something about the world almost ending makes me want to see him in one form or another, and my last encounter with Trickster left me even more eager to show some respect.

Besides, I'm so exhausted, all that awkward pain I felt earlier is almost gone. That is, until I walk up to the door and he opens it.

"Wade," Dad says, a face, a voice, not from a dream but from deep, deep memory. "I've been worried sick. It's all over the news, your webcast is everywhere. I was afraid they were going to catch you . . . but . . ."

He lunges forward and I think he's going to hit me,

but he just grabs and hugs me. I struggle a bit, then let go. I hug him back, mostly to keep from crying.

I break the clench and stammer. "Uh-uh-uh-uh . . . mind if I breathe now?"

He steps back, wipes his eyes, and nods a bunch.

"Did the good guys win?" he asks.

"Yeah. Definitely."

I walk in, sort of past him. I can tell he's hurt I'm not saying more. I try to make it easier. I bite my tongue and use the word, "Dad?"

"Yeah?"

"I'm beat."

"I'll bet."

"Could I tell you about it later? Right now I just need to . . . to . . ."

"Be home?"

Home. Right. I slouch toward the stairs.

"Wade? Tell me just one thing?"

"If I can."

"Are *you* all right?"

Geez, *I* am. I'm fine. But OG? His son? For all I know Klot killed him in my world. "Dunno," I tell him. "Do I have to know right now?"

He shakes his head. "No," he says. "Guess you don't. We can always call a lawyer in the morning."

Up the carpeted steps, into the hall, I feel his eyes on me. He says something about taking the day off tomorrow and making pancakes. God, his pancakes always sucked. Like cardboard. I grunt and keep walking. He doesn't say anything else.

Takes me a second to realize which bedroom is

"mine"—then I realize, of course, it's the cleaner one. Everything in its place. Where's my frakking guitar? OG didn't sell it, did he? Not under the bed. Closet?

Yeah, there it is. Way in the back with the rest of the toys he was probably trying to forget about. I stomp extra hard over some expensive-looking shoes to get to it. After I've got the guitar, I stomp on the shoes again, for fun.

Poor guitar. There's dust on it. It hasn't been touched in years.

I tune her up, strum a few chords, hum, but that's all I got. I lay it against the wall, face out. It's the wrong way, but screw it, it's not *my* guitar. I slip into bed, still wearing the Maintain-ant's overalls.

The mattress is one of those space-age foam things, curving up around me, filling every little space on my back. And above me? A window in the ceiling, showing sky. I see a big old cloud, lit up by a full moon behind it, stars here and there. Slowly, the moon emerges, a Trickster moon, playing peekaboo, hiding the stars, not because it's swallowing them, just because, right now, just for now, it thinks it's brighter than any of them.

But it's not. Not really.

CHAPTER 11

CHAPTER 11

They say everyone sometimes dreams of a monster chasing them, but now one's caught me. Horribly pleased, he comes closer. Even if I didn't have his stolen toy, even if he hadn't cut off HIS pinkie, I'd still be paralyzed. There's something about him, the size of his head, the way his eyes are different sizes, the way his skin looks fake, that makes him seem as if he were *designed* to be a machine that generates fear.

Klot brings his giant head so close I have to lean back.

"Blew it again, kid. Officer Smelser, bless him, spent the last hour—the last hour, can you imagine—trying to convince me all I should do is take my car, maybe *one* more finger, just because you didn't call like you were supposed to, and go. Isn't that right, Officer?"

"I did my best," he says with a shrug.

"Then I'm told *you're* the one who took it in the first place, but they could be lying, so I come here to check it out myself, peer down into this crap-hole, and what do I see? You and your friend trying to take my car apart to sell the diamonds! That's not just a crime against me, that's a crime against the craftsman who built it. It's a crime against art. I mean, there must be some law against that, right?"

"Defacing stolen property," Officer Smelser puts in.

"You don't understand," I say. My voice is horribly shaky.

"What? What don't I understand?" He brings his head still closer, so we're almost touching. My skull aches, like I'm being drawn into its gravitational pull.

"It was broken. I was fixing it," I tell him. "The wheel . . . came off."

He claps his hands together like a delighted child. "Oh! You were *fixing* it!"

He leans to my left, puts his off-eyes nearer to the vise. "Ah. Fixing it." He reaches a finger over and flicks the car's wheels, one at a time. They all spin. "Bullshit, Clown-boy. You don't even know how to blow your nose. But that's not the most troubling aspect of this situation, is it, Officer?"

"No," Smelser says, "it's not."

"We *heard* you . . ." Klot raises a finger and jabs it toward his flat ear. "*Heard* you say you were going to try to trap me for the police. Now that, that's not just against art, that's a crime against nature. You know what the punishment is for a crime against nature?"

"A strangelet that devours the Earth?" I think.

Klot smiles. "A game. That's the punishment, a game. It's all a game, remember? Everything. Time to play."

He's already pinning me against the table, but Smelser steps up and grabs me, too.

"Leave him alone!" Po shouts, but he's scared and doesn't sound like he means it.

Klot takes the car out of the vise, pulls out a handker-chief, wraps it gently inside, and lays it in a safe spot on the table. He nods at Smelser. Together they force my right wrist into the vise and tighten it. Cold metal presses my flesh, squeezing the muscle to the bone.

I want to apologize, beg for mercy, but I can't get the words out.

Klot nods. The vise is finally tight enough for him.

"Clippers?" Smelser asks.

"Nah. Not for a crime against nature. Not good enough."

Klot looks around. He spies the rusty hacksaw and grabs it.

"Leave him alone," Po says again. This time he sounds more like he means it. Even Klot and Smelser have to admit maybe he does, because Po has his little gun pointed at them.

Smelser steps up, towering over a hunched Po.

"Back off. I'll kill you," Po says.

"Really?" Officer Smelser says. "Going to kill a cop, are you? You know what they do to people who kill cops?"

I don't know what someone willing to shoot somebody looks like, but I don't think they'd look like Po. He steps back, to keep some distance, and tries to put in a good word for me: "He's a stupid clown. Don't mean nothing."

"I know," Klot says. "He'll live. I just want to give him a lesson."

Po shifts, like he's cornered. "He's a guitar player. He needs his hand."

Klot shrugs. "A foot then, okay? We'll take a foot." Klot nods at Po, like, "That's okay with you, right? That's fair. I mean, we've *got* to cut something off, yes?"

My anxiety's finally infiltrated HIS body and taken command. I feel dizzy.

Smelser chimes in. "They can even sew it back on, like his pinkie. What do you say? Put it down or you'll both get killed."

Po shivers, shakes, then makes a noise somewhere between a laugh and a sob. He lowers his little gun. "Just his foot."

Smelser grabs Po's gun. In the movies they're usually gentle about things like that, afraid the gun may go off by accident. Smelser just yanks it away. Po slouches back into the wall, like a sack of dirt.

"Now," Klot says, turning back to me, "where were we?"

He lowers the hacksaw against my wrist. Could've seen that one coming. Po screams and rises. Smelser puts the gun on the table, then shoves him back against the wall, hard.

"Oh? Is this not his foot?" Klot says. "Too bad."

He tilts his planetlike head and grins at me, as if he's a magician about to do a really great trick and he's being nice enough to warn me that I should watch this next part very carefully, to keep him honest.

He presses the blade against my flesh. *My* flesh. *My* fear. So I do something HE would never do, something totally beyond HIS smug self-assurance, something I'm much, much better at, even better than I am at soldering.

I faint.

There isn't much of a to-do about it. My eyelids flicker and I go down. The weight of my crumpling body pulls the vise free from the bench. I hit the floor with my knees, then go forward on my face. Thud.

My nose may be broken. Hard to tell. The only thing I

see is the cool grayness of concrete. A dank, musty smell fills my nostrils, but feels dim and far away.

I hear Klot sigh. "That's no good. I want him to watch."

Po howls. I hear a struggle.

Klot tsks. "Hold the old idiot. I'll do this part myself."

The dark floor goes pitch-black as Klot stands over me. The airy sound of the basement muffles as he kneels. I feel his hands grab my shoulders and turn me roughly over. I see him, the monster, hazily through the slits of my eyes. I wonder if he sees me.

"He's out," Klot says. He doesn't. The monster doesn't see me.

"So shoot him," Smelser replies, voice strained. Po's putting up a struggle.

"No!" Klot says. "I know what to do. Take a second."

His hand vanishes into his pocket, returns with a small glass capsule. He crushes it between his fingers. Smelling salts.

"This'll bring him around," Klot says. "Wuss kid, fainting like an old lady."

He's right about one thing, I am a wuss. But he's wrong about something else. I didn't faint. I pretended. Details, right? *No fun for me if you don't stay awake.* Even though I was scared, I faked my collapse to buy some time, hoping Po would grab his gun from the table. But that didn't work out.

Funny thing, as Klot brings the salts closer, I really *do* start to faint. My heart jackhammers, the tiny slit of my vision starts to wobble, and that falling sensation takes hold. But as that big, ugly cow head hovers over me, something new happens. Something unexpected. The falling stops.

I still have the fear, but I feel like I've landed, hit

bottom. I've hit the bottom of my fear, and I'm still here, still in charge of myself. Is this what letting go is like? Or is it just that the longer I stay in HIS body, the more like HIM I become? Whatever. Something in me says screw it, screw it to the remaining fear, screw it to the consequences, and I obey.

The metal vise is still clamped around my wrist, so I pull my right arm back and whack Klot in the head as hard as I can with it. It's not as if anyone could miss a target like that. It feels like I'm smacking a side of beef with a sledgehammer.

His head shivers and lopes sideways. My right wrist feels cut as the vise slides off, but I'm not done yet. It's as though I've spent so much time listening to the "flight" half of my fight-or-flight instinct, that the "fight" half is dying to prove itself.

I'm still lying on the floor, but while he's staggering, I pull my knees up, roll my back, and slam my heels into his nose. Klot flies up and backward, led by his skull. It's a short trip. The edge of the table is closer than it looks, because even before I fully stretch my legs, the back of his head hits it hard. This give me an extra second to kick his head into the table again. And again.

Klot sways, head lolling to the side. The rest of him follows it to the ground.

"Son of a bitch!" he growls dizzily. "Get him!"

Before I can stand, Smelser's on me, holding my wrists with his hands, squeezing the wounded one, shoving his knee into my gut. His badge is right up in my face, glowing silver in the light of the bulb, filling my field of vision, reminding me that, damn it, this man is a police officer, he's supposed to *protect* people, this man is . . .

Wait. Wait a minute. I don't believe it. It *is* all about the details.

By this time Po has his gun back. "Get up! Get off him!" he says.

Klot is still on the floor, grabbing his huge head with two hands.

Smelser rises, hands up. He's panting from our struggle, but his posture remains perfect. He should have been a dancer.

Po looks shaky. "Look, just let us get out of here, okay?"

"We can talk about that," Smelser says. "But why don't you lower that thing? Don't want to shoot a cop, right?"

"No," I say to Po. "Go ahead. Shoot him."

"Eh?" Po says.

I stand, staggering, nervous, but clearheaded. "His badge. It's fake."

For a second, Smelser looks shocked, worried, but he buries it under a practiced mask. "You're hallucinating, kid."

"Po, look. The number on it is 007. 007? Think he's really James Bond? He's a jerk in a costume. Ask him for some ID."

Po's eyes narrow. "Officer" Smelser's terrified look returns, this time to stay. He tries one last lie, but you can tell even he doesn't think it'll work.

"Kid, you don't know what—"

There's a sound like a firecracker pop, and a rush in the air. Po fired the gun. Almost hit Smelser.

"Get out of here, now!"

Smelser stumbles backward, hands up.

Then Klot rises and straightens his bruised head. He's nowhere near ready to surrender, even if Smelser is.

Klot holds his ground, showing that furious monster-gleam in his oddball eyes.

"Give me a break, little man. You're not gonna—"

Klot's shoulder flies back like it's been hit by a wrecking ball. The hole in his coat is neat and round. The blood that gathers beneath it, staining the fabric, is not.

Realizing his partner's been shot, Smelser runs for the deep pile of cardboard blocking the concrete stairs. Klot wavers, glances at the blood like it belongs to someone else. For a second I worry he'll go after Po, wound and all. Instead, not so much the monster now, he pivots to join Smelser. They wade through the fetid cardboard, trying to reach the short staircase to the storm door.

Po fires into the ceiling, bringing down plaster. Smelser, moving even faster, reaches across the last yard of boxes and pushes open the door. The basement floods with sunlight so strong it pushes us all back.

Klot and Smelser look briefly relieved, but when Klot tries to put his foot on the steps, something under the cardboard pulls it back. He screams. He claws at Smelser, trying to use his cohort's straight back to keep himself from being yanked down. Still screaming—bellowing, really— he yanks twice more before a huge furry blur rises with his leg.

The rat.

Startled by the light, it lets go, revealing huge tears in Klot's pants and a deep toothy wound above the ankle. The hairy blur disappears into the cardboard as if it were water, then makes two impossibly high leaps. The jumps are so high, the blur so big, it blocks our view of Klot's head as he and Smelser scramble up the steps.

The rat, its hiding place hopelessly destroyed, scampers after them.

I stand there, shocked and fascinated, until Po pulls at me. Together we make our way through the trash and up into the alley. Klot and Smelser are still running, Klot limping, his wounded shoulder sloping down.

We shake our heads in wonder. Po starts to say something, but doesn't. He stands there, swaying, staring. For a second I worry he accidentally shot himself. Then I see what he sees. We're less than two yards from the rat.

Not caring about us, it jumps halfway up a brick wall, then shimmies up and over. Po and I creep to the wall and look down. Far below, there's a vast junkyard that looks sort of familiar. We see the rat slip among the garbage, a living shadow in the harsh daylight. It passes a huge dog that stops gnawing on a bone to stare at it, too, as if it's seeing Bigfoot live and up close. Might as well be. The rat's nearly as big as the dog.

Soon the rat vanishes among the hills of garbage.

"There's something you don't see every day," Po says.

"Got that right," I tell him.

Po trots into the street and I follow. Klot and Smelser race toward a yellow Hummer. I think it's all over, but then I remember something Po said.

"They've still got Anthony! We have to at least get their license-plate number!"

Po fires a shot into the air above their heads.

"Leave the car," he tells them. They do. They leave it and run down the street.

"So, go get the license number," Po tells me. "And see if there are keys."

Obeying, I walk up and look inside. No keys but, in the backseat, I see what looks like a pile of clothing, only it's a pile of clothing with a head of hair and two dreadlocked antlers.

"Anthony!" I scream at Po. "He's not moving!"

He trots up. "Don't stand there like an idiot, get him out!"

I tug the handle. Locked.

"I'll shoot it open," Po says.

I hold down his gun wrist and say, "No, no, no. I've got it. Thanks."

There's half a brick lying at the edge of the building. I slam it into the window. The safety glass shatters. The air fills with a bleating car alarm.

I open the door and claw at Anthony. In my rush of concern it's a little easy to forget how angry I am at him—well, how angry I am at *my* Anthony. This one looks much the same, a little sloppier maybe, but I even recognize the shirt his mother gave him. He's bound, gagged, and blindfolded, but alive, shivering because he still can't see who I am. For all he knows, I'm Klot. I take the blindfold off first, untie him, and pull him out.

He staggers to his feet, breathing heavily. Putting aside everything he did to me in my world, I put my hand on his shoulder, happy to see him. He does not feel likewise.

"Don't touch me," he says.

What? He's mad at *me*? About what? The things HE said to Klot? What could it have been? Before I can ask, Anthony hobbles off. It's just as well. How would I have explained?

I look at Po, helpless. He grunts and catches up with

Anthony. They talk. Po hands him some cash, then comes back to me.

"Boy, he's pissed at you," Po says.

"I figured. Will he be okay?"

Po shrugs. "Gave him cab fare. He wants to go home, show his mother he's alive, then call the real police. Sounds like a plan to me."

We head inside. After calling a cab for Anthony, Po actually calls his own mother, just to tell her he's alive. He's kind of likable, in a way.

Then he calls the Rivendale police. I understand what he's saying to them, since we just went through it together, but he doesn't seem to be getting anywhere. I take the phone and give it a try. The first thing *I* talk about isn't Klot or Officer Smelser, it's the fact that I have a diamond-studded Hot Wheels car. Someone must be looking for it, right?

Twenty minutes later, a squad car shows. Two clean-cut, polite, professional, and, happily, *authentic* officers emerge. Once they see the shiny little diamond-car, they're more than eager to hear all about Klot and "Officer" Smelser. Especially Smelser. They take copious notes. Ask many questions.

"We don't like it when someone impersonates an officer. It's bad for everyone."

"You're telling me," I say, holding up my pinkie.

"You willing to testify?"

I hesitate, not because I don't want to, I'd love it, but I'm not sure what HE would say. If we switch back, it'll be HIS problem, not mine. But Po elbows me sharply, so I agree. It *is* the right thing to do.

Before they're done, they get a call about someone with a huge head showing up at the clinic with a gunshot wound and a rat bite. Apparently he's being treated for rabies. I hear rabies injections are pretty painful. No sign of Smelser yet, but his fake uniform was found, and the police seem pissed enough to find him.

Once they leave, I turn to Po. "Doesn't anyone around here know who the real cops are?"

He shrugs. "That's the thing. We don't *get* many real cops around here."

He cooks us a meal (*after* he agrees to let me wash the dishes and the utensils first—I'm calmer but not crazy), and we talk.

"Think I'm gonna paint a new sign. Put a big 'no' symbol through the rat."

"This place was named after the rat in the basement? I figured it was just short for *Ratskeller*, German for 'pub.'"

He looks at me like I shot his best friend. "Don't tell anyone that, all right?"

"Fine," I say. I also don't tell him I'm not exactly who he thinks I am, but once I wash the dishes, I think he suspects. After eating, we're beat, so I head upstairs for a rest. He gives me a new blanket and a pillow.

"So, Po, thanks," I tell him. He grunts. "I mean for everything."

He raises an eyebrow. "Sounds like good-bye. Going somewhere?"

I shrug. "Don't think so. 'To sleep, perchance to dream.'"

He furrows his brow and heads home himself. The place is quieter without him. Hell, *I'm* quieter. The constant fear is gone. My world might still be in danger but, somehow, knowing for sure I can't do a damn thing about it helps me . . . let go.

Upstairs, I find a closet door I remember from my dream. Looking inside, I wonder how HE could live here, even for one night. Then I wonder how many nights *I'll* be here. Despite my clever Shakespeare quote, I have no reason to think I won't see Po tomorrow morning and every morning after that. I was hoping that with HIS problems solved, I'd be heading home, but I could just as easily be trapped here. It's possible home was the dream and *this* the only reality. At least Denby's here. Can't wait to see her in any world. Anthony I've got problems with in both places, but what can you do? Then there's . . .

. . . something I have to do before I go to sleep, something I'm not sure HE'd like. I'm pretty sure HE wouldn't. Too damn bad. If we switch back, who knows what I'll find waiting for me? I'll probably wake up in a jail cell. And, really, it seems like *the right* thing to do, like testifying. Totally. So I do it.

I head downstairs and make some calls to old family friends. Finding him is easier than I thought, and feels even better. When I'm finally really finished with this screwy day, I pass through the main room, wander by a pile of wood that might pass for a stage, and spot HIS guitar. Mine, actually, same one I had three years ago. I think it's still in my closet somewhere.

For the hell of it, I snatch it up and try to remember a few chords. I sound terrible. No lie. Really terrible. The pinkie wound doesn't help. But some lyrics pop into my head, and a half-assed tune. Something I wrote, tried writing, a long time ago, before Mom died. Which maybe means *we* wrote it. Finding the stub of a pencil and a piece of scrap paper in the kitchen, I scribble down what I remember from all those years ago, change it around a bit.

As HE likes to say, "Whatev." I shove the pencil and the mess into my pocket.

Exhausted, completely, I head up to the closet mattress and pretend to get comfortable. It's worse than Schapiro's couch. Still, it is familiar, downright homey, in a completely awkward way. Head crunched against the wall, finger throbbing, I fall into a deep, dreamless sleep. Depending, of course, on what you mean by "dream."

CHAPTER 12

I wake in the dark, head scrunched sideways. My neck and shoulders feel like all their blood's been replaced with Silly Putty. It hurts to move them, it hurts to keep them still. I open my eyes. They're clingy with gunk. I see enough, though, to realize the skylight's gone. No windows, either. No big space-age bed. I'm in a space the size of a closet.

Heh. I'm back, baby.

Then I notice the intense pain in my pinkie. The bandage looks new, cleaner, but it's wet. During the night the wound must've opened up, or OG did something to it he shouldn't have. I've even got some kind of cut on my forehead now. I still love it. My dark dirt's better than his clean walls any day. Hey, playing Super-Wade and saving the world was cool, and maybe he could teach me a thing or two about stuff like math and having money, but, really, no thank you. It's too great to be in my own crumply clothes.

Something jabs me, a pencil stub in my shirt pocket. I fish it out and find a folded piece of paper in there, too. Handwriting's kind of mine, only neater. OG left a note? No. Lyrics. Well, look at that. It's a song I started a million years ago, a song *we* started, before the split. After all those years, OG tried to finish it. Just can't stop fixing things, can he?

He should be happy when he finds out he was right about the world being in danger. That's like his favorite thing, I figure, and you don't get much more right than that. Hope he doesn't mind how I left things. Then again, hope I don't mind whatever he left me. Ant could be dead or I might be married to Denby. Weird having remembered so much of his life from my dreams, not knowing what he did while I was away.

I'll find out soon enough, but right now, this in-between place, half-awake, not knowing, works fine for me.

So what's with this song? The lyrics are lame in spots, but they work their way into my head. Next thing I know I'm violating my own rules, making notes. I run out of space, so I snag an empty paper-towel roll from the trash and scribble some more. I'm at it until I hear footsteps and voices below.

My beloved Rat is gathering. I hear Po call, "You coming down?"

I grunt back, take another minute to finish, then head down to see what's left of my life. A familiar face greets me, a familiar body blocking the bottom step. I feel totally happy for the first time in years. The duck on my head? Gone.

"Denby! Uh . . . we're not engaged, are we?"

She ignores the question. "You bastard! You could have called! Po had to tell me everything worked out. Thank God!"

It worked out? Good! I flash her a grin. "You knew it would."

She shakes her head. "No, I didn't. Neither did you. They could've killed you!"

"Denby . . . you're right."

She eyes me like she can't believe I'm saying that twice in the same week, then changes the subject, like it's too much to consider. "You hear the latest or you been asleep all day?"

"Asleep." And hey, haven't even heard the *oldest* yet.

"Klot confessed." He was caught. Now that's an exhale. Denby continues. "The rumors about him being a sculptor were true. He got the commission for a statue at Prometheus before it was closed by that lawsuit. It was supposed to be his big break. They say that's when he lost it."

K on the plaque. Huh. Smelser's cousin. We both saved our worlds from Klot in a way. OG from Klot's finger chopping, me from his oogly art.

"And Smelser? I couldn't believe . . ."

He can wait. There's a more important question.

"Denby, is Ant okay?"

"Still pissed at you, if that's what you mean. You crushed him, you know."

Now I really exhale. He's alive. "Great."

"What?" Denby says, ready to be furious. "You think that's great?"

"Relatively."

Po calls again. "You playing or what?"

What's with him? He was never this eager to hear me before.

"No, Denby. Sorry. What I did to Ant was not great. That's not what I mean. I'll explain later. After the set, want to get some dinner?"

She twists her head, curious, then feels my forehead like I've got a fever. "I'm *right*, you're *sorry*, and you want to leave The No-Rat and go out with me?"

The No-Rat? I decide not to ask about that one now either. I'm probably lucky I didn't come back and find everyone turned into a talking lizard like in those freaky time-travel stories. "Yes. Let's go out. I'll tell you everything I know, so you can be sure it won't take long."

She smiles. "Okay."

All eyes are on me as I head to the stage. Ant's at his table, somber as a statue. I'm surprised he's even here. I wave my fingers at him, even the bandaged one, but there's no response.

I mount the Center of the Universe and strum. Damn. It hurts to make chords with my pinkie. I'll have to manage. I clear my throat. I balance the cardboard beneath the mike so I can see the lyrics and sing the song that was years and a couple of dimensions in the making:

Now, sometimes I can fight like the devil
And sometimes I lay down and die
Sometimes I'm just testing the mettle
Of occasional passers-by

If I'm down and out, or on the mark
Or somebody's holding me tight
If I'm drowning in my memories
Or bathing in the light
Just to make it through—I really hate to
        choose.

Sometimes I can stand in a corner
Sometimes I run round and round
Maybe I'll be screaming my head off
Or I won't even make a sound
If I'm sticking to the bottom
Or skimming off the top
Sitting in the middle
Waiting for my shoe to drop—right next to you
That's the best that I could do—'cause I really
        hate to choose.

The Rat . . . uh . . . The No-Rat actually seems thoughtful as it applauds. I catch Ant clapping, too, but he stops when he sees me. So I try something different. I sing the song Ant liked so much when he walked in here the first time.

Turns out between my pinkie and a lousy memory, I suck at repeats. Too self-conscious. By the end everyone's just staring. Po's laughing so hard he ducks under the counter. Ant remains unmoved. He probably didn't recognize the song given how I butchered it. So I stop looking at him.

When I do, I see someone among the coffee-teen-tables I haven't seen before, someone older, fifties.

Friend of Po's? Clothes are loose, cheap, but clean. Face shaved, reddish hair neat, like he's taking care of himself lately but not used to it . . . Dad?

I think about running, but instead push through the crowd to get to him. Turns out, he's the one who runs. He heads right out the front door. I'm almost out after him when Po uses both hands to pull me back.

"Let him go, Clown-boy," he says.

"Po, that's—"

"I know. Said you tracked him, called to tell him where you were. Didn't think you had that in you. Good for you. That's respect."

I tracked him? OG. Bastard. Wish I could smash his car again.

I pull at Po's hold. "So let me go."

"He's not ready. He's six months sober, got a job for the last three. Wanted to sneak out before you spotted him, but he did want me to tell you he'd be back."

"Asshole."

"Look who's talking. Let him go. You already did. Three years ago."

I slouch. I sigh. I hate feeling helpless. "He said he'd be back?"

"When he's ready. Everybody does his time on a pig farm."

So that's why Po was so eager to get me down here.

Denby slides next to me and slips her arm in mine. "Weren't you taking me out?"

"Yeah," I say. She's probably in on the Dad thing. Po would've told her.

I walk her outside quickly, hoping to spot my father.

He moves fast for a drunk, nowhere in sight. My guts are in a knot.

Denby rubs my back and I melt a little.

"That was nice, singing that song for Anthony," she says. At least she recognized it.

"He's still pissed," I tell her. "And I don't blame him. But I'll work on it. Maybe I'll ask him if he wants to help record some of my songs."

"Really?"

"Yeah, why not?"

Funny world. Funny *worlds*? Right now OG with his comfy bed and Happy Dad is probably banging his head on the wall, thinking like crazy, trying to figure out how it all happened, how we split, how we switched, how we got back.

I figure it's probably something stupid and simple. Like everyone's got a story, and we wound up with two. What's the difference? I'm here, he's there. I, at least, sure as hell hope we never meet again, 'cept in dreams.

Whatever the hell they are, right?

CHAPTER 12

My face is warm, my eyes closed, but I see red through my eyelids. It feels like someone's shining a flashlight at me. Po? I move to swat it away, but my hand sweeps above my head without hitting anything. The blanket feels smooth as silk. Home?

I open my eyes, squint at the brightness exploding through my skylight. I relax into a soft mattress that conforms to the shape of my body. My pinkie doesn't hurt. I don't smell. I feel clean. An overwhelming sense of gratitude fills me, bubbles over into the room. *My* room. Home. And it hasn't even been eaten by strangelets.

As for that other life, I am never going back there again. Not if I can help it, no way, no how. I don't even care that I'm wearing Prometheus overalls instead of pajamas. In fact, I figure that's a good sign.

"Wade?" Dad calls from the stairs.

Dad! Does he know I was gone?

"Yeah?"

He bounds in, cup of tea in one hand, a newspaper in the other.

"Finally awake, huh? Thought you'd want to see this."

He swats me in the head lightly with the paper, tosses it into my lap, and puts the cup of tea on my night table.

"Good guys ten points, bad guys nothing. A shutout." He bows. "And once you're up, oh prince of the realm, I'm making pancakes."

"That a promise or a threat?" I say.

He never could cook. But I'm so happy to see him, I'm even looking forward to chewing on cardboard.

"Bit of both," he says, pleased with himself. "New recipe. Loved your singing, by the way. I knew you never should have given it up."

Singing?

He bows again and exits, obviously in a very good mood. Given what he said, I don't expect the paper he was beating me with will have news of my impending arrest. I am surprised, though, to see my photo on the front page, beneath a headline reading:

TEEN UNCOVERS CRITICAL COLLIDER FLAW
DR. JOHN FINLEY RESIGNS
JUDITH WILSON APPOINTED NEW PUBLIC LIAISON

Son of a bitch. The crazy asshole did it!

It gets better. Prometheus was shut down this morning for two weeks, to alter the shielding. Near as I can tell, they don't quite cop to the end-of-the-world scenario, referring only to a possible radiation leak. I guess a world-devouring negative strangelet counts as radiation, so technically it's true.

Judith Wilson worries me, but, hell, she may have been right about the whole inter-dimensional rift thing. And if she was smart enough to use the data to land herself that job, more power to her. Maybe I'll figure out the parallel life conundrum someday and win a Nobel. Meanwhile, though, much as I hate to admit it, I may, as Dad says, just have to let it go.

No mention of how HE managed all this, but I'm even feeling grateful for my alter ego. Maybe we are good for each other in a way. Maybe we each have pieces the other's missing. I could learn a thing or two about chilling. I could teach HIM . . . to wash HIS face, for instance. Wait, there's something about a car accident.

Car accident? I flip the paper open. Page two has a big photo of that beautiful atom sculpture smashed in half. And there, at the bottom of the pool is . . . my hybrid?

Forget it. Just forget it. Small price to pay . . .

My hybrid!

Damn. I throw the paper across the room. I am going back somehow, someday, just to find that idiot and kill HIM. *My car!*

I'm just wild about Harry!

Usually I'd answer immediately to avoid hearing the crappy song, but I'm so happy to hear it, I tap my toes through the first verse before I pick up.

"Wade? Anthony."

So much for toe tapping. "What do you want?"

"Listen, I am so, so sorry about those letters, man. I never sent one, I was never going to, I was just, you know, venting my dark place, trying to work it out, get it out of my system. You were never supposed to see them. No one was. No one ever would have."

I'm about to hang up, but he starts talking, fast and serious. Behind the flailing syntax and the wall of words, I hear genuine regret. "I'm sorry about everything else, too. I should have listened to you from the beginning. I shouldn't have sided with Finley. I shouldn't have told them you were in the building. I'm an asshole, a total, despicable tool and you should beat the crap out of me the next time you see me. But, man, you've got to understand one thing, just one thing: I'm not like you. I'm nowhere near like you. I'm not as sure about things as you are. I get that you were right to handle it the way you did, and Finley was being evil, but this was like just *one* thing for you. You're going to do a *lot* of stuff in your life, probably just like this, or freakier, and Denby's going to be by your side, I know it, but for me, I was thinking this was *it*, my only chance to ever really lead a different life. That's all. It was stupid. It was pure evil, but can you try to forgive me? I admit, I totally suck, but can you? Ahab? I'll give back the scholarship if you say so. I think Dr. Wilson said it was up to you. But . . . do I have to? She says she wants to meet with you, there's like an honorary seat on the board if you want it—"

I hang up. I sip my tea. I lean back in bed. I think about it. Screw it. I don't need to think about it right now. Right now, I just need to lie here and feel good about having a pinky and a decent haircut.

I'm just wild about Harry!

Crap. He's not giving up.

I flip the cell open. "Look, you stupid son of a—"

"Wade?"

"Denby? Sorry! Thought you were . . . someone else."

"I'm so proud of you, Wade. And who knew you could sing?"

There's that singing thing again. What *did* HE do?

"Thank you."

"Happy ending, huh?"

"Looks that way. Except my car."

"Oh, I got you something better than a car."

She sounds funny, like she's not really happy. "What?"

"Seems like the guy who saved the world should get the girl, right?"

Now she sounds even more tense. I think I'm starting to understand.

"I've got something very important to tell you," she says. "Can I come over?"

"Sure. Want me to come over there?"

"Oh, either. Actually . . . I'll just tell you. I didn't want to tell you over the phone."

"Whatever you want."

"Yes," she says. Now she's trying to sound happy. "I'll marry you. You win."

Win? Like a game?

"Uh . . . Denby, are you sure this is what you want right now? Totally sure?"

There's a pause. "No. But *you're* sure, and I'm sure I love you and I'm sure you love me and I want us to be together."

"Me, too, but wouldn't you rather wait?"

I hear her brow furrow. "*Yes* . . . but you don't want to, right? This isn't about Anthony, is it?"

"No, not at all. Maybe a little. Maybe it just made me realize how much I *can* trust you. I thought I didn't want to wait, but I want *you* to be sure, too."

"You're not breaking up with me, are you?"

"No! No way."

Long pause. "So I'll give the ring back for now?"

"Yeah. It's okay, really. I'll save it."

"For me, right? You'll save it for me?"

"Wouldn't *ever* give it to anyone else."

"Now I *really* want to see you," she says. "You stay put until I get there."

I feel the tension flee her voice. And they say these things only carry *sound*.

"Great. But . . . Dad's home. Won't be very private. And, uh, he's making pancakes. Not pretty."

"Well, after breakfast send him out for some espresso or something."

"I'll see what I can arrange."

"Ha!" she says. She says something else, too, but she's so excited she hangs up on herself before she finishes.

"Ha!" I repeat, to myself, to the room. If I had a mirror handy, I'd stick my tongue out at myself.

Hey, my guitar's leaning against the wall, face out. A good way to warp the neck. One guess who did that. I walk over, pick it up, strum. Hm. At least HE tuned it.

A weird thought strikes me. I ransack my closet, looking for an old notebook. I find it easy enough. Orange, spiral-bound, cover crinkled like tree bark, pages not yellowed but blurry. Mom bought it for me when I was thirteen, to keep my lyrics in.

A few flips through scattered notes and I find it, the song, the one I . . . *we* wrote before we even knew Mom was sick, the one I worked on last night. There were a few verses I forgot. Hitting the easy chords, skipping the D, I croak softly to myself, hoping Dad can't hear:

Sometimes I'll be lost in the forest
Where no one else can see

Won't know whether to follow the map
Or to let it follow me
Do I flow with the momentum
Or swim against the stream
Argue with reality
Or dream another dream—of me and you?
Don't know what to do—but I really hate to choose.

Sometimes I'm afraid for the children
Sometimes I couldn't care less
Mostly I just never could tell
What to make of this ungodly mess
If the jury's out or in my head
Then why do I feel so alone?
Am I waiting for the axe to fall
And leave a message at the tone?
Haven't got a clue—but I really hate to choose.

Something like that, anyway. I lean the guitar against the wall, back out, the right way.

Maybe I *should* meet with Judith Wilson, sit on the board. It might be easier to keep an eye on things from the inside. Then again, once they get me inside, it might be easier for them to change me, make me paranoid like Judith Wilson or numb like Dr. John Finley.

No. I think I've run the gamut with the change thing for now. After all, I'm not particularly worried about the world ending. Then again, a comet could always come along and wipe us all out. Did I read something about that in the paper recently?

That was a *joke*. I'm trying to get better with the whole joke thing.

ACKNOWLEDGMENTS

My responsible half would like to express my deep grati-tude to my wonderful editor Stacy Cantor for her terrific help and continual support and advocacy for my work. This was a tough one to edit, what with all the parallels and double dialogue. In addition to Stacy, copy editor Chandra Wohleber did a great job making sure things were properly synched. Thanks also to first reader Christie Suave for reas-suring me that the whole thing made sense. As always, thanks to my lovely family, Sarah, Maia, and Margo, who provide my life and my work with endless joy and meaning.

My irresponsible half doesn't want to thank anyone other than myself, because first of all, hey, I did all the work, and second of all, I have a really tough time paying attention to anything for very long. Ooh. What's that pretty light outside? Gotta go.